THE JAGGED SIDE OF
MIDNIGHT

A Horse's Tale of Love and Loss

Patrick DiCicco

Bertie; you'll never look at a horse in a pasture the same way again.

2017

iUniverse LLC
Bloomington

THE JAGGED SIDE OF MIDNIGHT
A Horse's Tale of Love and Loss

iUniverse books may be ordered through booksellers or by contacting:

iUniverse LLC
1663 Liberty Drive
Bloomington, IN 47403
www.iuniverse.com
1-800-Authors (1-800-288-4677)

ISBN: 978-1-4917-1967-1 (sc)
ISBN: 978-1-4917-1969-5 (hc)
ISBN: 978-1-4917-1968-8 (e)

Library of Congress Control Number: 2013923791

Printed in the United States of America.

iUniverse rev. date: 01/06/2014

There are clouds coming
Across the mountains,
Some never seen before;
Some so dark, they can
Make dim lights bright.

Pretty from a distance,
But yet bring no
Comfort to the darkness
Of night.

Where have the green pastures
And the mighty oaks gone
That once gave me comfort?
What is under my hoofs
Now that I cannot feel?

How did I get here?
Why am I dead on my feet?

CONTENTS

The Birth of a Champion 1

Friends in Low Places 15

My Teenage Years..29

The Premonition 40

My Education 48

The Tornado..63

The Two Year Old Wonder...68

Las Vegas 81

Three Years Old..92

The Triple Tiara 105

Turmoil On The Farm 113

The Race 134

Life without Lauren..149

Debts Due and Payable 159

Close Call 179

Actions have Consequences 188

The Investigation..198

Ohio 205

Stallion Springs 212

Darkness Blue Moods and No Moon 225

The White Owl...230

PROLOGUE

So there I stood, in the middle of nowhere with total strangers, each one of us on his last leg, each one of us not knowing if we were to be "rescued." "Rescued—what a misnomer that is," I thought. Rescued from what? Rescued to another stressful situation? Rescued and to be picked up by someone who knows nothing about how to take care of me? Rescued to stick me in their back yard and to be looked at from a window, just because they wanted a horse they couldn't afford to buy? Rescued to be fed only once a day, or worse, every other day? Perhaps fed with inferior food and without a shelter or companion again? I've been there and done that; all I want now is to be left alone, alone with my memories. I'll always have those. The good memories keep me going, but unfortunately the bad memories are the ones I can't run from. They linger and loom over me like a gloomy dreary black cloud, like a storm relentlessly pounding on my brain with waves hitting and slamming the rocks on the shore, giving me no rest or relief from the shadows of the horrifying feelings and haunting occurrences that have followed me since that dreadful day in New York. Just when the crashing wave leaves the rocks and goes back out to the foamy sea and you think you're feeling better, then bam, another wave hits my brain again, dropping me to my knees. Over and over the cycle repeats itself until it erodes your very soul and drains you of everything, then it slams you into the ground and there's nothing left.

I won the championship that rainy day in July years ago; yeah, I won it alright. That day and every day since then has been a staggering loss, a living hell. The dream I had prior to that race was a premonition, but I was too stupid and proud to realize it or act on it at the time, and because of it I pay the price for it on a daily basis. I guess this is my Karma. "Karma for what," I thought? I was good; I had a kind heart. I never hurt anybody intentionally; I shouldn't have had such a miserable life. Maybe it was my pride that brought me down. I think Dad was right; pride and vanity are indeed sins and they can kill you. Dad was always there for me when I needed to talk, but Dad is gone now too; I don't know where he is or if he is even alive. I only wish I could see him again and talk to him again; he was always wise and understanding and really cared about me.

Although I had walked the long fence at night many times before, this night seemed eerily different. The full moon was covered tonight with ominous clouds, indicating an impending summer storm. The locals called it monsoon weather. The scattered Joshua trees and the barren desert landscape I stood in exposed the majestic snow capped Sierra Nevada Mountains in the distance. In the opposite direction and west from here I could also see the Tehachapi Mountains with the wind mills turning on them and reflected on my time in Stallion Springs. The Mojave Desert is vast and empty and went on for hundreds of miles and was a concise reflection in contrast to what I have experienced, almost an analogy. The brightness of the full moon and the aura of the city lights of Palmdale and Lancaster were soon obliterated by the rain that began to fall, cooling my hot and dry skin.

Just then I heard and saw a huge lonely white owl flying high above, slowly circling me overhead, and producing a surreal moment. It looked almost majestic with its large white wings outlined by the cobalt blue clouds. As it screeched, the darkness and the still of the night awoke my inner senses and brought out innate emotions in me that I hadn't felt, or knew existed, in a long time. It was almost as if the owl was calling out to me, as if the owl was occupied by another spirit, a spirit greater than its own. It continued to circle me overhead and call out loudly to me, as if it had a message, as if it was trying to talk. Confused, I watched and listened to it for a while and then looked around at my empty surroundings, now realizing I was standing out in the middle of this desolate field in the desert by myself. A single Joshua tree standing alone in the desert is as starkly expressive as the vast wasteland it represents. I looked up at the screeching owl again and then I looked around at my dismal new home.

Like a dark and dirty window that was just opened for the first time; I saw my reality very clearly. And although I had been in a depression and in denial for more years than I can remember, I fully understood the consequences of death now. I now understood how when life becomes bleak and there isn't a promise for tomorrow, when all hope is gone and each new day is a repetition of the past, how one can succumb to the dark shadows of depression. It was very sad and yet, very eye opening; but it was all perfectly clear. I knew in my heart that I had finally given up. I just put my head down and closed my eyes.

But it wasn't always this way; I wasn't always this depressed. I was once like you. I had a great life once, full of fun and love and was the talk of the horse racing world. It was a life that many wish they could have had, but like all good things, it came to a crashing end. After all, what goes up soon comes down. Let's go back a few years to a kinder and gentler place, where there was fun and hope and every day brought something fun and new to do.

THE BIRTH OF A CHAMPION

The dark blue and purple clouds rolled slowly over the hills and valleys, as lightning displayed its entertaining and deadly dance in the sky. The strong winds broke mature tree branches and easily bent the young saplings, making the birds and animals scramble for shelter: Flashing intermittingly across the ominous sky, amazing display's of bright irregular bolts of lightning and loud thundering crashes shook the souls of everyone and startled the meek, making the horses in the pasture run for cover. The big house on the hill was outlined by clouds that mourned for light. Although it was the middle of day, the darkness of the storm made it feel like night. My mom was standing alone in the meadow at the time, and it was under these conditions I was born.

Race horses are born every day, but my birth was a highly expected event. I was sired by a National Champion and my birth was looked forward to with great anticipation. Although I was pelted by a seasonal storm when I first came into this world, the lightning dancing around me made me experience fear for the first time. My mom was the first thing I saw when I first opened my eyes, and my legs trembled underneath me as I stood up. She towered over me and gently nuzzled me while I tried to catch my balance, and then lovingly looked me in the eye while licking off the fluids from my birth, which were covered with rain. While other horses were running in fear from the lightning, she was very kind, duly nurturing and protecting me, making me feel more secure. As the warm and noisy storm slowly passed, the hot southern sun gradually shone on me with a brilliance that reflected in my mother's big black eyes. She looked down on me with a love that was genuine and hard to describe.

The rolling hills' of Kentucky are a wonderful place to live, especially if you are a race horse. The gentle hills are alive with luscious Kentucky Blue Grass and statuesque oak and magnolia trees with slight winds, so that when they blow, can stir the senses and make a horse's nostrils flare. This was horse country, and the farms were breeding grounds for the best in the world.

Roberta Windsor, the owner of Chestnut Mountain Farms, was a very nice woman and she soon rushed down to visit me with the farm's veterinarian. When she saw my beautiful red coat glistening in the sultry rain, she quickly named me Summer Storm. My first impression of her was of a very caring woman with a big heart. She and the farm's veterinarian examined me closely and said I looked healthy and that I was beautiful and had great confirmation. Roberta lived on the farm in a stately manor. It was a big brick, two-story colonial house with four white columns outlining a large porch that had a grandiose ceiling painted the right shade of blue, the colors of the farm. It sat prestigiously on a large meticulously landscaped knoll overlooking her realm. I heard people say the house was more than 150 years old, nestled in tall stately trees, with dogwoods and azaleas beautifully placed in the shadows. It looked like a beautiful European castle peering out when the fog would settle in and around the pastures below it. The house and area was rich in history, being built long before the Civil War.

"The Big House on the Hill"

Our farm was huge and consisted of about ten square miles with a tall white split-rail fence that surrounded and crisscrossed it every so often, separating one pasture from the other, one grazing area from the next. It had a racing facility too, with a full time contingent of jockeys, trainers and veterinarians on staff. It was one of the most famous horse farms in the world, having bred many champions. The long and winding asphalt driveway that led up the hill to her house was over a half a mile long and was lined with beautiful, tall cherry blossom trees that were beautiful and fragrant every spring. She would frequently walk over to my mom's paddock and admiringly say; "She is going to be a good one; look at how tall she is for her age." But even though everyone who saw me admired me, I never knew what she meant.

My mom nursed me and I would stay by her side all the time, whether in her stall or out in the meadow. I was too young to eat grass yet, so I would follow her everywhere and lay next to her when we slept. As I would grow, Mom would take care of me very well, always guiding and teaching me what I should know and what I should be aware of about life on the big farm that we lived on. Her name was Sultans Bride and she was a retired race horse, having been bred to my dad, Bold Czar, who was one of the greatest stallions that ever set foot on a race track. Dad lived on the farm too and was a champion chestnut Thoroughbred, standing an impressive seventeen hands tall. Mom was a white Arabian, with great confirmation. I got my long legs and my glowing, reddish color from Dad, and my white socks, upright tail and head, and my long mane from Mom. Some say I inherited my endurance and looks from my Arabian mom, while I got my speed, size, and heart from my dad. Regardless, everyone said I was the most beautiful filly they had ever seen.

"Mom in her prime"

As I got older, I would roam the large green pastures that surrounded our barn and always enjoyed running and playing with the other colts and fillies that lived here. I was always the fastest one, even outrunning the colts, some of which were older than me. Everyone said I was all legs, as I grew faster than the others and looked quite gangly when I was young. The long, wooden, white fence that corralled and outlined the farm seemed to meander for miles through the woods and green rolling hills, and we would run and play in them every day, exploring and visiting each part of our pasture. It was a fun time in my life; everyday brought out something new to do and new to see. Every day was exciting and stimulating to my senses, which seemed to get more refined on a daily basis.

"White fences Forever"

Lauren, Roberta's daughter, was pretty too; she looked just like her mother. They both had blue eyes and long blonde hair. She was a petite seventeen years old, stood 5'2", and weighed about 100 pounds. She was still in high school and had a lot of friends, some of which played a big part in her life. My first impression of Lauren was a young woman with a soft voice. She had a big heart like her mother and was very kind and caring. She used to spend time with me every day when she got home from school, talking to me and combing and brushing me. She was taller than me then, but that didn't last very long, as I was growing fast. I always looked forward to her visits and would always give her my complete attention, as I could tell she really liked me and she liked spending time with me as much as I liked spending time with her. Of course, the treats she gave me were nice too.

When I was three months old, Lauren took me down to the tack room in the main barn and fitted me for a bit and bridle. The tack room was huge with large wooden beams exposed on the tall raised ceiling and the walls were lined with knotty cedar. We had to enter from the side of the building, because in the entry, the floor was comprised of tile with famous horses of the farm engraved in them, etched with the dates they had won important races. It was the late 70's now and the sport of horse racing was at its pinnacle. My dad was the most famous horse on the farm and one of the most famous horses in the world, and they honored him too. You might say he was the straw that stirred the drink here. When you entered the tack room, there was a big diamond shaped marble inlaid tile at the entry, larger than the rest, that bore his resemblance and the words that said; "Home of Bold Czar, Triple Crown Winner." The shelves were filled with saddles of all types, and sizes and bits and bridles for every size horse. The farm's colors of blue and white seemed to monopolize the room, with all blankets being those colors. There was a full time employee running the tack room, mainly because there were over eighty horses on the farm that needed attention. After fitting me, Lauren then put the equipment on me, which I fought to no end, and then started to walk me. Lauren was the first one to walk me, and after a while she wouldn't let anyone else walk me. She said I was hers. I would always follow her through the stables and paddocks that lined the pasture and she would always give me a treat of tasty carrots or oats when we finished. And little by little, always following her, we'd go for much longer walks, often visiting her girlfriends on the other horse farms that adjoined our property.

Lexington, Kentucky, was horse country, and the green rolling hills consisted of many farms that raised the best race horses in the world. They were all adjacent to each other and the white fences that bordered them stretched on for miles. I always enjoyed our quiet walks together and I felt very special, mainly because Lauren didn't spend any time with any of the other horses and no other horse was allowed off the farm for a walk but me.

Time seemed to go by fast, and when I was about eight months old she put a small saddle on me for the first time and at first would lead me and walk me with it. I really hated when she cinched up the straps around my belly and put the bit in my mouth, fighting it when I could, but I gradually got used to it, because she never hurt me. She always talked and explained everything to me in a soft voice, comforting me in the process; and because of that, I learned to trust her completely. It wasn't long and Lauren was training me and riding me around the farm, much to the disgust of Angelo, the farm's trainer. Angelo was in control of every horse on the farm, but me, and this angered him to no end. Unfortunately, I would soon find out this would only be the beginning of Angelo's anger.

The older I got, the more I saw of Roberta. Roberta was forty five years old but looked much younger. She was a pretty woman who stood about 5'3", with long blonde hair and a pretty smile, who always dressed in pretty clothes and smelled nice. People said she crashed the "Good Old Boys Club" years ago when she inherited the farm and business upon her father's death. When she began this new career more than fifteen years ago, it was unheard of for a woman to breach the all-male world of horse racing, yet be as dominant in the sport as she was. When she would look back on her and her family's time in the business, she was always proud of an unblemished record in an arena where various forms of corruption had landed others in prison, or perhaps even worse, brought down their family and their farm. She was smart enough to know that it took generations to build a reputation and vast family fortune, and she also knew that it only took one mistake to bring it all down. She blames simple greed and compromising professional ethics for the corruption that took over the industry and not only felt a watchdog agency should have been put in place years ago, but she lobbied for it as often as she could. She was a feminist in every sense of the word and surrounded herself with women who were smart and independent. Consequently, the most important positions on the farm were filled by women with the exception of her trainer, whom she inherited with the farm. Angelo had worked here for years and she felt morally obligated to keep him on, even though his soiled reputation was voiced to her by her father before his death.

She has barreled through one gender barrier after another, but never lost her femininity. Today she stands in front of me clad in white casual slacks, a tight powder blue cashmere sweater, a white silk scarf, and a pair of white Gucci pumps. Her long hair has a stylish coiffure with finger nails that are always manicured and her figure was one that a twenty year old would have envied. She is unapologetically feminine, but yet determined and quite sure of herself. Roberta was the only child of John and Cheryl Windsor and had attended Vanderbilt University in nearby Tennessee when she was young, majoring in Business. She was a shrewd businesswoman and had a prior history of working in the banking business and subsequently made a fortune in the stock market, chasing IPO's, as she had connections on Wall Street and the business world. Later on, she became the Vice-President of the Federal Depository in Atlanta, before she inherited the farm, which was an appointed job from the then current administration in Washington. These positions of prominence came along because of her father's influence in the political world; (he was the Governor of Kentucky for eight years when she was a child.) Because of that, she associated with big-wigs from every facet of business and had many friends in high places. She used to tell Lauren that racing was a business too, not a hobby, and that she shouldn't get too attached to "that horse." You see, Lauren told me Roberta was raised on the farm as a young child with beef and horses. She said her dad would always tell her, "Don't ever get attached to something you might have to sell or eat." So when Roberta used to call me "that horse," I didn't really know what she meant. I actually thought Lauren and I were friends and we were just having fun every day, kind of growing up together. I knew Lauren simply loved spending time with me and beating everybody, like I did, when I ran. I also knew in my heart that my relationship with Lauren was more than business, no matter what Roberta said; we were friends. In conversation, Roberta was terse but eloquent. She was raised "old school." If she looked you in the eye and shook your hand, it was as good as a contract.

Her secretary, Pam, was always at her side, always taking notes, always recording my progress and the other horses on the farm's progress too; she was a walking computer before computers were invented. Pam was taller than Roberta, standing around five foot eleven with brown eyes, long straight brownish-blond hair, and very classy looking. She, too, was always dressed up nice and was soft spoken. She was of Italian and Irish heritage and was also very business-oriented. When Roberta would be out of town on business, Pam would take over the operations of the farm and have Lauren run me and exercise me. When we were done, she'd stop at my stall and give me some carrots too; I really loved those carrots, they were so sweet and tasty. Pam, though classy as she was, drove a beat up and noisy gold colored 66' Mustang that had sentimental value to her; she said her dad gave it to her before he died. You always knew it was her when she'd drive up. It had a hole in the muffler and the exhaust would bellow out blue and smelly smoke. When people would tell her to restore it, she would frown and say she wanted to leave it the way her father gave it to her. She too had values.

"Mom and me in the pasture"

Lauren was very popular and had a lot of girl friends. On many a weekend, they would come over and have a sleep-over in my stall.

Gina and Tawnee lived next door on a huge horse farm, while Andrea and Jennine lived on a large horse farm across the street. Brittany was younger than the rest of them and lived on another farm a few miles down the road. They all had a lot in common; they were all raised on a horse farm and had gone through 4-H together, as well as elementary school and high school. To say they were privileged would be an understatement, as all their parents were well off. The girls would play the radio, eat s'mores and laugh and talk girl talk all night. They would put their sleeping bags on the cedar chips that covered the floor of my stall and depending on how many girls stayed over, sometimes the stall would be completely full. That was saying a lot, because I had a large stall. When they got tired of talking and listening to music, the girls, their horses and I, would all go for a long walk under the bright moonlight, just walking and talking. Because all of her friends lived close by and each one owned their own horse, they all rode their horse over for the sleep-over, and would board them in the large barn next to mine. Even at night the farm was beautiful, with the bright moonlight glowing off of the white stately fences that framed the dark blue grass and stately magnolias and oaks, looking much like a framed picture. We'd slowly walk the paths of the shadowed woods in a long line, while the girls talked and digested the quiet and peacefulness the forest bestowed. I was Lauren's prize possession and she spent a lot of time with me, even when she had company.

On my first birthday, Lauren surprised me with an adorable baby goat to keep me company, which she named Winnie. Winnie had soft white curly fur and was full of energy. Winnie used to talk to me all the time, bleating and bleating; though I didn't understand her, it was great having a real companion in my stall, because I used to hate being alone at night. The night had never been my friend, it brought out an eerie loneliness that for some reason haunted me. Winnie always enjoyed the sleep-over when we had them too. The girls always pampered her and brought her treats of fresh produce that she really enjoyed. A pretty black tuxedo cat named Princess stayed in my stall during the day light hours too, but she would always be gone hunting at night, so Winnie's company was a blessing. And even though there were 47 other horses in my barn, some of which were my mother and three brothers and one sister, I felt much more relaxed and happy with

Winnie in my stall. We enjoyed each other's closeness, often lying against each other when we slept. Winnie's name was supposed to be short for winning. With Lauren still in high school, my little friend made it more comfortable for me on a daily basis too. Not only would she sleep next to me at night, we would always eat together too; she was a great companion. When I would walk out to my paddock in the morning, she would always follow me. I think she thought I was her mother, because she was so young when Lauren bought her and gave her to me. Because of that, we connected and bonded very early.

"My friend Winnie"

I grew strong quickly and when I was about a year and a half old they brought me down to the track for the first time and let me run the practice oval where Mom and Dad used to train. The farm was huge and the race track we practiced on was a real one mile race track. It also had a small grandstand area where visitors and the press could watch. They started me off trotting at first, and after a couple of weeks I was running short sprints of about 2-400 yards. After a couple of months and after my muscles began to develop, I became much stronger and was learning to run around the oval, instead of just running in a straight line. Lauren insisted on being my rider and we got to be great together. She knew I liked to set my own pace, so she never pushed me. I also appreciated her kindness and understanding when we ran, because she never hit me with the whip like I saw other jockeys do to their rides. I could tell she really loved me as she treated me very kindly; she really did make me feel like I was hers and this only made me want to do my best for her. Roberta and Angelo, at first, wanted to put an experienced jockey on me, but Lauren insisted that she could ride me and being Lauren was her only daughter, Lauren often got her way. She was a little smaller than the jockeys in our stable, but very head strong and just as tough. All of the other horses had a groomer, but Lauren not only was my jockey, she was my groomer too. I looked forward to her daily visits and the way she pampered me, always bathing me and brushing me after a workout or walk. Her voice was always very soft and comforting; I never saw her get angry at anyone and she was always calm around me, talking to me in a soft whisper when she spoke. She used to take me for casual rides every day when she got home from school, often visiting her girlfriends, Tawnee and Gina, who lived on an adjacent farm. Tawnee went to school with Lauren and they would visit each other often. She was small and pretty like Lauren, with long black hair and green eyes. She rode a white Arabian mare that was twenty years old and was quite easy going; her mare reminded me of my mom. The mare's name was Lady Light and she treated me like a daughter, always telling me what I should look out for when we walked through the woods, as there were copperhead snakes in the area and they were very poisonous. I was much taller than she was, but she could tell that I was part Arabian because of my erect head and tail when I walked. I told her my mom was Arabian too, which endeared her to me even more. We looked almost regal together when we walked together, side by side.

"The Practice Oval"

Gina was about five foot two and had brown eyes with long and curly strawberry blond hair. She was a year older than Tawnee and Lauren and attended college at Cal Poly, San Luis Obispo, studying Animal Husbandry. She wanted to be a veterinarian, specializing in race horses, as her mom and dad raised race horses too. Gina rode an older roan Quarter Horse gelding that was about sixteen hands high; his name was Checkers and he was an ex-race horse too. Since she attended school in California, she was only home for the summer months and the holidays. And when she was home, she often spent time with her boyfriend Joe, who also lived down the road.

Tawnee and Gina had an older brother named Bryan, whom Lauren had a crush on for years. I think that was one of the reasons we ventured over to their farm so often. He was a star football player at the State University and came home every weekend that he wasn't playing an away game. He was very handsome, tall and rugged looking, and had brown hair and brown eyes. Although they had known each other since childhood, Bryan and Lauren had been dating for only a couple of months. They spent a lot of time with each other every weekend and corresponded by phone every night. Bryan would often come to my paddock with Lauren when he was in town and we would often go for long walks together. Bryan's parents owned the adjacent farm and Bryan would ride a Thoroughbred gelding of a chestnut color. His name was Star and we got along fine; the geldings had no interest in me, and I none in them. Lauren would look forward to each weekend, but I didn't, mainly because Bryan would take her away from me sometimes. You see, Bryan had a pilot's license and would often take Lauren on small trips out of town for the weekend. You know; day trips. On some weekends they would disappear completely, and on others, Bryan and she would spend the entire weekend with me. I never knew what to expect.

FRIENDS IN LOW PLACES

Angelo, an ex-jockey of Italian descent, instructed Lauren on riding me and had a dubious history, to say the least. He was the farm's head trainer and had worked here for quite a while, originally hired years ago by John Windsor, Roberta's father. He was my dad's trainer too, when Dad won the Triple Crown ten years ago. Angelo was about 60 years now, old, thin and wiry, and originally came from Palermo, Sicily. He wasn't very dark, as some Italians are, and said he got his blue eyes and light skin from his mother, who came from a small town outside of Milan in northern Italy. I once overheard him say that his family was in the Sicilian Mafia and his dad was a Don and a real power freak. The money meant nothing to his dad; it was all about control. He controlled everything, everything from his family to the docks and shorelines of Italy.

He talked about his father a lot. In fact, I overheard and learned many things about Angelo while he talked to the groomers and jockeys around me. On this one particular occasion, Angelo's roots and heritage were discussed, as he was proud of his heritage and the country he came from. He practically divulged his life history, rambling on and on for hours it seemed. I heard him say his father Pasquale, amongst many things, was a slightly built man and drove a black Cadillac sedan that was given to him by Sammy "The Nose" Luccido, his close friend and ally in New York. Owning a Cadillac was a big deal in Sicily in the thirties, as there weren't any American cars there at all, yet a big Cadillac. It was all decked out with concealed bullet proof armor plating and bullet proof glass. Sammy took good care of Pasquale, mainly because Don Pasquale Raffaniello was the main supplier of Luccido's Olive Oil importing business in the states.

You might say Don Pasquale was a "Mustache Pete," a name given to Mafia members from the old school. He was a true Sicilian and took "Omerta," the vows of silence, very seriously and would die before giving up anything to the authorities.

While I stood there snacking on my oats, they talked about Sicily and the mob a lot. Sicily was originally a dumping ground for criminals from the mainland of Italy, much like Australia was the dumping ground for Great Britain's criminals. This "dumping" of criminals on the island of Sicily led to street gangs and later La Cosa Nostra, or the "Black Hand," as the locals called it. In America, La Cosa Nostra was substituted for "this thing of ours." Sicily in those days was not only the main supplier of olive oil to the mob in America, but it supplied them with "soldiers" too. And because of these commodities, the New York mobs fought over both the imported oil and the importation of soldiers with the Chicago mob for years. The Mafia wasn't a decorated street gang; it was very structured and set their regime up like the Roman legions of their fore fathers years ago. There were the bosses (Dons), the capos (Captains), and the soldiers. And unlike street gangs, members of the Mafia were liked by the local populace and were looked upon as noble rogues because they took care of their own. They protected the people who were down trodden with nowhere to go for help, as all municipalities were corrupted, and they provided services that weren't readily available, some of which were illegal. Of course, with these "favors" came an indebtedness that never could be paid off, thus becoming parasites to their own people. Doing "favors" wasn't personal, it was just "business" to them.

He said because of the power and influence he had in Palermo, Pasquale was forced to fight over the lucrative olive oil exporting business in Italy and all of the other fingers of crime that the Mafia controlled there, including the ports, booze, drugs, and prostitution. Because of the ongoing war on his family's home turf in Sicily, Angelo had to eventually leave after there were a rash of killings in his small town of Ciccio that eventually threatened him and his family. Car bombings were a very popular tool the Mafia used for eliminating their foe and obtaining justice, as well as executions, which were mostly carried out with a garrote, up close and personal, or from a distance with a sawed off Barretta. You see, shock and awe originated in Sicily years ago and found its way to the streets of America with Mafia immigrants in the twenties and thirties.

He bragged that retaliation was a common practice in the Mafia, and if you were on their horizon, no one got a pass. So on a hot and sunny Sicilian summer morning, Angelo and his mother unfortunately witnessed his older brother's death in a car bombing outside their church. He said after Sunday Mass was over, his older brother Matteo went to retrieve his vehicle, in order to drive around the front of the church to pick up Angelo and his mother. Matteo was in his twenties and had been running the docks of Palermo for his father and was being groomed to take over his father's operations some day. Because of this, he had acquired many enemies, as Palermo was the biggest port in Sicily at the time and many goods shipped in and out of there.

The church of Santa Lucia was over four hundred years old and was situated on a hillside overlooking the town of Palermo, in the southern part of Sicily. It was made of white adobe and red tiled roof with antique stained and arched glass windows. Tall Italian cypress trees dotted the arid and rocky terrain around it and parking was down the hill from the church on a flat cobble stone area. Parishioners were walking down the cobbled path to the small town when Matteo turned the key to start his Fiat, the blast from the explosion instantly splitting him in two. The enormous blast threw his torso into power lines that were suspended above the street and blew out the stained glass windows on the church, one hundred yards away, his legs and feet remaining in the car. The blast was so powerful, people standing one hundred feet away were knocked down, and no blood was found in the car or dripping from his body; it was simply vaporized by the sudden heat of the blast. Flies had already begun to feed on his body in the sweltering heat, when his upper body was removed from the power lines. After seeing the carnage, a broken Don Pasquale took him to an undertaker in town that owed Don Pasquale a favor. The undertaker tried in vain to repair the damages to his face so that Matteo's mother could see him one more time before he went away. But this was to no avail, as the blast made Matteo unrecognizable and he had to be in a closed casket at his funeral, much to the dismay and sadness of his mother.

Pasquale felt a terrible remorse for not allowing Matteo to take his armored Cadillac to church that day and instantly vowed revenge for the death of his oldest son. This started a Mafia war in Sicily that would never actually be settled, as each side would retaliate for each new death that occurred, essentially creating a revolving door of death, carnage, and revenge. Because of her oldest son's death, Angelo's mother Josephina pleaded with Pasquale to hide Angelo, fearing the death of her only remaining son, her "bambino." Pasquale then arranged for Angelo and three body guards to hide out with some friends and relatives in the rugged but picturesque hillsides of Apecchio until things cooled down. The mob couldn't get to Pasquale, as he was surrounded by a contingent of body guards at all times, so the best way to hurt Don Pasquale was to kill his sons. As is the practice in the Mafia, this type of behavior only extended their war and the ensuing bloodshed for many years to come; after all, vendetta is an Italian word and has been carried out for years.

Apecchio is located in northeastern Italy, hundreds of miles from Sicily and half way between picturesque and historical Florence and the Adriatic Sea. It is quietly nestled in the southern foothills of the Italian Alps, far removed from the hot, rugged and dry Sicilian town he was brought up in. It is a pretty town with meandering rivers that wind down from the surrounding rugged limestone and basalt mountains and pass gently through the center of town. The town was originally founded around the river about 900AD and is very remote with only one highway feeding it, essentially one way in and one way out. It also has no access to the complex rail system that serves most of Europe and Italy, making it all the more unreachable and inaccessible. Because of the hilly terrain and the cool winter climate, it is a wonderful place to grow truffles and is known as the Truffle Capital of Italy, drawing tourists from all over the world at harvest time.

Pasquale knew a wealthy Swiss family living in Florence that owed him a favor; the Mafia existed on "favors." The Gustafson's also owned a small Villa in nearby Apecchio where Angelo was welcome and could lay low for a while. Pasquale and Otto Gustafson had history together and were "business" partners years ago; they used to control the Port of Gioia Tauro. Pasquale supplied the muscle and Otto was the Consiglieri for the Don; he supplied the brains. The port of Gioia Tauro is located on one of the busiest maritime corridors in the world and is on the route midway from the Suez Canal and the Strait of Gibraltar in the Mediterranean Sea. It is located on the "toe" of the foot of Italy, right across from the Island of Sicily and is the main harbor on the Mediterranean for imports of all goods entering Italy and southern Europe.

During a fight over control of the Port, Otto was subsequently killed in a car bombing by the orders of a Mafia chieftain from Naples. The mere fact Otto was Swiss, and not Italian, made him an "Associate," and not a member of the mob. This fact contributed heavily to his death, as well the fact there was a war over control of the Port and the surrounding area and Otto played a big role managing stolen cargo there. Upon his death, Otto left his wife Inga the Villa in Apecchio and a vineyard outside of Florence, which she and her daughters visit regularly. Don Pasquale had been taking care of the Gustafson family since Otto's death, which is Mafia tradition; they always took care of their own. Inga Gustafson was now a widowed woman with three beautiful daughters, one of which Angelo subsequently fell in love with during his short stay there. Her name was Morgan and he talked about her all the time. She was eighteen at the time and had beautiful Swedish features; beautiful long blond hair with big, wide, blue eyes, a chiseled face, with high cheek bones and a tanned gorgeous figure.

He had to abruptly leave her behind when the La Costa Nostra got wind of his mountain location and closed in on him, with them actually killing one of his bodyguards one day when he was sent into town for groceries. Someone had actually hid on the floor of the backseat of his car and used a garrote on him when he entered the car and sat down. His windshield was kicked out from his violent struggle and his head was almost decapitated from the force applied to his neck from the garrote, which was composed of piano wire attached to two wooden handles. After that occurred, Angelo had orders from his father to leave the town immediately. And so, on the eve before his departure, he and Morgan went for a long walk in the mountains with his remaining two armed bodyguards accompanying them. They walked closely behind them with sawed off Berettas, scanning the rocky landscape as they walked. Angelo and Morgan nervously strolled the bright moon-lit and rocky hillside of Apecchio for over an hour and promised each other their undying and everlasting love. They both cried on each other's shoulder as Angelo promised her he'd return soon to get her and bring her to America. But he had no choice but to leave, because In Italy you can run a long distance and you can still be in the crosshairs of a gun.

As the Mafia tightly closed their grips on the area, he said he was forced to flee the town under the cover of night and was brought to the Port of Naples under armed guard, where he anonymously purchased a ticket on the Andria Doria. He said at the time, the Andria Doria was a large Italian Liner as luxurious as the Queen Mary. As the ship left the harbor, he stood on deck and sadly watched the hills of Naples disappear in the distance. He soon passed the Isle of Capri on his way to the Mediterranean and had a tear in his eye; he thought of Morgan and his family and didn't know if he would ever be able to return to his beautiful girlfriend and country. He was eighteen now and because he was seeking to downplay his status and notoriety, he rode in the steerage section of the large ocean liner with poor Italians seeking to become immigrants in America. Steerage was located in the bottom of the ship and he said it was very hot and humid and stunk of body odor, as steerage occupants were considered low class and didn't have access to showers or other luxuries as the other passengers. They had no access to the rest of the ship at all and their food was actually brought down to the steerage area on a dumbwaiter. The area where they were housed was next to the boiler room of the ship, which also contributed to the noise, heat and humidity they experienced. He also had to sleep in a large dorm like room, full of bunk beds stacked close to each other with no privacy and little space for moving around. He said they were treated like cattle and occupied a part of the ship that nobody else wanted, but he chose it to keep a low profile.

He said he had ample time to think about his fate while crossing the Atlantic. He spent most of his time in a top bunk just staring at the ceiling and the hot steam filled heating ducts that were exposed. He knew what he was leaving behind, but was unsure of his future. Oh, he knew where he was going alright, but he had never been to America and didn't know what obstacles lie before him; in fact he had never been out of Italy. He was only eighteen and would miss his mother, as they had been very close, but it was better to miss her than to die in Sicily. His father wanted him to lay low for a while and come back to "learn" the trade. But after seeing eighteen years of violence, Angelo made a conscious decision to forego that lifestyle. He had enough confidence in himself and would make his own way.

After a long and sweltering two week journey across the Mediterranean and the Atlantic, he was finally allowed up on deck. He saw the Statue of Liberty peering out from the foggy waters of gigantic New York Harbor as they approached the Island, with the busy bustling city in the background, and was in awe. It was the first time he had been up on the deck since he boarded the ship two weeks ago and he really enjoyed the fresh air. He watched the busy happenings of the tug boats in the bay and reflected on the quiet but dangerous life he left behind. After finally landing on Ellis Island in New York, he said he was at first treated badly upon entering America, as most Italians and eastern Europeans were in those days. He said that when he gave his name to the immigration officer at the desk, it was shortened because the man was too lazy to write it down. His real name was Ricardo Angelo Raffaneillo, but it was changed to Angelo Raffello. After hearing his name spoken, he said he incredulously looked at the immigration officer and spoke in Italian.

"That's not my name! Why are you doing this to me?"

"It is now dago," he said, having heard this before from other Italians. "Move it on or I'll call the Police," said the officer in English, with a rudeness implying he had apparently done this many times before.

This was a cultural collision and it came hard to Angelo, as he only spoke Italian, so he didn't get very far with his argument. Changing names was common practice at Ellis Island then, as he would learn, as the immigration officers had no respect for southern Europeans, and because of that, many names were changed. Upon entry, the immigrants were also looked down upon and often had to take work that no one else wanted. Work was hard to come by in the late twenties and early thirties, as America was going through the Great Depression at the time and all foreigners were deeply resented. No one wanted to lose their job, especially to an immigrant. There were very few opportunities for young Italian or Irish immigrants then; you either became a gangster, a priest, or a cop.

He told the groomer Sammy "The Nose" met him at Ellis Island and immediately took him under his wing. Sammy was a big player in New York, running one of the five New York families that controlled the area. The government inadvertently made him and other gangsters rich by passing the Prohibition Act in 1919, thus making it illegal for the public to buy alcohol. Because of this law, bootleggers became popular and rich by providing the outlawed service, running Canadian Scotch and English Whiskey out of Canada and filling the "Speak Easy's" with booze and entertainment. The twenties and thirties were the "Golden Era" of crime in America and the money they derived from bootlegging made the mob strong. This was also the time of "Murder Incorporated," the enforcing faction of the mob. They ultimately ended up controlling the docks, the unions, city construction contracts, trucking, Race Tracks, gambling and the Boxing Commission. As an example, if you owned a company and didn't play along, you weren't awarded the contract and if you were a boxer and didn't play along with them, you would never get a title shot. Because of the inordinate sums of money the mob brought in, they also controlled the Police, Politicians and Judges. It was also rumored that J. Edgar Hoover was a cross-dresser and the mob had photographs of him in compromising positions, thus blackmailing him. This contributed greatly to their success because Hoover denied the existence of the Mafia to the day he died and left them completely alone.

It was Sammy's obligation to shelter Don Pasquale's son in America, but Angelo wanted no part of the underworld and its way of life. He turned down the job of running numbers and wanted a real job, a job with no mob influence. He saw enough of that life style in Sicily; after all, he knew number running was the first rung on the ladder of crime and only led to theft, larceny, and murder. Numbers running, or "the bug" as the locals called it, was actually a lottery before the lottery became legalized. You bet any amount of money on three numbers which were derived from adding the winning times at all of the race tracks on the east coast. It could be a nickel or a dollar or more; it didn't matter; the Mafia took it all. You could also "box" it, which meant any combination of the three numbers you selected could win, but of course if you "boxed" it, the odds of winning were greater and your winnings would be less. For example a horse won in a time of 1:34 minutes at Aqueduct Race Track in New York in the first race. That was only one winning time of one race at one track. All times and all races from eastern race tracks were totaled with the last three digits, say 742 being the total for the days' race times. People would bet at their local bar, card club or grocery store, anything from a nickel on up. Bets and winnings would be collected and paid out daily by the number runner; the mob always made good on your winnings. They looked at themselves as friends to the community, providing services that everyone wanted but was against the law. Since the mob controlled the tracks and controlled the jockeys, they also controlled the winning numbers. Numbers running was only the beginning of the food chain for a mobster. "Thanks, but no thanks," he told Sammy. Angelo wanted no part of "The Life," as made members called it; he saw enough of that in Sicily, where it all started and where crime ran rampant. What they were doing in New York was child's play compared to home; after all, Sicily was where the Mafia was started. Luccido was initially upset at Angelo's attitude, but said he understood, even though he had promised Don Pasquale that he would look after his boy.

With virtually no money in his pocket, he soon left the protection of the Don and soon found himself stranded and sleeping on the streets of Bensonhurst in Brooklyn. Bensonhurst was also known as "Little Italy" and was comprised mostly of Italian and Jewish immigrants at the time. Brooklyn, as a whole, was a large melting pot of nationalities from all over the world, but was comprised mostly of Europeans and Chinese at the time, each living in their own segregated area, each sheltered and comfortable with their own people. They had their own churches, grocery stores, newspapers, and even radio stations that catered to them. However, nobody catered to them when they went to work or school; they either learned English or they didn't get plugged into the system.

They talked about New York like he was there yesterday. Adjacent to Bensonhurst, in Brooklyn, was Hell's Kitchen, where the Irish mob ruled. They were called the "Westies," and under Mickey Spillane, were in direct competition with the Italian mob. And although competition for the dollar was tough, they mostly respected each other and left each other alone. The main difference between the two was the Italian mob killed for "business" reasons, while the Irish mob killed for money. None entered the other's territory.

After a few days passed and Angelo didn't return, Luccido got worried about Angelo and sent out some of his cronies to look for him. He was hard to find, mainly because he moved around so much. Some nights he would sleep in a vacant house and some nights he would search for a car that had been unlocked and slept inside. After touching base with their contacts, they subsequently found him sleeping with some bums in the subway near Manhattan. Luccido took him in and offered him a job at a local horse racing track that the mob controlled, with the caveat that he could come back any time he pleased. You see, in the back of his mind, Luccido figured Angelo would soon tire of working for beans and come running back. But Angelo was a hard worker and very persistent, getting his first job mucking stables at a New York race track and making the best of it. Angelo's main goal was to be respectable and earn enough money to send for Morgan; he simply didn't want the life style of Luccido or his father and didn't find the job of mucking stables beneath him. Seeing his brother get ripped in half and the agony his mother went through was the last straw for him.

Angelo said he also had some experience with horses, having raced horses through the cobbled streets of Palermo, Sicily on Saturday nights for money. Sicily at the time was a very poor island with no race track and very few amenities, so horse racing was done through the streets of town. Racing through the streets of Palermo was much like from the wild, wild, west in America and was a source of gambling revenue for the Mafia and of course recreation for the locals, which they were always happy to provide. In addition to collecting revenue from the race, the Mafia would sell liquor, drugs and women; at the end of the night everyone was happy, except for maybe the women.

He liked his job at the track, figuring if he worked hard enough he would improve his station there and perhaps race some day. But respectability came slow to Angelo in America, however, mainly because Luccido just didn't control the race tracks, he controlled the trainers and the jockeys too. After gradually working his way up in the stables from mucking, Angelo started grooming and walking the horses, and then much later on he learned to ride professionally and finally became a jockey. Luccido was instrumental in getting Angelo his first ride and started visiting him more often after that, thus starting a new career. The career came with "favors" owed to Don Luccido, of course; favors that can be cashed in at any time or whenever the Don desired. As he soon found out, being a jockey wasn't as wonderful as he thought it would be, mainly because the mob virtually controlled the outcome of every race and the "favor" that The Don granted when he got him his first ride would never be repaid. You see when a "favor" is granted by the Don, paying it off could go on forever.

He said the mob controlled the outcome of a race like this. The betting windows were closed as the horses came onto the track and slowly walked to the starting gate. Slowly is the imperative word here. After spending a little time on an adding machine, they knew which horse had the most money bet on it and the number of the horse they wanted to win would be flashed down or radioed down to the steward on the track bringing up the last horse to the gate; that's why it takes so long to get to the gate once the windows are closed. The steward would simply call out the number to the jockeys in their gate instructing them on who was to win; "number four," for example.

All the other jockeys would hear it and would play along with the outcome, always making it look interesting. You played along, or if you didn't play along and you were lucky, you just got hurt; it was that simple. It was the old story of silver or lead that got its start in ancient Rome; you take the bribe or you take the bullet. You couldn't use your skill as a jockey, but instead you'd have to play along with the outcome. This outcome was controlled by doping the horses or threatening the jockeys and trainers, either way the gambling stakes for each race were controlled and essentially earned the mob millions each year just at the track. There was also collateral income derived from off-track betting at every bar and nightclub that the Mafia controlled, years before off-track betting became legalized. If you didn't play along, you could get hurt real bad, as it was very difficult to ride a thoroughbred with a broken arm or a deformed leg. That was your first occurrence. The second time you just disappeared, it was just business to them; "you took a trip."

Boxing was also controlled in this manner, only with different players. You paid off the trainer and the fighter. As a special precaution, in case the fighter's ego got in the way, you'd pay off a judge or two. All championship fights were handled in this way and still are. If you didn't play along, you'd never see a title shot. Hearing this scared me. "What did he mean by "doping" the horses? Is he going to dope me too," I thought.

Then he said years went by before he refined his trade, and thanks to Sammy, became very successful in the process. Sammy was never very far removed from his life, however, and earned him good money on the side, getting him rides at the tracks he controlled with Angelo returning the favor by losing a race every now and then that he was favored to win. When he was thirty and had been a successful jockey for six years, he unfortunately broke his hip, falling in a horse race at Hollywood Park, California. He was thrown from his falling horse and run over by a following horse, almost crippling him for life. Unfortunately, he wasn't able to return to Apecchio until after the operation and physical therapy were completed and he was doing better. Because of this injury and the time it took to save enough money for his trip to Apecchio, plus the length of World War II, which occurred shortly after, a long twelve years had gone by since he left Morgan and a longer four years since he last communicated with her.

When the war ended and he finally returned to Apecchio, he said he was shocked to find out that Morgan was killed in an air raid bombing of her hometown during the war. They had always corresponded by mail, but when the war began, Mussolini put an end to the mail service, making it four long years that he hadn't heard from her. And because of the War, he had to delay his trip to pick up Morgan too. It was unsafe to cross the Atlantic during World War II, as U-Boats were sinking everything, including hospital and cruise ships. When he received the bad news of Morgan's death; he went to her family's Mausoleum on a barren windy bluff, overlooking the Mediterranean, and knelt and wept for hours. He kicked himself in the teeth for not getting there before the war started and vowed to her his undying love and hoped that they would be together again someday. Her family told him that Morgan loved him dearly and had only lived and prayed for his return. It broke his heart, to this day, as he still thinks about his love that got away and the innocent beauty of their short relationship. You see, he remembers her as a teen, young, beautiful and vibrant, the way he saw her last on that beautiful moonlit night in Apecchio. I think the combination of her untimely death and his debilitating injury made him very mean and resentful. He had tragically lost his first true love and he was unfortunately taken off the track while he was still in his prime, a profession that he loved. When he lost his job and lost his love, he submissively fell into the intricate web the mob created.

Because of his misfortunes, he always languished in the past, always telling me stories about the fast horses he rode, always telling me I wouldn't and couldn't measure up to them. He was very tough on me at times, pushing me, pushing me, pushing me, and I would learn to hate it when he was there, as I would only listen to Lauren. This often infuriated him beyond his self control, as he had a short fuse anyhow and he drank a lot. He would often yell at me for no reason at all, with Lauren catching him yelling at me sometimes. She then would argue with him about his behavior towards me. She would comfort me and tell me not to worry and to pay him no mind as he was jealous of her relationship with me, mainly because she got more out of me than he was getting out of the horses he trained. I was always the fastest of the horses that raced on the farm, and was never pushed by Lauren, while he pushed his horses and jockey's relentlessly. For some reason, it was not uncommon to see one of the horse's Angelo trained hurt or lame.

MY TEENAGE YEARS

I eventually started racing against other fillies and mares on the farm's oval and I always won. The two older brothers and younger sister I had were beaten too; they never were happy about that. Showing off and rearing up after every race became common, as I would proudly kick my front legs high in the air. The first time I reared up Lauren got really afraid and almost fell off of me. I didn't mean to scare her like I did, but the act really surprised her by me doing it without warning. Each time I won after that, I would rear up with Lauren gradually becoming accustomed to it. Eventually, Lauren actually grew to like it too, because she knew I liked to flaunt our victories. It was almost as if I was saying; "Hey, look at me! I'm the alpha female here!"

"I should have known you'd do something like that; I remember your dad did the same thing after every race he won too. I should have been more prepared; it must be in your genes. You know, your dad was one special horse. He lit the candle here and started it all. He's the one who made this farm famous." Lauren said.

"My Dad"

My big moment came when I was two years old. Every race horse has a birthday on the following January 1ˢᵗ, no matter what part of the year you were born. That is how they set up races for two year olds, three year olds, etc. It supposedly equalizes everything and simplifies everything for the races and titles. I was to race in a "Maiden" race against other two year olds, all fillies, and had run many times around the practice oval preparing for this event. I found out we would have to fly to New York for the race and being enclosed in that big silver plane scared me to death.

Most race horses are "shipped" by air to the race tracks. Lauren said that shipping is very stressful to the horse and there are various ways to ship them. She said some are enclosed in crates, or air-stables, and put on the plane with a hydraulic lift. The more fortunate horses are shipped in built in stalls on the plane, often with cedar chips or hay to lie on, proper blanketing, and their own groomer; the experience is to replicate home as much as possible. Each can contain one to three horses and an area for the groomer. Either way, a groomer must accompany the horse because a horse can become claustrophobic and go berserk. The noise and vibration of the plane is stressful to the horse, as well as the enclosed environment. She said that in 1960, a horse named Markham had to be destroyed in flight on the way to the Rome Olympics. She said most planes used for horse transportation have a loaded gun on board too, just in case something like this happens. A large horse can endanger everyone's safety and cause panic in the other horses on board. Although euthanasia is rare, nevertheless, sometimes there is no other choice. It is better to sacrifice one horse than risk the safety of the airplane, as a large horse is very powerful and can do a lot of damage. When she told me about the gun, I got scared to death.

Lauren said even though horses are shipped this way, we had our own plane. It was a DC-3, one of the most reliable planes ever built. It was bought and paid for by my dad, who made millions for the farm. It had seating above for thirty people and an area below, in the cargo section, designed to replicate our barn at home. There was also a medicine cabinet for equine first aid, as the farm's vet traveled with the horse too. She usually sat above in the coach section and would be called below if needed. Roberta liked to flaunt her entry to the airports race tracks, and would usually fill the plane with staff and friends.

I didn't know what it was when I was led up to it; it was huge and shiny, with the sun glistening off of it, and very loud, hurting my ears. It was cold and dark as I was led inside and it made so much noise, a noise I had never heard before, a noise that droned loudly and wouldn't go away. The noise just went on and on and really bothered my sensitive ears. Lauren insisted that Winnie come with me and stay with me, much to the disapproval of Roberta, but her presence helped me relax and feel much more comfortable, and she knew that. Lauren wanted to stay with us too, much to Roberta's chagrin, so we all lay down in an enclosed stall with a big bed of fresh cedar chips while we flew. As we laid there, Lauren laid her head on my neck and comforted me as she talked about our upcoming race and what we had to do when we landed and what we had to do when we got to the track. She covered all of us in a warm blanket, because it was very cold in the plane and the blanket helped calm me because I was tense too. She talked about a lot of things while we flew and seemed to confide in me about the current gossip on the farm and her private moments too. Bryan's name would always come up, as she loved him dearly. It made me a little jealous sometimes, but I liked Bryan too. He always treated me nice. She would just talk and talk as she believed I understood; little did she know that I did understand. I understood everything. Winnie would just stare at her and listen, letting out an occasional bleat. Everything was going fine, but little did I know that things would soon change.

And change they did. The plane trip took almost three hours and I was more than glad when we got there. It was cold and raining in New York when we landed and the sky was gray and dreary and looked smoky, a bitter smoke that partially hid the tops of the tall surrounding buildings. I found out later, while listening to others talk, that it looked smoky because it was smog, a word I never heard before in the pristine hills of Kentucky. Oh, we had fog in Lexington, a light hazy mist that enveloped the white rail fences and looked beautiful from the top of the hill with the tall magnolias and oaks protruding from it, but this stuff smelled nasty. Upon landing, we were picked up at the airport by a special trailer and taken through the busy freeways and traffic to Belmont Park. I could smell the dirty air as we drove to the race track grounds and didn't like it at all. It was so different from Kentucky's clean air and the beautiful countryside I just came from. The air actually made my eyes water and it burned my lungs when I would breathe. I don't know why, but there was just something about New York I didn't like. It just wasn't the noise, depressing weather, and the biting air that bothered me, it was deeper than that, but I couldn't figure it out. The aura of it haunted me the whole time I was there with a feeling I couldn't forget. It was almost as if something overshadowed me and hung over me like a pendulum, getting closer and closer, a feeling that wouldn't let me rest while I was there.

When we arrived at the race track, they put me and Winnie in a stall next to horses I had never seen before, horses from all over the east coast. I learned that they were all here to race too. I was surprised that Lauren stayed with us through the night, but I was happy too. I was in a strange place for the first time in my life and I nervously paced my enclosure while she tried to soothe me with her quiet words.

The next morning Lauren rode me around the track in the cold, foggy, and smoggy damp air while Angelo timed us and Roberta, Pam and Kate watched. He always had that timer with him, always yelling at us to do better. When we were done practicing, we walked past Roberta and Angelo on the way to my stable and I overheard their conversation.

Angelo was tense and wanted to approach Roberta about changing jockeys, but didn't know how to do it without offending her. He was terse and definitely lacked tact.

"I don't know Roberta; her time isn't as good as back home."

Roberta, sensing his voice fluctuation, knew what he was getting at. She had watched him during the speed trials at home and saw a sense of urgency in him. He was definitely getting to her.

"It could be the travelling or it could be the weather, but if she doesn't look good in this race, I may have to replace Lauren. She thinks this is just a hobby, but we have a lot riding on this horse's future. We'll let her run one race, and then we'll take it from there. We'll let her get it out of her system."

Hearing that, Angelo became totally relieved. This is what he's wanted from the start. He knew he could control everything if he controlled the jockey.

"It's good to hear that coming from you. I didn't want to intervene, because I knew she was your daughter, but I think I could get more out of Bell with a different jockey, somebody experienced. I think her times could be improved greatly."

"Let's see what happens here first; then I'll decide," Roberta said, as she looked him in the eye. She was very assertive and wasn't one to be rough shod over.

"You're the boss!" Angelo said, noticing her assertiveness, but then blurted out a slip of the tongue. "But what happens if she wins? I'm sorry; I mean I just want you to know I'm here for you and want the best for you. I'm ready whenever you want to make a change."

Roberta turned and stared at Angelo. She sensed something in Angelo's voice that she was wary of, but couldn't put her finger on it. She knew he wanted complete control of me, much more than just being my trainer. But he was too anxious, way too anxious. She had noticed him getting more edgy and controlling lately in their practices too and wondered why. She also remembered what her father told her about Angelo before he died. His words kept echoing in her ear.

Angelo then turned his head and saw two friends of his calling out to him. He acknowledged them and walked away with them into the crowd standing outside the barn. The racing facility was a big complex with many barns; there were also a lot of people milling around, friends of trainers, owners, gamblers, etc. He had been in the business for years and had a lot of friends at the tracks, so she thought little of it. Roberta watched him walk away and then entered my stable and told Lauren to do whatever it takes, but we would have to have better times than we were recording. I heard her and understood what she wanted, but I wasn't used to running in mud, as it was slippery and it made my feet feel very heavy. I didn't have much time to practice either, as the race was just two days away. I then heard Roberta nastily say it was going to rain all week, so we'd better get used to it or she would have a jockey from our farm ride me next time. I felt real pressure for the first time in my life, and I didn't like it. I got a knot in my stomach when I heard that because I had never seen Roberta act this way. I could see that Lauren was under pressure too, but she never said a word about it. She just comforted me and told me not to listen to them and that we were doing fine. She held my halter and looked me in the eye.

"We know more than anybody what you're capable of, so don't let them worry you. You're getting stronger every day," she said, as she stroked my neck. "They'll find that out soon."

This really motivated me to do better, because I didn't want anyone else to ride me but Lauren, and I didn't want to disappoint her either, mainly because she had so much faith in me. I wish there was a way to let her know about the conversation I overheard between Roberta and Angelo.

The time went by fast and it soon was race day. There were thirteen horses scheduled to run today, but one was scratched at the last minute, leaving twelve. It was raining very hard when we walked out on the track for the race at two o'clock that Saturday afternoon. The sky was so dark that they had the lights on, illuminating the track like daylight. The rain was coming down hard, creating large puddles on the track, impressions that the tractor had previously smoothed out. The light shining on the muddy track and puddles was like looking at a lake from afar. Belmont Park is one of the most prestigious race tracks in America, and it is here that Roberta wanted me to get my feet wet. Getting my feet wet was an understatement; I had never raced in mud before, even though I practiced in it all week. It weighed my hoofs down and it was slippery; I surely couldn't imagine running in that slime. I had never been in front of a noisy crowd before either, and I wasn't used to the continuous loud roar they expelled, but Lauren was always very comforting.

"Why are they yelling?" I thought, as I stared at the crowd and pranced to the gate, wanting to rear up. "Why are they so excited?"

She then rubbed my neck as we were led to the starting gate and whispered in my ear again.

"Summer Storm, you look great in these colors. Your dad made blue and white famous when he ran. Because of your dad, every race fan in the world knows those are the colors of our farm. Let's have a good day and make your dad proud when you get home. You've already made me proud."

I scanned the competition as we walked and noticed Lauren was the only female jockey in the race. It made me feel special again, mostly because of our close connection to each other. Lauren always used to say that I looked so proud when I walked, mainly because of my erect head, and the long mane and erect tail I inherited from my mom. When she complimented me, I raised my head and took a deep breath, flaring my nostrils. It made me even prouder and it showed in my gait. I pranced to the gate like I was invincible; at least that's how she made me feel.

"The starting gate"

As they closed the gates behind us in a driving rain, I got very nervous and tried to rear-up; I never did like being enclosed. I looked down at the slop I was standing in and tried to prepare myself for a good start. As Lauren tried to calm me, the gate slammed open with a loud noise and all the other horses were off, with me starting late and bringing up the rear.

"What a terrible way to start a racing career," I thought as Lauren whispered in my ear. I wished I hadn't got so nervous.

"Come on Summer, just settle down; I'm here with you. Let's do this; it's no different than practicing at home. Let's go baby. You can do this."

It was my fault that we had a late start and being I had never been behind in a race before at the farm I had trouble dealing with this. I now heard Roberta's voice echo through my head again: "If you don't do better, I'm going to have to put a male jockey on her next time." I didn't want that to happen. I've seen male jockeys race many times, and each one of them would flog and hit their horses with a whip, which Lauren never did. The whole field was in front of me and I was in a panic as we started passing up the other horses one by one. My eyes, nose, face and chest were getting splattered with thick and slimy mud that the other horses were kicking up in front of us as they ran. Since I had never been behind before, or ever had mud kicked in my face and eyes, I didn't like what we were experiencing at all. Not only did it make it uncomfortable to breathe, it made it very hard to see, as the mud and rain kept pelting my face as we ran. The race was only about 5.5 furlongs long, a short distance of 2/3 of a mile, mainly because all twelve of us were young and this was our first race, our Maiden Race. I gradually tracked them down and eventually passed seven horses, which were all bunched together, coming from the outside, and now there was only one horse in front of us. She was hugging the rail as we went into the stretch. The crowd got very loud as we caught her on the outside and approached the finish line. I was still behind by a half a length with only one hundred yards to go, but I was coming on strong; I was making up ground and outpacing her with every step. Lauren then rubbed my neck and whispered in my ear again as she rode.

"I love you Summer. You can do this. Come on baby. Stretch those long legs for me. Let's do it, let's do it!"

I then pinned my ears back and caught the other horse, a black filly from another farm in Lexington, passing her at the finish line and beating her in a photo finish.

This was my first official race and my first official victory. Lauren was so happy, she leaned over and hugged and kissed me with tears running down her face.

"I knew you could do it, baby; I knew you could do it! Let's see what they have to say now."

I was exhausted! I had given it everything I had to make up for my mistake at the beginning of the race. The raucous crowd continued to roar as we slowed down, with everybody standing up and clapping their hands as they yelled. We were both covered in mud, but I didn't mind it now. After a little trot in the rain to cool me off, we then walked over to the winner's circle where Roberta, Kate and Angelo were standing under umbrellas, along with a contingent of photographers busily snapping pictures of us. Roberta smiled proudly at us, while Angelo was turned around and was being interviewed by the press. As they patted him on his back, he looked happy, but a little perturbed too. I think he wanted me to lose so he would be in charge of me. Then a lady put a large ring of red roses around my neck and everybody took a lot of pictures while Lauren rubbed my neck and whispered in my ear. I felt so proud, not only for me but for Lauren too, as we both worked very hard for this, and I also felt Lauren had proved herself to Roberta and Angelo. I knew what I heard before the race and didn't know if Lauren was aware of it. I only hoped that Roberta wouldn't make a change.

After a nice warm shower and a good nights' sleep, we had to board our plane in the morning for the flight back to Lexington. It was still raining when we left and I was happy to leave it all behind; I just felt weird here for some reason. I was so glad when we got home; I really didn't understand what was going on and I was afraid Winnie and I would have to stay in New York forever. I was so happy to be home; that night I slept like a baby. I saw my mom in the pasture the day after I got back. She licked my face and nuzzled me and told me she was so proud of me. Her friends all said that I was tall like my dad and would probably win a lot of races. I soon found out that we would always have to travel in planes for the races, except when we raced at Churchill Downs in Louisville, which was just down the road from us, about an hour and a half away. But thankfully, I found out no matter where we raced, we would always come back home.

I spent most of my youthful days running, playing and grazing in the tall Kentucky bluegrass of our meadows with Winnie and my friends, who were colts and fillies my age. Some of my friends were old enough to race and were racing too, but everyone used to whisper that I had the most promise, that I was the biggest and fastest filly they had ever seen. Lauren graduated from high school that summer and visited me every morning. She would comb me, groom me, and every day we would go for a ride to see Tawnee on the farm next door. And every other day, Lauren would come to my paddock early in the morning and we would train at the racing oval with Angelo and his beloved timer. When we would go for our long rides to the neighbor's farm, Winnie would have to stay behind, which she didn't like at all. When we would return, she would ramble on and on with her bleats, always letting me know how unhappy she was to be left alone.

Roberta and her attorney, Kate, had set up a schedule for me and I would be entered in a race every six weeks this year, preparing me for the big races of three year olds the next year. Kate had been originally hired by John Windsor, about five years before he died. She was a pretty woman with dark hair, dark eyes, and a pretty smile, who was world savvy and always displayed a lot of class. She was very business oriented, headstrong and independent; she and Roberta would often clash over my schedule and my earning capabilities, as Kate was Roberta's financial advisor too. They complimented each other well. Roberta was very goal oriented and Kate was more calculating. Regardless, they both had a good business sense and made a good team.

My next race was set up for Hialeah Park in Miami, Florida, again against other two year old fillies. I was scheduled to race every six weeks that summer and fall, with races at Arlington Park in Chicago, Churchill Downs in Kentucky, Pimlico Race Park in Baltimore, the Meadowlands in New Jersey, Saratoga in New York City, and then finishing at Santa Anita in California at the end of the year. These races were pivotal and designed to differentiate the best two year olds from the others, in preparation for next year, and they were to weed out the ran's from the also ran's. Each race got progressively tougher. Angelo said; "The cream always rises to the top."

THE PREMONITION

It was a cold and grey rainy morning with the low clouds hugging the tops of the tall trees that were scattered throughout the farm. I awoke in my stall to a loud and piercing thunder storm with lightning flashing its deadly dance on the green meadow in the distance. I was terribly frightened as it was very bright and loud, and it seemed to be very close. The hair on my body was rising from the static electricity in the air. My mother was in a stall further down in the barn and was blurting out words of caution in hushed tones.

"Don't go there." She said.

"Don't go where Mom?"

"You'll know when it's happening and you'll know you shouldn't be there. Others will warn you too, but you'll be faced with many obstacles, and people you trust will betray you. You'll be injected with drugs too, but listen to your heart. It'll tell you not to go."

"Don't go where Mom? Who will betray me? What are drugs? What are you talking about?"

"Your brain will fool you honey, telling you you're alright. But you won't be; you'll get hurt and you'll never be the same again. And sadly, most of all, this will just be the beginning for you. You'll never be the same or feel the same. You'll be haunted with guilt and depression for years to come and I won't be there to help you. No one will be there to help you. You'll be all alone. You were born on a rainy day and you will have much more rain in your future."

The rain continued to come down in buckets, with large balls of hail now pounding on the roof above me and in the paddock outside my stall, and the winds whistling and slamming against the wooden doors.

"What is she talking about?" I said to myself, as I wondered where this expression of emotion was coming from.

"Are you okay Mom? You never talk like this."

"I'm sorry Summer Storm, but it was so real. I just had a nightmare honey and I don't want to talk about it; it must be the storm that bothered me."

Just then Lauren came rushing into my stall wearing her blue and white jockey uniform, which was all covered in mud. She looked tense, as if she wanted to tell me something.

"I came to comfort you baby, I knew the storm would bother you," she said. "But we have to get ready anyway; our plane leaves in four hours. This is a big event; you're the darling of the country. You'll be the focus of attention."

"Why is she so muddy?" I thought. "She's always dressed pretty before our trips; this is weird."

She then combed and brushed me while I ate. As she brushed me, she said she was going away after the race, but we would be together soon. I looked down at her muddy clothes again while she talked and then I nervously flicked my tail. I didn't know what she meant because she never left me. Just then, Angelo arrived holding a big syringe and inspected me all over, picking up one leg at a time. He then looked me in the eye and then looked at my right front leg.

"Something doesn't look right! This leg looks swollen and inflamed. Did she bump it or something?"

"She's been perfectly healthy Angelo, unless she bumped it in her stall during the storm this morning."

"Well, let's play it safe and give her some steroids and keep an eye on it, this race is important." He then injected me and left the stall.

After Lauren brushed me, she put a blanket on me for the trip that I had never seen before. She said it was my dad's "Good Luck" blanket and he wore it when he won the Triple Crown. She said it would bring me luck and she couldn't believe how well it fit me.

We then drove off in the trailer and arrived at the terminal in Lexington thirty minutes later, amidst pouring rain.

"You'll be flying alone today Summer Storm; I won't be with you. You're a big girl now. You'll have to get used to being alone. There will soon come a time when I won't be with you any longer and you'll be travelling alone all the time."

She then walked me and Winnie into the plane, kissed me goodbye, and promptly walked out. It was very unusual, as she always flew with me, but today I had a groomer fly with me. I got very nervous, and after we took off the plane seemed to be noisier than usual, probably because Lauren wasn't there. The vision of her dirty uniform and her callous words echoed in my head during the flight. When we arrived in New York three hours later for our big race, it was raining there too. We always arrived five days before the race to get acclimated to everything, the stall, the track, the weather, etc. Roberta visited me at my stall at the race track and said I better get used to the rain, because it was going to rain on me for a long time.

She looked at me in a confused way and said; "I'm not going to be here for you forever; but you'll get along. You're tough."

"What is she talking about," I wondered? "What are they trying to tell me?" "Why are they talking like that?" This was too weird.

Angelo came in to inspect my leg again and told Lauren to take it easy on me before the race. We had five days to prepare in this slop. Then he gave me another shot.

It continued to rain all week. The race would be one and a half miles long and would be run in a quagmire, a distance and a track condition I wasn't used to. I took it easy all week, mostly just walking and trotting in the raining early hours. We ran the track just one day and I hated running in that heavy mud. I almost slipped and fell while we were practicing, which scared me to death. I was afraid something might happen to Lauren. We were to race on Saturday and it seemed forever until Saturday came, as I was getting edgy being confined to my stall. It was even too wet to visit the paddock, which was located just outside my stall.

Blue and white: the colors were all over my stall. Lauren always wore a blue and white silk suit on race day, and I would wear blue and white colors under my saddle too. Saturday finally came and we were to go off at five thirty. It was the feature event and was the last race scheduled for the day. My leg wasn't swollen anymore and I was ready to go. I always anticipated race day and became quite edgy before each race. Lauren knew how to comfort me, but today she was sick and much to my surprise, wouldn't be riding me. I was told she got food poisoning the night before the race and they had to fly a jockey up for the race from our farm in Lexington. He was very experienced and rode my dad to all of his victories when he was racing. This turn of events completely shocked me, as Lauren was the only one to ever ride me. I never had another rider, never, not even in practice. His name was Jorge and seemed to be nice, but he had a deep voice and was all business, whereas I was used to a soft voice and kindness. This unexpected news made me extremely nervous and I paced my paddock while we waited for our time to walk out to the track. Jorge had never ridden me before and now he was supposed to race me in this big race. Lauren came down to see me before the race with mud all over her blue and white suit again and looked white as a ghost; only this time, she had a brace on her neck.

"That's odd. Nobody told me about her neck. Why is she muddy? What's going on here? You told me she was sick," I thought.

She was still sick and very quiet, but told me she was sorry she couldn't be with me. She then told Jorge; "Don't hit her with the whip; she doesn't need it. She'll get you there; just treat her like a lady and she'll be good to you."

Jorge just looked at her and me in a confused sort of way and nodded at Lauren in agreement.

It was time to leave the safe and dry confines of my stall and walk out to the paddock for the traditional photographs and pre-race jockey instructions. Angelo told me to run my race and everything would be okay. When Jorge finished his pre-race instructions with the other jockeys, he walked over to where Angelo, Lauren and I were standing. We all posed for photographs and then he mounted me for the first time. It felt really weird, as no one else had ever ridden me, and I noticed immediately that he was heavier than Lauren. We then left the paddock and were led out to the track by a steward on a gelding. Each horse entered in the race was led out of the large paddock one at a time, about twenty feet apart. I was the only filly entered in the race and was a slight underdog for the first time. It was a field of colts and only one of the colts was favored to beat me. This was the first time I was listed as an underdog. As I surveyed the field, I noticed one of the colts was ridden by a female jockey that Lauren knew; her name was Tisha. Tisha was from northern California and had been riding for ten years. I pondered that for a minute and wondered if Tisha and her horse had just as close a relationship as Lauren and I had.

It continued to pour as we walked in the thick mud. As we were led into the starting gates, one by one, I noticed a colt from California looking at my leg and shaking his head.

"You shouldn't be here today Summer Storm; this is no race for you. You don't belong here with us; this is the boy's club," he said.

I just looked at him, nervously pinning my ears back and wanting to rear up, but Jorge pulled on my bit tightly, preventing me from doing that. I was fortunate enough to draw the pole position for the first time and considered that very lucky in this weather, especially since I was the only filly here racing against colts. The lightning and thunder had passed over a few hours ago and now it was raining in sheets, fed by a driving wind that was completely drenching us. Although it had been raining all day, the large crowd erupted with a loudness I had never heard before, and came to their feet when my name was announced when I walked out on the track. They had been standing in the rain all day just waiting for this event and had anticipated it greatly. This race would be on national television and had been publicized for months; today would be the culmination of a year's hard work. Everyone wanted to see the filly beat the colts, but the fact that I had a new jockey on me for the first time lowered my odds of winning even further.

I enjoyed standing in the gate at the pole position, but the downside of it was I was the first horse in the gate and had to wait for all the others to enter. All of a sudden I felt very comfortable. I looked down the row at all those studs lined up in their gates and I knew I could do this; I knew they were going down! While I felt focused and at ease in my gate, I could smell the virility and testosterone in them and sense their tension, as they nervously thrashed about and waited for the race to start. Then bang, the gates slammed open and we were off, zero to thirty in two seconds. Jorge had a different style of riding me, but I was more focused on the favored colt that ran alongside of me, the one from California that spoke to me earlier. I held the rail going into the first turn and as we cornered I gradually pushed him further outside, making him have to work harder to keep pace with me. It is a huge advantage holding the rail, because you can force the other horse running alongside of you outwards, making him tire quicker, and hopefully leave nothing in his tank for the end of the race. I had to be careful though, this race was a long mile and a half and I didn't want to get spent too early. Jorge was standing in his saddle, bent over my neck as we ran and doing what he was instructed to do, just let me run. At the quarter mile pole I was leading by a neck, with five other horses closely behind us. At the half mile pole

I maintained the same lead with everybody just keeping pace, with no one wanting to go yet; it was too early. Both of us in the lead were just pacing each other out and waiting for the stretch because of the weather and track conditions, mainly because you could get tired very easily in this slop. At the three quarter mile pole, the colt with Tisha rode up alongside the California colt running next to me. There were now three of us running for the lead with four horses now running closely behind and gaining. Both of the other horses alongside of me were getting whipped by their jockeys while Jorge was just bent over and talking to me in my ear and letting me go. At the mile pole we were running neck and neck and I could hear the crescendo of the crowd increasing as they yelled with great excitement. The three of us made the final turn together and were closing in on the stretch with only a quarter of a mile to go. A fourth horse then joined the party on the outside and was out striding us ever so gradually. Now there were four of us, running side by side with the colt on the outside ahead now by a neck. It was time to go. As I pinned my ears back and dug in, the colt with Tisha riding it dug in too and took the lead with less than fifty yards to go. The horse on the outside and the California horse next to me both fell back a little, getting spent in the process, leaving me a close second to Tisha's horse. I was only behind by a nose now with each one of us changing the lead back and forth, as our strides were different. Back and forth the lead changed, and as we crossed the finish line the winning horse yelled out in pain and fell to the ground, tumbling over her jockey, Tisha, and breaking her neck. Tisha was then run over by a horse running closely behind her, putting the finishing touches on her. Jorge and I then trotted over to the exit gate while the ambulances came onto the muddy track. There was no noise now as goose bumps consumed my thin, wet skin as I witnessed this. Both Angelo and Lauren met us at the paddock and comforted me, as I was terribly shaken. I just observed a terrible accident and I had lost my first race too. Jorge told Angelo we probably could have won if he was allowed to flog me, as this was the first race I had lost and was in great contention to win. There wasn't any Winners Circle for me, no flowers, no hoopla, no photographs, just death on the track and a quiet walk to my stall; I wasn't used to this. I was young and didn't even think this could happen. Somehow, my feeling of invincibility vanished that day.

Lauren walked with us down to the stall and took my saddle off while tears ran down her face. She felt terribly sad that her friend Tisha was killed and said she was glad I didn't fall because they had to put the horse that was injured down. He was a beautiful colt who had only lost one race in his career, but today he lost his life. She then took me over to the shower area and quietly gave me a good cleaning and then walked me back to my stall and fed me a little. I wasn't very hungry. I was never behind anybody in the race, so I was mainly dirty in my under belly from the mud I kicked up on myself. She told me I ran a great and respectable race, being I was the only filly running with colts and said she was sorry she wasn't with me, because together we probably would have won. She said that Jorge weighed more than her and that was probably the biggest contributing factor in my loss. She then left and for some reason the path she took out of the barn was gleaming with golden rays of sunshine glistening through the falling rain. I stared at her walking away in a peace that almost defied disbelief because it was so tranquil and pretty.

Just then a lightning flash went through my stall with the crashing of thunder and awoke me from my crazy dream and brought me back to reality. I stared at Winnie and rehashed the dream in my mind, trying to get my bearings. It seemed I was dreaming all night, the events in my dream stopping and starting, as though I was curious about the outcome, but afraid to face it.

"It was exciting. It was tragic and sad; yet it was beautiful and sprinkled with love. But it was so vivid it carried a strange omen and scared the hell out of me," I thought. "What did it mean? Is there something in particular I should pay notice to, or should I pay attention to the whole dream?" It was very confusing to me.

I relived the race and the nasty weather conditions and the fact I had a strange rider on me for the first time. But I couldn't forget the strange messages that everyone in my dream were throwing out to me. I pondered over them and their occurrences in the dream for days, but never did totally forget them and wondered quite frankly what their meaning was, if any.

MY EDUCATION

It was the beginning of summer now and the weather at Chestnut Mountain Farms was wonderfully warm and calm, with an occasional thunderstorm which I hated to no end. The flash of the lightning would scare me to death, making me bolt and run in fear. If the thunder and lightning occurred while I was in my stall; I would frantically pace the perimeter and occasionally rear up, while Winnie would just sit there and watch me; it never bothered Winnie, but Winnie's presence made it easier for me, as I was wound way too tight and the lightning reminded me of the lightning in my dream. The trees were emerald green again, after the cold winter and spring, and the magnolia's huge fragrant flowers were blooming in their beautiful white color against their dark glossy green leaves. The dogwood's beautiful white flowers looked stunning amongst the magnolia's and azalea's in front of Roberta's house. The rolling hills of bluegrass were a dark splendid green again, dotted by grazing stallions and mares, colts and fillies, and framed by the miles and miles of white rail fences and large trees that enclosed them. The large pasture and barn I shared was with older mares, fillies, and young colts, as they kept the stallions away from the fillies and mares at all times. Every one of them was bred for racing; every one of them had a dollar sign attached to their head. I rarely saw my dad, and I didn't even know who he was for quite a while, but one day Mom pointed him out to me in the pasture bordering theirs. He looked so regal and proud, holding his head up high, his nostrils flaring while his chestnut coat and flying mane and tail were shimmering in the sun. You could tell he was the alpha horse of the farm, as all the other stallions looked up to him and kept their distance. When Lauren and I would enter the farm's main gate from their long walks to their neighbors, we would always pass a large bronze statue of a reared up stallion at the entrance; I didn't know it was a statue of my dad until Lauren pointed him out to me.

"Do you see that horse there? That's a statue of your dad. He was one of the greatest race horses that ever lived. Maybe one day there will be a statue of you on the other side of the driveway. What a beautiful bookend that would make, framing the entrance. You and your dad! I really think you're that good."

I just stared at the statue and felt in awe.

"Gee. My dad! He rears up just like me!" I thought, as I tried to imagine my statue up there with him. It just boggled my mind, so much so that I had to stop thinking about it; it was just too grand to imagine.

"Ain't I pretty?"

I would soon find out that is why Angelo, Roberta and Kate expected so much out of me; I was his heir and came from championship blood lines. My dad had won the Triple Crown as a three year old, the most prestigious award in horse racing, and in doing so guaranteed Roberta millions of dollars in breeding fees. They looked at me as their next cash cow. I was a walking dollar sign in their eyes.

I awoke early one morning to find Roberta directing Angelo, outside of my stall, on how he should train me for the upcoming race in Florida. I should say they were arguing; they were both head strong and neither one of them liked to take orders or suggestions from others. In fact, I guess all four of us were that way. Lauren then opened the door to my stall and fed me just a little, while they argued, because we were to work out hard today. I would eat good later, after my practice and bath. She then saddled me up and slowly led Winnie and I down the long path to the paddock near the oval, gradually warming my muscles as I walked. When I would be working in the oval, Winnie would graze in the paddock adjacent to the track and watch me; she was never far from me. The oval was about a half a mile from my stall, which was more than enough distance to warm up my legs and joints as I walked. The oval had a distance of a mile and was set up with an electrical timer every furlong, which was approximately every 660 feet. This was the place my dad built, if you know what I mean. After I would warm up, I would get into position to leave the gate and to be timed. We would be running seven furlongs this time, one furlong further than the distance of the upcoming race, which made the upcoming race a little easier than the distance we practiced on.

Lauren mounted me and we trotted a little before she walked me to the gate. After being enclosed for about ten tense seconds, the gate opened with a bang and I broke out quickly, hugging the rail as I ran. Lauren was standing on her stirrups and bent over me, rubbing my neck as I ran, just like she always did. We sped through the course at a speed of 1:09:03. It was so fast that Angelo said we should run it again because he didn't believe it. Lauren insisted that we wait until the next day, because she didn't want to see me get hurt. Angelo reluctantly agreed, and so the next day I ran it again at the speed of 1:09:07, which completely floored him. Roberta was told of my time the previous day and came down to the oval to watch me this morning. She said that the time was so fast; she might start entering me in

Stake races against colts, which were more competitive and paid more money than the filly races. Angelo quickly agreed, but Lauren said I wasn't ready yet, and that was the end of that conversation. Angelo got perturbed and just stared at Roberta.

"Are you going to let her control everything? You make me feel like I don't know anything anymore. What did you hire me for?"

Roberta, totally aware of Angelo's selfish motives, tried to be polite.

"Angelo, I feel like she's bringing her along the right way. There's no hurry here. Let's give that horse a chance to develop. She's getting stronger and more confident with every race. They're good together; they have a good chemistry. Can't you see her grow?"

Angelo just shook his head, and angrily walked away. He sensed his days on the farm were numbered, as Roberta didn't listen to him like she used to, but he needed to make some quick money; he owed Vinnie ten large and he needed a way to pay him back quick; the vig increased the debt ten percent of the balance every week whether he made a payment or not.

About five o'clock, when he was done working for the day, he got into his old 53' Buick and drove down the country road to his favorite watering hole. It was a small country bar, located by itself on a small two lane road and nestled in the woods between the farm and the outskirts of town. It was dimly lit with a horse shoe shaped bar, several booths, a jukebox, two pool tables, a dart board, and sawdust and peanut shells on the floor. There was a stone fireplace in the corner with two adjacent tables and the walls were adorned with saddles, halters, and photos of famous horses and jockeys from the area. It was the late seventies, but this bar was a cross between Archie Bunker's Place and a sports bar before either one was popular. Everyone knew him here and using the phone was a natural occurrence for him because he didn't like to use the one in his room. He put a fifty cents in the slot and called Brooklyn.

"Hey Vinnie, it's Ange!"

"Hey, paison, what's up?'

Angelo was in debt up to his ass with Vinnie, but Vinnie kept him alive because of Summer Storm's potential. He knew there would be a big payday someday, so he played along to save his ass. He also knew he had to be careful with Vinnie. Vinnie was a Mafia Don in New York and was used to getting his way. He was a man of not too many words, but he ruled with an iron fist. Vinnie believed in the Golden Rule; simply put, the man with the most gold makes the rules.

"Hey, we got a live one here Vinnie. This filly's got a lot of promise. She's only a two year old, but she was sired by Bold Czar and she's posted some damn good times at home. She's only run one race, but was fucking impressive, slipping at the gate and coming from behind in the mud to win."

"Yeah, I remember her; that's the horse I saw a few months ago. Before we go any further Ange, where and when can I see her go again?"

"Her next race is at Hialeah next Saturday; you always liked it down there!"

"Okay, I'll pay you a visit. Make sure it's worth my while!"

Angelo smiled. He knew he had Vinnie believing in him again. He sipped on his beer bottle and looked around, making sure no one could overhear him. He then fiddles with the cord while he whispered into the phone.

"Hey Vinnie, this horse is the real deal. I told you she's good; don't worry 'bout it. I guarantee you'll be happy."

Angelo got off the phone and grinned as he walked back to his stool, knowing he had a money maker here. He promptly ordered a boilermaker and a meatball sandwich while he munched on some peanuts. After he downed his shot, he stared at the mirror across from him and smiled at himself, thinking he finally had some big paydays coming. It's been a while since he's had a horse with so much promise. His only obstacle was Lauren. Somehow, he had to take over complete control of Summer Storm, but he didn't know how. Control over Summer Storm would insure his fate and future. He somehow had to convince Roberta that it was "for the good of the farm" to have a male jockey with some experience on her.

"Hey, Billy Joe!"

Billy Joe was a local hero of sorts. He was about thirty years old now, stood about 6'3" and weighed about 220, his high school weight. He was an All-State quarterback at the local high school, and had offers of scholarships from all the major schools. Because of his girlfriend, he decided to stay home and attend the State University, starting first string in his freshman year. In the third game of the year, he suffered a debilitating injury, getting speared by a helmet in the back of his neck, paralyzing him momentarily, but leaving his future tenuous, to say the least. Because of his prognosis, and the fear of paralysis, he had to give up the game he loved. He has been bartending for his dad ever since.

He called the bartender over, wanting his opinion on how to sway people over to his way of thinking and how to get them to go along with him. He knew Billy Joe was young, but figured he knew how to deal with people, being he was a bartender and all.

"How would he handle this?" He wondered.

"What's up Ange? Do you need another shooter?"

Angelo couldn't divulge his motives, but beat around the bush. He avoided eye contact and looked at his shot glass while he spoke.

"Billy Joe, if you wanted someone to go along with an idea of yours, to agree with you; how would you go about it?"

"Well Angelo, I'd make the presentation look like it was good for the other person, like it was something he couldn't pass up. You can't act selfish, but you have to make it look like they can't live without it."

Angelo pointed his Budweiser in his hand at him and stared at him.

"Yeah, I see what you mean. I've tried that, but I haven't touched the right nerve yet. I haven't been able to get to first base."

"What are you talking about Angelo? Can I help you?"

"No, no; I was trying to get a raise at the farm, that's all."

"Hell! You've got to be kidding! With Summer Storm, you're problems should be over."

Angelo stared at his empty shot glass, nodded, and cupped it in his hand. He then lifted his head and looked at Billy Joe, knowing they were talking about two different things.

"Yeah, I guess you're right. I guess I shouldn't be so damn impatient."

Angelo ordered another boilermaker while he pondered his plan. Summer Storm was the key to his future and he had to control her somehow. It wasn't unusual for him to drown his sorrows at the bar; it was terribly lonely in his room. He closed the place that night and drove the dark winding country road back to the farm, all the while thinking of how he could get to Roberta.

It wasn't very long and we had to leave for the Hialeah Race Track in Florida. Lauren wanted Winnie to travel with me again, so the both of them rode with me in the plane and stayed with me in my stall that night. It was a long flight, but having Winnie travel with me made me very happy, as we bonded immediately when she was a baby. Besides, Lauren had come to the conclusion that Winnie brought me good luck.

The weather in Florida in June is hot and humid; it never cooled off at night like home in the hills of Kentucky, and it took some time to get used to. The Hialeah Track complex was simply beautiful. It had palm trees that lined the track with little ponds scattered around the landscape with big, beautiful, pink flamingos wading in the water. The skies were an amazing azure blue. It was far removed from the race tracks in New York's congested metropolis. Every morning, before day break, we would practice in the cool air and walk the track, preparing for the race on Saturday. The field consisted of twelve horses, all fillies, some in their maiden race, and two other fillies that I had raced and beaten at Belmont Park in my maiden race. Every race we entered became more and more competitive, as some horses were weeded out for lower paying races and the best horses moved on to the Stakes races, which paid more money and gathered more publicity. It was a long journey to determine a three year old champion next year, essentially the best of the best.

"Lined up for dinner at the track"

Well, Saturday soon came and I was my nervous and jittery pre-race self. I paced the stall while Lauren tried to calm me, all the while thinking of the upcoming race. Winnie never did understand why I got so uptight before a race; she just used to sit there and watch me, letting out an occasional bleep. She didn't know how competitive I was and what I had to go through on that track. She was laid back, which was the polar opposite of me and was good for calming me; she complimented me in every way. Roberta and Angelo came to my stall to visit me and watched while Lauren put on my saddle and my proud racing colors of blue and white. We then walked out to the paddock where hundreds of fans and photographers were waiting, before moving on to the track and the introduction to the roaring crowd. The noise of the crowd still bothered me. It was still new to me and I really didn't understand yet why everyone got so excited.

The weather was hot and humid and the track was dry and fast. Angelo was looking for me to post a great time today, as the conditions were perfect for racing. My senses were high and my nostrils flared as we walked onto the track and the Steward blew his bugle introducing us to the crowd. I could smell the other horses as they came out on the track too; each one had their own distinct odor. There is a fine line in the preparation of a horse for race day; you want the horse nervous and on edge, but at the same time you don't want him too edgy, you want him under control. Lauren knew just how to bring that out in me. We were slowly placed in our gates, one by one, and nervously waited for the race to begin. As I waited, you could sense the apprehension of the other horses and jockeys. The horses would anxiously bounce around between the gate that they stood in and the jockeys would be talking smack to each other while trying to prepare their horse for the opening of the gate. Everyone looked for an edge. Each horse wanted to win and each jockey was chasing the dollar. I had the three slot today and anticipated a good start so I could grab and hold the rail, as holding the rail controlled the race.

The gate finally broke open, and we were off. I quickly took the lead and made my way to the rail, holding it by myself. A Chestnut filly tried to challenge me on the outside, but I gradually increased my lead, leaving everybody lengths behind. No one was going to kick dirt in my face again, not today at least. Lauren rode me to the finish line at a time of 1:08:51, less than a second off the world record, and

I won by 8 lengths. As we crossed the finish line Lauren stood up in the saddle and turned around to see the field running behind us. She then hugged me and whispered praise in my ear as we slowed down and walked over to the winners circle. Roberta, Pam, and Angelo were waiting for us and were very proud and excited too, with Roberta joyfully announcing to the crowd that I would soon be racing against the colts, because the fillies weren't competitive enough for me.

Angelo agreed with her and said; "I'd like to put a male jockey on her to race the colts, and I'd like to start some serious training with one of our good jockeys."

He wanted to control her, as controlling her controlled his income with the mob.

Roberta looked at him and then looked at Lauren and smiled in a motherly way. She then spoke in a slow manner with her southern accent.

"I think she's doing just fine; I think they're both doing just fine. They're growing up together. They have a chemistry that I think is unbeatable."

Angelo just looked down and shook his head and said; "I don't think Lauren is capable of riding against colts. She doesn't have enough experience, nor is she strong enough. She's only run two races so far. Summer Storm needs a "real" jockey on her when she goes up against real competition. It could get real mean out there. There will be a lot of bumping. You wouldn't want her to get hurt, would you?"

Roberta was perturbed now and looked at Angelo while she took off her sun glasses. He was beginning to bother her now with his constant pestering. A frown creased Roberta's elegant features. She wasn't used to being criticized either, especially in public.

"This is not the time or the place to talk about this Angelo. We'll discuss this further when we get home."

Angelo then walked away without saying a word and met up with two friends who were waiting for him. He was angry and felt he should be getting more respect from Roberta than he was getting, but knew he was dealing with her daughter, and family ties were strong with these southern "blue bloods." He also knew he'd have more control at the track and would be able to make more money "on the side" if he had his own jockey on her, but he still didn't know how to approach Roberta. He has been rebuffed on every attempt he's made so far.

Roberta watched him as he walked away with his friends and then looked at Lauren with contempt in her eyes. She then spoke with a strong southern accent.

"Young lady, do you know what modesty is? A famous coach from Green Bay once said; 'If you win, say nothing; if you lose, say less!' Don't you ever stand up in the saddle and turn around to look at your opponents again! That is showing off and displays poor sportsmanship. We never want to put anyone down. It may come back to haunt you some day."

"I'm sorry Mom, she ran a good race and I was just curious to see how much we won by; that's all! I wasn't trying to show anyone up."

"Well okay! But please remember what I said. We run a class operation here and don't want to be remembered that way. It just looks distasteful."

"Okay Mom! I said I heard you!"

After Roberta was finished with all the post-race photographs and interviews, she and Pam went up to the dining room in the Players Club that overlooked the track for dinner. It was a large secluded area with glass windows overlooking the track. Waiters in tuxedos worked the area, each one bearing a silver tray with deep-fried hors d'oeuvres. It was a place for those who could afford elegance mixed with the privacy only a few could indulge.

As Roberta perused her menu, she couldn't help but think of the attitude Angelo displayed after the race and she felt an urgency in his voice that alarmed her. She couldn't help but think of her father and what he told her before he died and wondered if Angelo had an ulterior motive in wanting to change jockeys on Summer Storm. "He has been quite persistent and acting quite odd lately," she said, half to herself. She also wondered who his shady looking "friends" at the track were, as she had never seen them before.

Roberta then put down her mint Julep and looked at Pam while she stroked her long blond hair on her shoulder; "I can't help but get paranoid about Angelo's motives about wanting to control Summer Storm. It really is bothering me. He just doesn't let up!"

Pam looked at her while studying her face. She saw the worry and concern in her eyes; she and Roberta had been together too long.

"I wouldn't get too concerned Roberta. Summer Storm appears to have a lot of potential and Angelo has always had full control of all the other horses. It's just natural to want to have full control here too. I think it's just a matter of ego. There would be a lot of notoriety for him if Summer Storm is as good as we think she is."

"Yes, you're probably right Pam. I shouldn't be so suspicious," Roberta said.

While the two women sat there leisurely enjoying the post race and victory dinner, Roberta couldn't help but think how much Pam meant to her through the years. She was very loyal and her personality complimented hers very well. She looked at Pam with affection in her eyes and spoke.

"Yo'all know me too well. You have a way of comforting me when I get upset. Let's get to the airport before I want another Julep."

They both laughed and had the Maitre d' phone down for their Limo.

When we returned to Chestnut Mountain the next day, Roberta and Kate came down to my paddock late in the afternoon and talked to Lauren for quite a while, argued with her, I should say. Kate was a very successful business lawyer with licenses in New York, Kentucky, Illinois, Florida, and California, which was set up that way because those were the sites of the major race tracks in America. She had been the family's lawyer for over twenty years. She was able to arrange the contracts for each race in each state and worked with Roberta in setting up my schedule. Roberta wanted me to stay the course and continue racing fillies, saying it was possible I could win the "Triple Tiara" for three year olds next year, which was the Triple Crown for fillies, if we continued on our planned course; that is building my confidence and endurance gradually. While Kate wanted to make as much money as we could, running me in every race she could.

Roberta looked at Kate and said in a subjective and justifying tone; "Even though she's posted world class times; she's still a baby and has room to grow and improve." "I think this is a special horse and if brought along properly, could bring us far more riches down the road. If she takes after her father, she'll be growing fast and filling out slowly. God knows she has his heart."

"I know Roberta. It just appears we have a money maker here and we should take advantage of it. This is a rare opportunity we have."

"Let's be patient people. Sometimes a bird in the hand isn't worth two in the bush. Sometimes you have to look at the big picture; let it develop."

But even though she voiced displeasure, Roberta's feelings were extremely ambivalent; she also thought I should be tested against the colts now because a horse like me doesn't come around very often, plus there was more money in the colts Stakes races as opposed to racing the fillies. Lauren said that racing against the colts could leave me injured because I had a competitive nature and didn't like being behind, plus I wasn't fully developed yet. I was still growing.

Angelo quickly agreed with Roberta and said I'd give the colts all they could handle. He also repeated his fervent plea to change jockeys, which fell on deaf ears again.

Lauren overheard all of this and felt a need to speak. She knew Angelo wanted to rev up my workouts and wanted a male jockey on me.

"She doesn't like to be behind Angelo, and if she did get behind, she may get injured trying to outrun them. Besides, colts are built stronger and mature quicker and that's why fillies are outnumbered by a margin of 19-1 in these races. Let's wait awhile; let's let her get stronger. We have time." Lauren said, as she pleaded to them with urgency in her voice.

So there I stood, listening to everything, as the discussion continued. Lauren didn't want them to overwork me, because she knew my competitive nature better than anybody. Kate then argued that this was a business and that I would bring more money at breeding time if I was tested better. Well, to make a long story short, everybody kind of got their way. That is everyone except Angelo. They agreed that I should continue racing fillies and mares this year, all the while getting gradually stronger through the winter months. I would then race colts after I turned three years old next year and was more mature, and in doing so, still left me eligible for the Triple Tiara towards the end of next year. What was important to me was the fact that Lauren would continue to ride me. When they finally walked away, Lauren turned to me.

"You know Summer Storm; many people go to a bull fight and cheer. Everyone has an opinion. Everyone thinks they're an expert in killing the bull. Everybody stands up and yells and tells the matador how to kill the bull, though they've never stood in the arena and faced one, not knowing what the matador feels and the fear he experiences. But only one man fights the bull, and Summer Storm, you are that matador. It's you that races the race, and it's you that knows what's best for you and what your limitations are. I know and sense your limitations when we race. No one can push you where you don't want to go. I won't allow it."

I stared at her and listened as she brushed me. "Why didn't they know that," I thought. I then knew she only wanted the best for me and that we truly were a team. I respected her more than ever and wanted to do my best for her.

The next race was set up at Arlington Park in Chicago in six weeks, and was to be 6.4 furlongs, or 8/10 of a mile. We started training almost immediately and increased our distances on the track gradually. We then went to Arlington Park and I won by seven lengths on a sunny day and on a fast track. I was never challenged, taking the lead at the onset of the race, and running by myself to the finish line. Lauren didn't stand in her saddle and turn around at the end of the race. This was beginning to be fun.

THE TORNADO

The summer went by quickly and I gradually got stronger and faster; I was 16 ½ hands high now, quite tall for a filly and almost as tall as my dad. I was starting to be looked up to by the other horses at the pastures on the farm, not because of my height, but because of my ability. It seems I had the best start and the fastest times of any two year old, including my dad. I was indeed an alpha female and commanded respect.

Our next race was scheduled at Churchill Downs, not far from our farm and the site of the Kentucky Derby every year. It was right down the road from us and it was nice being trailered to a race instead of going through the airport routine and flying out of state. We arrived in Louisville three days before the race and slowly got acclimated to the track conditions. I knew my father had won the Derby here and I was impressed by the history and the plaques and statues on display of all the past winners; it was like walking through a museum. I was in awe as Lauren would walk me past the barns and paddocks explaining everything to me as we went. She even showed me a large bronze statue of my dad, with an inscription telling us when he won the Derby. Everything was pristine and kept in immaculate condition, much like my barn at home. As we walked, people would photograph us as we went, as I seemed to attract a lot of attention. The more they stared, the more I exhibited my proud Arabian characteristics, i.e. my head and tail erect.

The weather was hot and humid all week, and on Saturday, the day of the race, we had thunder showers around three o'clock in the afternoon. My race was scheduled for five thirty, the last race and the feature race of the day. The wind increased dramatically as the storm approached and I nervously paced the stall as the thunder cracked loudly, appearing to get closer and closer every minute. Lauren rushed into my stall and said we had tornado warnings and we would all have to move to the complex which was built under the concrete grandstands. It was used mainly by veterinarians but could house many horses. As the barn was cleared out and we hurriedly walked to the area, fans and spectators were rushing about, all seeking shelter from the driving rain and high winds. The sky was a dark and an ugly purplish green and I was pelted by dust and debris and hail as big as golf balls as we hurriedly trotted to the shelter. Lauren had a hard time controlling me as I was really afraid. The hail felt like bullets as it pounded against my thin skin, and the lightning was crackling and lighting up the dark sky all around us with thunder that was very loud, hurting my ears.

Just before we entered the building, a purple funnel came out of the sky in the distance, throwing dirt and debris everywhere, and then the rain and hail suddenly stopped. All I could hear was a loud noise that sounded like a train coming out of the clouds and people yelling and screaming as trees and cars were being tossed about like matchsticks. After a frantic run to the building, a steward quickly closed the door behind us and it became quiet again; we were finally safe. The shelter was below the concrete grandstands so we couldn't even hear the storm above us. The electricity went out momentarily and it was dark for a minute or so before the auxiliary generator kicked in. It turned out we had to stay down there for about four hours with about fifty other horses, as there was a cluster of tornados that swept through the area that day. Lauren called it a tornado outbreak and they wreaked destruction that I had never seen before. After it was clear and safe to return, we were escorted back to our barn, which miraculously, was one of the barns still standing. Because of the storm, our race was rescheduled for the following day, a Sunday. This had never been done before here.

The storm gradually passed and we had a very noisy night. Construction workers were cleaning up debris and repairing damage and all I could hear was the noise of tractors and trucks running all night long. Race day dawned and the track was a little muddy, not fast like the previous day and I was tired from all the construction activity all night. There was a lot of pre-race hoopla, interviews, photographs, and announcements we had to endure, but finally we got down to business. The sun was shining brightly as we walked onto the track with the bugle playing, announcing our arrival. I got goose bumps as I surveyed the track. The track, the crowd, the noise, and the clear blue skies filled my head with an awe and reverence that was indescribable. I was acutely aware of my surroundings and I could even smell the mint juleps in the crowd. My dad won the Derby here, and now I was racing on the same track he raced on. I had to win, I had to go home and tell him I won. Nothing else would do. I wasn't happy about the mud though; for some reason I was afraid of it, afraid I might slip. I kept thinking about yesterday's lightning and that damned dream I had. It haunted me almost every day.

Out of the twelve horses running today, my post position was the seven slot, so I hoped seven would be my lucky number. I would be in the middle of the field. I would have much preferred to be closer to the rail, but that's the luck of the draw. I was fast enough to get to the rail and I knew what I had to do to get there. I knew I was a little tired, but I also knew everyone else had to be too. We all had to put up with the construction noise here last night. We finally were escorted to our gates and as we all stood there waiting, we all anticipated the start of the race. Lauren leaned over and whispered in my ear, while my feet moved up and down anticipating the opening of the gate. I knew what she wanted, I was ready. The gates slammed open and as we thundered down the track, I eased myself closer and closer to the rail, gradually passing everyone and outpacing everyone. I got to the rail and held it.

"No mud in my face today," I thought.

I was never challenged and won by six lengths on a muddy track in front of a roaring crowd. It was nice going home with my head held high. I was an heir to one of the greatest horses that ever lived and I didn't let him down. It was also nice going home in a trailer instead of dealing with the wait at the airport and the coldness on the plane with the drone of the engines for hours on end. I had to share the trailer with Winnie and three other horses from our farm that raced today, but I didn't mind. They raced in three of the other seven races, but I was the only winner. As we drove home, I looked out the window in the trailer and was surprised to see all the damage from the storm. The countryside was littered with fallen trees and telephone poles, their wires on the ground and an occasional house removed from its foundation, its contents littering the countryside like shreds of confetti. After this carnage I didn't know what to expect when I reached my farm. I thought about Mom and Dad and hoped they were alright. Winnie was with me, but my little friend Princess was left behind at the farm. "Was she okay," I thought?

As we entered the imposing brick and iron gateway to the farm, we drove up the long and winding tree lined road that led to my barn. I could see destruction everywhere. Some trees were down and a large part of the white rail fences was in the process of being repaired. I saw Dad's barn without a roof and the ground was littered with trees, roofing, and splintered wood. No horses roamed the pastures and there was a veterinary truck parked at every barn. Everyone was busy, everyone was scurrying about and trying frantically to get everything back to normal. I looked over to the main house on the hill and saw it was okay, but the little white fence up the hill and to the right of the house was down. The fence contained white patches of gravestones and a Mausoleum, which was where Roberta's family was buried. Lauren's pickup truck and Roberta's Jaguar were still parked in the circular driveway. Kate was visiting too, as I saw her white sports car parked there.

After we parked, Lauren walked me out of the trailer to my barn. As I slowly walked down the sandy path that was strewn with debris, I noticed one of the adjacent barns was heavily damaged and part of the roof was gone, but thankfully, my barn looked intact.

"Good," I thought. "That means Mom and Princess are okay. But, I wonder how Dad is? That's his barn that's damaged," as I scanned the area in fear, not knowing what to expect.

When I got to my stall, Princess was there and sleeping in the loft as if nothing happened. The "cat bird" seat Angelo called it. I whinnied out to my mom, whose stall wasn't far from mine, to see if she was alright. Thankfully she answered and it gave me great comfort hearing her voice. She told me four horses were killed yesterday, but my dad was okay. Two of them actually were raised from his barn when the roof was sucked off. The storm's vortex literally lifted them up and threw them down about a quarter of a mile away, killing them instantly. The other two died from falling beams when part of the roof collapsed. Many were injured, including my sister, but thankfully she survived and was to be treated daily by the vet. I saw my dad the next day and he said he wished he could have been there to see the race, but he said he had all he could handle. It was a living hell waiting out the storm, not knowing if he was going to be the next one sucked out of the barn. Even though he had endured a catastrophe, he was still interested in me and asked me about the race I ran. He inquired how I felt in the gate before it opened and told me how important it was to stay in the moment and not let my emotions control me, as you can get hurt thrashing about in anticipation of the gates opening. He always gave me good advice. I think he wanted me to win as badly as I wanted to win. It was comforting to know he always had my back.

The fences were all fixed in a few days, and we were then allowed to roam the pastures again. The construction on the barn lasted all summer, though. We soon had to prepare ourselves for the next race amidst this carnage and reconstruction. It was to be held in Baltimore, which was only about two hours away by plane. The time went by fast and five weeks later we went to Pimlico Race Park in Baltimore and I won by nine lengths, missing the track record in the mile by :02 of a second.

THE TWO YEAR OLD WONDER

Meanwhile, as I was winning on the east coast, a two year old filly named California Miss was making a name for herself out west. She was a strange looking horse to me, part Thoroughbred and part Appaloosa. She was undefeated too and winning by large margins on the west coast, as her name was often brought up at my practices. Angelo continually stressed to me that she was undefeated and very fast and told Lauren that they'd meet her at her home track at Santa Anita towards the end of the year and we had to be ready. Not only was she winning, California Miss was breaking records on the west coast and all the tracks she raced on in the southwest; she indeed was a force to be reckoned with and perhaps my only threat. I casually brushed the stories aside because I figured it was easy to race on a dry surface, mainly, because California Miss had never run in mud like I did. She didn't have the summer rains to contend with in California and Arizona; her racing conditions were always ideal. So I just sort of shined Angelo on, as I really wasn't bothered by her reputation yet.

However, first things first; the Meadowlands in New Jersey was next. It was a one mile race, which was my longest distance run so far, and it consisted of a large field with fourteen fillies and mares entered. The track was muddy again, as it had rained for three days prior to the race, but I was getting used to running in the mud. I didn't like it, but did what I had to do. Some of the racing sportswriters started to call me a mudder, which I didn't appreciate at all. A "mudder" is a derogatory term given to a horse that could only run and win in mud, a horse that couldn't run against the best on a fast track. What an insult, I thought. I could run and win anywhere. It just happened to be a wetter summer than usual.

Because of the wet week we had, the track was mired in a thick fog the day of the race. As we were escorted on the track, the fog was so thick that my visibility was only about twenty five feet in front of me. I couldn't see the grandstands but I could hear the crowd in the distance and the announcer broadcasting the prerace hoopla. When we got to our gate I surveyed the field in their gates, and because of the weather I knew I had to get off fast and hold the rail. This would ensure me of a safe trip down the foggy track, as the rail was the only thing I could see and it would give me my bearings. It didn't turn out to be a problem, however, as I took the lead immediately and held it. I hugged the rail as I ran, as the thick fog continued to blanket the oncoming track. We couldn't see more than twenty or thirty feet ahead of us as we ran, a distance I ate up every second. Although we couldn't see, we could still hear the hoofs pounding the turf behind us. Going into the stretch, the fog lifted at that part of the track and I could finally see the finish line and the crowd ahead of me. The crowd roared loudly as I came into view. I easily won again by ten lengths, with no mud on Lauren or me, and Lauren and I were the talk of the horse racing world. Roberta was happy making money and Angelo was gaining acclaim from my victories.

Angelo said that when we finally broke into view, it was like a beautiful mirage with Lauren and I running out of the clouds all alone. No one in the crowd knew who was leading the race until the absolute end, as the fog obliterated most of the track from the fans. We were then written up in a national sports magazine as "A Horse for all Generations." Angelo hadn't had this much notoriety since he trained my dad and he acted accordingly. He started to drink more, and for some reason he would often get lost at the track for hours at a time. Sometimes he would be seen talking to the same people I saw at other tracks; they seemed to follow us everywhere. He always seemed happy though, so I never thought much about it. At least he wasn't bothering me. There were only two races left this year, Saratoga and Santa Anita. Traveling wise, this meant we had to fly almost three hours to New York City, and later on, a long five and a half hours to southern California. That's how I looked at the races, not by the competition, but by how much time I spent in that dreaded cold and noisy airplane.

Next was Saratoga, the oldest race track in America, and it was full of history too. I didn't like racing in New York, but I made the best of it. It was now the end of September and the race had a distance of one mile, and this time the weather was hot and humid and the track was dry and fast. I blitzed through the field with a time of 1:34:57, a little more than a second off the track record, set by the late, great Ruffian, and won by seven lengths. The fanfare after the race was tremendous, as I was starting to get comparisons to the great Ruffian.

Ruffian was perhaps the greatest filly to ever race; but she was unfortunately killed in a match race with Foolish Pleasure, the fastest colt and the Triple Crown winner of the same year. He was the Triple Crown three year old winner that year and she was the Triple Tiara three year old winner, and because of their times, everyone wanted to see them race against each other. The race was advertised as being a two horse race, the best colt in the world against the best filly in the world, just the two of them confronting each other on a mile and a half track. The race had been publicized and anticipated for months in advance and brought great interest to the sport as they raced on national television on a Saturday afternoon. Ruffian immediately took the lead from the beginning and had stretched her lead to a half a length, half way through the race, before she broke down horrifically. She had never been behind in any race she ran, including this one, until she snapped the sesamoid bones on her front leg. She was so competitive; she even tried in vain to run after the injury, even after snapping her front leg and limping on three legs. When she couldn't take the pain any longer, she succumbed and fell to the ground in agony. That day was the saddest day in horse racing history; when she fell, all horse racing fans fell and cried with her. She gallantly tried to stand and finally did before the ambulance arrived and took her away. Later that day, the horse racing world was in shock when they found out she had to be euthanized; she was a tall and beautiful filly, but her strength and character was just too intense and wouldn't let her rest or relax. She didn't know how to quit, and she had so much spirit she wouldn't let herself rest enough to be healed. Everyone said there would never be another Ruffian; she had a heart as big as the sky. I found out horse racing could be just as dangerous as it could be cruel. The dream I had months ago and the fate of Ruffian used to play in my mind like a record I didn't want to hear. Because I was being compared to the great Ruffian; her accident literally scared me to death.

I was glad to leave New York and go home, as my front leg was sore, but I didn't let anyone know. I never favored it. I had kicked it against the gate when the gate opened at the start of the race and ran the whole race in pain. Dad had warned me about keeping my composure in the gate and I foolishly ignored it, thinking I knew everything, thinking if I anticipated the gates opening I would have an advantage, kind of like a sprinter anticipating the sound of the starting gun while crouched in the blocks. Lauren said our next race wasn't until December 26, in Santa Anita, California, which meant I had three months to heal and prepare for California Miss. To me, I figured I would surely be ready because three months seemed like an eternity, plus I felt invincible. Heck! I was undefeated!

It was the end of September when we got home and my leg was really bothering me. I was too proud to limp, so I just walked around the farm slower than usual and continued to train in pain for Santa Anita. Fall was coming to the countryside of Kentucky, as the icy morning frost eventually made the maples trees turn a brilliant red color on the hills surrounding our majestic farm. The morning air was cool, with a light misty fog every morning which cradled the white fences and low lying areas, making the bluegrass look like a frozen white blanket of dew. The cool air also made training a little easier on me. But Angelo, not knowing I was in pain, soon revved up my workouts and increased them almost weekly, much to the disgust of Lauren, as I think she sensed something bothered me and wanted me to rest. All Angelo talked about was California Miss and how she was still undefeated like me and that she was our main threat to the Triple Tiara next year.

After Lauren watched me practice lackadaisically for a while, she told Angelo; "She doesn't have the fire in her eyes like she usually has; I think something's bothering her. I think we should rest her awhile."

Angelo looked at me and then surveyed my body with a scowl. He took his hat off and scratched his head.

"Do you see any difference when you ride her; has anything changed; her gait or pace? I can see her times on the oval are off a little."

"I do see her lack of intensity; maybe we've been working her too hard," Lauren said.

Angelo then looked me in the eye and looked worried. He said to Lauren; "Alright, let's cut back her workouts a little and I want a full report on her food intake daily. We still have time to get it right. There's still two and a half months before the race."

Thankfully, after both conversing, they decided to cut my workouts back and allow me to regain my strength, as they both thought I was tired and was being pushed too hard. So instead of a workout every day, I was working out every other day. One day to break down tissue, and then one day to repair it and gain muscle mass. I spent my off time grazing in the pasture with Winnie, my mom and friends on my days off. Some days, if Lauren wasn't busy, we would go for long leisurely walks in the hills surrounding our farm where it was always calm and peaceful.

The coldness and beauty of winter soon came and with it came very cold mornings with an occasional snowfall. When it snowed a lot, we would be confined to our stalls which were always kept warm. It was like living in a palace for horses; we had the best of everything. I had every comfort you could imagine, plus I had Princess and Winnie for companionship and my mom in a stall not far from me; I was very happy. When the snow melted, we would resume our training with Angelo. For endurance, he continued to run me one furlong further than the actual upcoming race, which was supposed to make the actual race easier because it was shorter than the distance I ran in practice, but the extra distance in practice was harder on my leg.

"Pretty Princess"

As December brought an occasional snowfall, I longed for the upcoming race at Santa Anita. I was feeling better again and my edginess was returning. I wanted to rock. The holidays were quickly approaching, and we soon would have to leave for California. The race was to be run on December 26, the day after Christmas, so we left six days before Christmas. This gave me plenty of time to adjust to the new time zone and the weather, and not have any jet lag the day of the race. Because I lived in the cool hills of Kentucky, my blood was thicker in the winter than the California horses, and I had grown my winter coat. So that meant I had to acclimate to the warmer weather and get my body conditioned and my blood vessels thinned for the race so I wasn't lethargic. Brock was out of school for the holidays and made the trip with Lauren, sitting down below with us on the plane. The plane ride was a dreadful five and a half long hours and the drone of the engines seemed to go on forever, but the weather was beautifully warm and sunny when we arrived. It was much warmer than Kentucky and instantly brightened my spirits. When I stepped off the plane and smelled the warm air; it invigorated me almost immediately and made my nostrils flare as I lifted my head and smelled the new surroundings.

Each day I absorbed the beautifully warm sunshine with the majestic snow covered San Gabriel Mountains serving as a backdrop for the track. We practiced every morning and then every evening about five o'clock, which was the time of the upcoming race. Angelo wanted my competitive clock in order. I liked it out here. It wasn't as green as home, but it was far nicer than the noise and congestion I endured at the New York tracks. Instead of looking at tall buildings and factories belching out smoke, I was looking at the snow covered San Gabriel Mountains and palm trees swaying in the wind that outlined the track. It was a more relaxing atmosphere. Everyone seemed more at ease here, including Angelo.

On Christmas morning, the day before the race, Bryan surprised Lauren by coming down to the stable and helping her with my pre-race preparations. While Lauren was brushing the left side of me, Bryan got on his knees on the right side of me and started taping my legs. While they talked and Bryan was out of view of Lauren, Bryan reached in his pocket and pulled a small jewelry box out of his sweatshirt pocket and put his arm behind his back. While still on his knees, he then moved to the front of me and looked up at Lauren, trying to get her attention.

"Lauren, what's this here on Summer's leg?"

Lauren stopped brushing me immediately and turned to the front of me where Bryan was kneeling, looking very concerned. "Where? Which leg? I don't see anything!"

Bryan, his right arm concealed by Summer Storm, then reached into his pocket and hid the box in his fist; "Here it is," he said, moving his tight fist around my leg and opening it, producing a ring. "Will you marry me?"

Lauren dropped the hair brush and screamed with excitement as she jumped up and down. She held her hands over her face and started to cry with joy. Bryan then stood up and held her in his arms and comforted her while they hugged and kissed.

"Of course I will. Of course I will. Oh my God, how I love you. I dreamt about this moment for such a long time and now it's come true."

She then reached up and put her arms around his neck and kissed him again while tears of joy ran down her cheeks. They held each other for what seemed like minutes and talked about telling her mother, to which Bryan said he had already asked her first. He was a complete southern gentleman and knew that was the proper thing to do.

Although they had almost grown up together and known each other for fifteen years, they had only been going together for a year and a half. Bryan was going to be graduating from college in June and they were to have a summer wedding. She used to confide in me of their plans on our walks and our quiet time while we were together on our trips and insisted we would always be together, even after they were married. They really were happy and looked so good together. They both then looked at me and showed me the ring.

Lauren then looked me in the eye and comforted me, talking to me like she thought I understood what was happening; "I don't want you to worry honey; I'll always be with you too. We'll just be adding Bryan to our family. You'll always be with us."

I looked down at her with complete trust. We had been together too long and I trusted her implicitly. She never lied to me and was always open with her feelings.

Then Lauren said with a surprised look; "Summer, it's Christmas day and I have a present for you and Winnie too."

She bought me a silk blue and white blanket for Christmas, and Winnie a wool blue and white blanket with a blue collar and leash. I got some carrots and Winnie got some fresh produce. They gave it to us in our stall at Santa Anita. It was a very happy day for all of us.

After almost a week under the warm Californian sun, race day finally came and the extreme apprehension that always comes with it. Lauren arrived around noon and then fed me a little and brushed me, all the while talking to me and giving me words of inspiration for the race. We were scheduled to go out to the paddock about forty five minutes before the race, where sports writers, photographers and fans were anxiously waiting. It was like every other track in America. The pre-race procedures were the same everywhere.

This race, although it was the final one of the racing season for me, was the beginning date for the horse racing season at Santa Anita Park. Because of the long and hot California summer, their season always starts the day after Christmas and goes through the spring and ends in early summer. Then Hollywood Park, Los Alamitos and Del Mar would open and the horses would transfer there for the summer months, where they were near the coast and cooler. This race was to be a distance of 1 1/8 miles, my longest distance raced so far. There were fourteen horses in the field again, with the best fillies from all over the country entered this time, which was the last race of the year for two year olds. Next year, when we were all three year olds, the best of us would be considered for the Triple Tiara, so that alone made this last race of the year all the more important. Angelo said that I was a slight underdog today, with the filly from California that I had heard so much about arriving undefeated too. Her name was California Miss and this was her home track; I think that's why she was favored. She was a fan favorite out here and everyone wanted her to beat "that big filly from the east coast." She came from good blood lines too and was tall like me, but I would soon hate to hear her name mentioned.

Competition to me was everything. I lived for the adrenaline rush before each race and how my senses came alive when I was announced to the track; it was a feeling of supremacy that touched my very soul. My dad said you can judge your competition by looking them in their eyes; it was that simple. You knew how you stood then and who would be a force; their eyes told you how much spirit they had, and their gait confirmed it; it was like reading a book. The more spirit I sensed, the more adrenaline dripped into my blood. For some reason, being it was my genes or my spirit, or perhaps both; I knew I was unbeatable. I just knew it. I never looked a horse in the eye and experienced fear. I knew they all had a weakness and I eventually would find it and expose it. The level of my competition was always lowered by my presence and I flaunted it with my proud Arabian gait. I could also tell by my presence that some of my competition was already beaten before we started. If you weren't impressed by my mere presence and you chose to display some heart, I would pound it out of you on the track. You would learn who the alpha female was.

When Lauren left the stall for her pre-race instructions, Angelo quickly came in and gave me a shot of steroids, he called it. He said it would help me and I trusted him. As he was leaving, Lauren returned and we prepared for the race.

"Angelo, what are you doing here?"

Angelo, afraid he was caught giving me the shot, looked scared and bewildered.

"I just came by to check on her. It's an important race and I was just checking her out. I thought you would be here."

Angelo then left the stall and hurriedly walked down the long corridor of the barn. Lauren stepped out of the stall and followed him with her eyes, shaking her head at his odd behavior. After being saddled, Lauren and I spent about forty five minutes in the large paddock with the other horses entered in the race, where we were observed and photographed by adoring fans and journalists, as well as gamblers scanning the horses, looking for a weakness, any kind at all, before they went to the betting windows. After the fanfare and hoopla was over with, we then passed through a long dark tunnel that ran under the Grandstands before being escorted onto the track, about twenty yards apart. As was my nature, I observed and perused everything. I was extremely alert and aware of everything as I walked onto the track. The California sun had gradually faded over the mountains in the distance and being it was December, darkness came early. It was getting dark and cooler; the lights of the track were on, illuminating the area brightly. Even though it wasn't quite dark, the temperature was still nice and about fifty five degrees. We were to go off at five thirty, being the premier race of the day and this race was anticipated by many fans, not only here, but all over America; it was my first race to be televised nationally. The track was lined with tall palm trees lining the rails, that blew in the distance, with the smell of fragrant flowers that grew around the infield that made it smell like spring. The track had been cultivated and smoothed out by the tractor and was dry, but spongy as I walked on it. Lauren patted me as I walked and I took everything in, my head and ears erect. California Miss was in front of us as we walked and the crowd roared when they announced her name; for the first time in my career, a horse got a bigger applause than me. I understood that, mainly because this was her home track. As we slowly walked to our gates, I checked her out closely. She had long legs and a proud gait and she pranced around like she owned the place. Then she turned around and looked me in the eye.

"I heard a lot about you. This is my track, my home track; you don't have a chance here," she said as she turned and stared at me.

"We'll just have to see, won't we? I just don't talk the talk, I walk the walk. You'll see. It'll be over real soon," I said, as Lauren stopped me from rearing up.

But even though I spoke with bravado, I felt a little weird; I was getting much more tense than usual and couldn't wait to go. It was as if my mood changed and I was getting intense and irritable; I couldn't describe it or know why I felt so different than usual. Was it the shot that Angelo gave me? I didn't know, but this was the first time he had given me a shot before a race and this was the first time I felt so weird before a race. I didn't know what was happening. But I knew one thing, I was full of energy and I wanted to explode. I wanted to explode right now.

When we finally were escorted to the gates, California Miss turned and cockily looked at me again before she entered her gate. Our eyes then met in a long gazing stare, with my nostrils starting to flare and me wanting to rear up and show her I was the alpha horse here. It was almost as if we knew each other was a force to be reckoned with; no one else in the race mattered. It was just me against her. I was oblivious to the others. I just stared back at her as I walked slowly to my gate. I knew by the look in her eyes that she had heart and she was ready. My head and tail were standing erect as I strutted and I let my proud Arabian characteristics show. I drew the seventh hole today with

California Miss getting the third slot; she had the better pole position, advantage to her. I was extremely tense as I waited in the gate, resisting the urge to rear up like I wanted to, remembering how I got hurt in the starting gate in New York and what my dad told me; "It's important to stay in the moment." I wanted to beat her bad. I was tired of hearing her name and I was tired of Angelo crowing about her. I didn't like her smart mouth either. Today I would show him how fast she was. Today I would be the only two year old still undefeated, or so I thought.

"And they're off!" The loudspeaker blared loudly as the gates slammed open. I had a great start, quickly catching California Miss at the rail, with both of us running side by side, running nose to nose, and leaving the others behind. They were cooked already in my mind! After waiting to come out of the first turn to turn it on, I passed her on the straightaway and took the rail away from her. At the half way mark, I was four lengths ahead and pounding the turf as I ran, displaying an exorbitant amount of speed.

"Take it easy baby. Save it for the finish;" Lauren whispered in my ear.

I heard Lauren, but I couldn't slow down. I was full of energy and wanted to run. Going into the stretch, I couldn't hear Miss' hoof's any more, but I could hear her jockey hitting her with a whip and yelling at her. Lauren was bent over me, calmly patting my neck as we ran, just letting me go. I felt an unusual burst of energy today and won the race by a whopping ten lengths, running away from the field, and missed the Santa Anita track record by less than a second, running it in 1:44:38. As Lauren slowed me down, California Miss went by and looked at me with contempt in her eyes. I just stared back at her and put my head up high and stopped trotting. I then reared up and kicked my legs out at her. She knew what it meant; I was the alpha female here. I was now the only undefeated two year old filly in the country and was voted the Champion Two-Yr-Old Filly of the Year and eagerly looked forward to next year, as this racing season was over for me. I had not only beaten California Miss on her own track, I humiliated her. This made Angelo, Roberta, and Kate very happy, not to mention the pride I felt. After the festivities were over, Brock followed us to the stable and happily picked Lauren up off the ground, giving her a big hug and kiss. As Lauren took off my saddle and started to walk me to the bathing area, I saw Angelo in the paddock outside my stall talking to the same two men he was talking to at the end of my maiden race. I thought that was a little unusual because my maiden race was in New York several months ago and we were now thousands of miles away in California. As they talked, I saw one of them hand Angelo an envelope or something. I couldn't really make it out, but Angelo had a big grin on his face as they shook hands and departed.

LAS VEGAS

The next day, everybody departed for Kentucky except for Angelo. Roberta came down to my stall before we departed for the airport and mentioned to Lauren he had arranged to stop in Las Vegas on the way home to meet a "friend." Not be known to them, it was a "business" meeting arranged by Vinnie and designed to spur extra income for the mob across the nation; it was a "sit down." Angelo commented to a friend, in front of me, that he was extremely nervous about the trip, but said it might be advantageous to him if he played his cards right. Vegas was only an hour ride by plane from LAX, just enough time to take off and have a drink before it was time to land.

Upon reaching Las Vegas, Angelo looked down on the desert floor, looking at the dotted buildings surrounded by a vast expanse of what seemed like nothing. The valley floor was surrounded by mountains that gave off a shimmering red glow in the sun. Years ago, Vegas was just a train depot in the middle of the desert, a place to change trains for troops travelling from one place to another. But, with 1980 looming around the corner, things had changed considerably. He couldn't believe how large the footprint of the city was as he got closer to the strip, which was adjacent to the airport.

Las Vegas to Angelo was like Disneyland to a kid. Though he had never been here before, the gambling mecca was foremost on his "bucket list." He had heard so much about it through the years and knew this is where the big players went. He knew about the mobs involvement here and looked at it like a history lesson while they flew overhead looking down on the strip. He had met Bugsy once in Sammy's bar in Manhattan back in the forties, with Bugsy making an impression that was hard to forget. That was Bugsy though; his reputation and swagger arrived before he did. When Bugsy was subsequently killed by the mob for taking money under the table, Angelo felt like he had lost a friend. That was the personality of Bugsy, very impressionable and hard to forget, very dynamic and charismatic. Angelo wanted to see the Flamingo, the place Bugsy built and the casino that started it all in Vegas.

When he arrived at McCarran Airport early that afternoon, he was surprised to see a chauffeur standing in the baggage area with a placard that said "Angelo." He was then escorted to a black limo where his friend Vinnie was waiting in the car. They departed west on Tropicana Drive and then went north on Las Vegas Blvd. to Caesars Palace, which was further north on the strip. While they rode, they talked.

"You still drinking Crown, Ange?"

Vinnie grabbed a bottle from the bar rack. He wasn't there to just wine and dine Ange, he was using him as a pawn and setting the framework for a big payday next year. He was greasing the pig.

"Yeah, that's my fav. I've been drinking it for years. Just on the rocks Vinnie. No water."

Vinnie lit a cigar and casually looked at Angelo, turning his head to blow the smoke out the window.

"Do you want one Ange? Their Cuban, picked them up in Havana personally."

"Sure Vinnie, how can you turn down a fuckin Cuban Cigar? How in the hell did you get to Cuba anyway? It's off limits"

Vinnie looked at Angelo and just smiled.

"Ange, I could go anywhere the fuck I want. We got ways!"

He then poured himself a seven-seven and bent over to talk to Angelo, who was sitting across from him. He knew Angelo was wary and tried to relax him.

"Boy, we kicked some royal ass this weekend Ange. It looks like you have a real winner there! When can I see her go again?"

"Yeah Vinnie; I juiced her for the first time, just like you wanted. We kicked some major ass. Blew that California horse away on her own fucking track!"

Angelo looked at him and stared out the window, thinking about the ramifications of his question. He knew how much he owed Vinnie and he also knew he wanted something. He also knew this horse could bring him some big paydays down the road. He didn't want to cross him, but ethically, he knew he had to be careful with Summer Storm because of her potential. This wasn't just another nag racing in a stakes race; she had the capability to go all the way and he didn't want to see her hurt. Yes, he still had some ethics; they all weren't compromised yet, but damn he was greedy too. He knew he owed Vinnie money and Vinnie wanted more control of the outcomes.

"Well Vinnie, she's gonna be resting for a few months. The racing season is over back east. She's damn tall for a filly and if she fills out like her Dad, she's gonna be a great one next year. Roberta and her attorney Kate set her schedule, not me. I got nothin to do with it. Then they give it to me and I get her ready. I do know they're designing a program for a run at the Triple Tiara next year; she's that good. She's championship material."

"Oh yeah! Hell, I see that! Keep me posted on everything about her. I want to know when you know. You hear me? We got to go with this one!"

As they pulled off the strip and into the long Italian cypress lined driveway that led to the covered entrance to Caesars, Vinnie turned and looked at Angelo.

"Ange, there's some people in town I want you to meet while we're here. Got some big fucking players from all over the country in town. It's a big opportunity for you. You scratch our back, we'll scratch yours; cappeish? I got us a suite in the Forum Towers, hot running dames and cold flowing booze. Anything you fucking want."

"Sounds good! Where they from?"

"Where's who from? The dames or the people I want you to meet?" Vinnie said as they got out of the Limo.

After they got a ticket for their luggage from the Valet, Angelo stopped and took a good look around, absorbing everything. It was the end of December and the daytime temperature was a comfortable 72 degrees. While he scanned the Vegas skyline, he took a deep breath.

"Hey, I like this place. Reminds me of Italy; look at all the statues and gingerbread on the building and the cypress trees everywhere, just like Sicily."

Vinnie laughed and put his arm around Angelo's shoulder. "I knew you'd like it here Ange. You ain't seen nothin yet. Wait til you get inside. This place is fucking amazing; it's humungous, first cabin!"

They walked in the revolving glass front door into the large and spacious registration area and saw a huge bronze statue of Julius Caesar facing them with a large circular fountain in the background adorned with roman statues. The floor was laid out in beige marble and rich pink roman columns and mosaics of tile embellished the room and walls. Angelo was awestruck and taken aback. He had never experienced anything so grand. He couldn't help but feel a little homesick as he perused the area. Its architecture and aura reeked of Rome and Florence.

"Hey, this is just like a piazza back in the old country, only fancier. I love it!"

"Wait til you see the Sports Book; it'll fucking blow you away. It's as big as a city block! Hell, you could bet on anything here, probably even when the Pope takes a piss. Let's go upstairs and freshen up first. I got a couple of phone calls I got to make before we relax. Then we'll come back down and gamble a little; they must got a dozen crap tables here, all kinds of table limits. You can lose your ass here in no time at all!"

After checking in at the VIP lounge and evading the long lines, they walked across the casino and took the Forum elevator to their suite. Angelo was aghast when they opened the door. Their suite was huge with three bedrooms, three baths, a sitting area with a room with a bar and a pool table. It was adorned with roman columns and statues, marble baths, and a spa in the middle of each bedroom. He had never seen anything so luxurious. On the couch sat four beautiful women dressed in tight low cut sweaters, miniskirts and heels. There was a brunette, a redhead, and two blondes, who smiled and nonchalantly crossed their legs as Angelo and Vinnie came into the room. While they relaxed, Vinnie poured everybody a drink and made small talk. While Angelo was talking to one of the women, their luggage was delivered to the room, along with a bottle of Champagne. Angelo got up and walked over to the window and opened the drapes. He stared out at the Vegas strip with the red tinted mountains in the background and wondered why it had taken so long for him to get here; he loved everything about it. His "date" walked over to him and put her head on his shoulder and her arm around his waist while he looked down at the pool area, where scantily clad females were tanning themselves. She put her hand in his pants pocket and then gave him a kiss on his cheek, whispered in his ear, and led him to his bedroom, pulling him by his penis. Angelo was nervous, as it had been a while since he had been with anyone so young and beautiful. He poured another drink while she disrobed in front of him and walked over to him and sat on his lap. Her black nylons and garter belt and heels mesmerized him and nature soon took over, as she kissed and caressed him. And after a half an hour or so, Angelo was ready for a shower and some gambling. Angelo was anxious to go downstairs; he wanted to shoot some craps like he did on the streets of Brooklyn when he was young. It had been a long time. She kissed him on the cheek and told him she'd be here when he got back. As he and Vinnie got into the elevator, Vinnie put his arm around him, seeing he had him where he wanted him.

"Damn, what a nice surprise! How long are they going to be with us?"

"As long as you want Ange. It's your treat. Did you have a good time?'

"Hell yeah; I can't wait til we get back later. Remind me not to drink too much tonight; I want to be ready."

Vinnie laughed and patted him on the back.

"These guys we're going to meet are from Chicago, Miami, and Philly. They're connected and I want you to treat them with respect. They're all looking forward to meeting you. You're the talk of the town after yesterday! They're interested in what kind of "magic' you could help them with on their gambling interests. I already filled them in on our relationship and what you do for me."

"Sure Vinnie, but you never told me where there from when I asked you before. Why they interested in me?"

"Hey Ange, there in the business! You know what I mean? They like the control you could give them at the track. They're chasing the buck, just like we are."

They walked into the Forum Casino and took a long walk down to the bar which was adjacent to the Sports Book. Vinnie ordered a seven-seven, while Angelo ordered his Crown Royal and took everything in while he spun on his stool and looked around. The casino area was huge with the sound of craps players yelling and the ringing of slot machines going off in the distance. While they talked and played video poker at the bar, Sammy Castanno, Junior Piccolo, and Sal Lanzo joined them. They ordered another round and left the bar and found an adjacent table where they all could sit and talk in private. Their table was across from the Shadow Lounge, a bar where naked girls danced behind a lit screen, with only their dark and sexy silhouette visible on the screen; their "shadow."

Vinnie introduced his friends and lauded Angelo as a main player in his business, greasing his chain again, knowing after a couple rounds he'd have Angelo right where he wanted him. He also knew Angelo owed him for past gambling debts and he had him in the palm of his hands. Although Vinnie ran a mob family in New York, if he had gone straight, he could have run a large corporation, he was that smart. After all, he really was running a large corporation, only it wasn't legal.

"Ange, these are my associates and they have their fingers in all the major race tracks on the east coast, Chicago, and the mid-west. They want you to play ball with them and they'll make it worth your while; you savvy? Cappeish paison?"

Angelo stood up and shook their hands, noticing large diamond studded pinky rings on them. He suddenly felt out of place. He felt like a pauper. These guys were wearing tailor-made clothes with silk shirts and he was wearing a Dacron leisure suit and a cheap Fedora. As they sat down, Vinnie spoke.

"Boys, Angelo has access to everything you need to get your machine running properly, if you catch my drift. He's a paisano from Sicily, so you can trust him. His home base is Lexington, and it's only a day's drive from there to either Chicago, New York, or Philly. He can get you what you want and he can deliver it on weekends once a month. You just have to have somebody in your corner to administer it properly. I'm sure you got concerns; any questions?"

"What kind of stuff we talking about and how much is this shit?" Sal said, as he looked over to Angelo, while he puffed on his stogie.

Angelo realized what was up now and spoke freely, knowing he was amongst friends. He lit a cigar, leaned over the table, and started talking. He was nervous and spoke freely.

"You know; amphetamines, acepromazine, downers, steroids, herbal remedies, you name it. I can show you the dosage per animal pound and the results you might expect per horse, depending on their past times. I can make them win or lose, it's up to you. I have access to it all. Some of this stuff ain't new; but I can teach your trainers on how to administer them the right way. Some of this stuff ain't new and some is. The trick is I got it down to a science and I could teach your cronies the tricks. It's like a fucking graph; you'll catch on!"

"What kind of quantities we talking about?"

"Any amount within reason; we don't want to turn the Fed's heads in Washington. I got somebody in my corner that does the ordering and I can get you a month's supply at a time. Any more than that might raise a flag."

They all looked at each other for reassurance, and then Sal from Chicago spoke.

"Does weather have anything to do with the doses administered? Does weather affect the drug's results? Does it come into play? We have all kinds of weather up there, hot and cold. How does this shit work?"

"Naturally, if it is too hot, say over ninety, you should use less. If it's cold, you use a little more. It's a matter of ingestion. Other than that, weather shouldn't play a problem. The weight of the horse and the dosage is the most important thing. I'm speaking from experience here. Vinnie here can let you in on how using this stuff turns the odds in your favor. I know he's made a ton on this shit."

"What about testing? Is any of this stuff hidden or is it all detectable?"

"You're going to have to take your chances on that one. Testing is random at the tracks, but not mandatory. As of now, there's no mandatory testing; so it's a crap shoot when they test. I'm sure you know amphetamines and downers can be detected in a blood test or urine test, but acepromazine and some of these new growth hormones and herbal remedies can't be. They all have different characteristics. That's the tight rope you'll have to walk. If you play it safe and pay off the right people at the track, you won't have to worry about testing."

Vinnie motioned over to the waitress and ordered another round. He looked at his colleagues while he glanced at the moving nude dancing behind the screen and spoke.

"Those are good questions, but I can assure you I've made a ton of money on this shit. You can virtually guarantee the odds will be in your favor every race. If you do things right, chance is taken out of the picture. What do you say? Are you in or out?"

Sammy and Junior looked at Vinnie. "What do you want out of this? What's your take?"

"The usual vig. Ten percent of your gate. It's a small price to ask for what you'll be bringing in. Trust me." Vinnie said.

"I'd like to see how some of this shit works first. What's the difference between amphetamines and acepromazine? I never heard of that one."

Angelo picked up his drink and spoke. "Well it's real simple actually. You've probably been using amphetamines at the track for years. Amphetamines get your engine running, no different than what we've been giving to football players and boxers for years, but if used improperly, can kill or injure the horse. But acepromazine is a new drug that actually relaxes the brain and allows the horse to concentrate on the race instead of burning up the unnecessary nervous energy that amphetamines do. It's quite the opposite. It keeps them calm and focused. Amphetamines are detected in blood and urine tests, whereas acepromazine and some of the new growth hormones aren't, another plus."

"I'd like to try it out first; when can you get me some?"

"Just tell me what you want and where you want it delivered and I'll get it there," Vinnie said.

As they spoke, their drinks were delivered to the table by a beautiful blond waitress, scantily clad and wearing a tight Roman outfit, her creamy breasts bulging out of her silk bodice. When she bent over to place the drinks on the table, Vinnie slipped a c-note in her bra and kissed her cheek.

Vinnie lifted a glass; "Cendone my friends; a hundred years! That's it then; the deal is done."

Vinnie lit a cigar, passed around a Cuban to each of them, and looked at them. He could tell they still had questions, or perhaps they didn't want to pay the Vig, he didn't know.

"Look, this is only the beginning guys. Eventually we will be at every track in the country. We just hook up the right horse and the right trainer to the right jockey and haul in the dough. They all have to be coordinated or it don't work. I've been doing it for years. If the jockey or trainer fucks things up, we teach them a lesson. We have a "talk" with them. That's the only way to keep them in line. Angelo here can instruct your trainers on how to use this stuff, then the rest is up to you."

Vinnie looked at them and knew he had them where he wanted them.

"You guys asked how much this new stuff costs. It ain't cheap, but I can assure you what you bring in at the windows will more than compensate for the cost. It's a win win situation!"

They all looked at each other and said; "Then it's a deal. When can we begin?"

They looked at each other and nodded and then lifted their glasses and toasted the new deal. After finishing their drink, they ordered another round and turned around and watched the dancing shadow "show" on the screen, laughing about perhaps starting a show like that back home in one of their bars. After about thirty minutes of bonding, they walked down to the Sports Book. It was a large cavernous room, much bigger than an auditorium, with large movie screens circling the room with different sports venues on them, all televised live. Betting windows were underneath them and seats and tables filled the area with local horse races on individual screens. They virtually had every horse race from every track in the country, all live and all available for wagering at the window. The odds were posted on the walls that circled the "book" along with upcoming football games and whatever sport that was in season at the time. You could essentially bet on anything here, even on an event months in advance. Horse racing was the big attraction, though, as they raced year around, depending on what part of the country had good weather. Races in England and Europe were also televised and available for betting. Angelo was mesmerized as adrenaline was pumped into his blood system. He had a bad gambling problem and felt like a kid in a toy store.

After surveying the area and shooting craps for a while, they walked upstairs and picked up their dates for the evening. Then down the elevator again, and together they walked the Forum and ate at Spago's, an upscale restaurant with a Piazza with tables overlooking the cobbled street of the Forum. The Forum was the plum of Caesar's properties, which was a large walkway set up like the streets of ancient Rome with cobbled streets and outdoor piazzas and restaurants with a blue sky on the ceiling overhead that changed color with the time of day. The area was adorned with Roman statues and fountains. The street was lined with high end exclusive shops from all over the world. If you wanted luxury, you found it here. The cobbled street reminded you of walking the ancient cobbled streets of Rome. After eating and walking the Forum, they went back to their suite where Vinnie had set up some "recreation" with a couple more show girls, dancing and stripping to create the "mood." Angelo liked it here; he liked it a lot. Unfortunately, the clock would strike midnight for him and he would have to fly back to Kentucky the next day. The coach he had been riding would turn into a pumpkin and he would be confronted with the real world again. The shiny black limo would soon turn into the old beat up Buick and the suite would be forgotten when he returned to his one room apartment.

THREE YEARS OLD

The cold, crisp winter of Kentucky slowly passed and I continued to mature, growing bigger and stronger. I was bigger than all of the fillies and mares on the farm and was as tall as my father now, who was big in his own right. I enjoyed my time immensely on the farm, which was world renowned and located in Lexington. I overheard Lauren say that Lexington is known as the "Horse Capital of the World," and is nestled among many world famous thoroughbred horse farms, each one specializing in breeding and racing world caliber race horses. The city is rich in history, being founded in 1775, with Kentucky becoming a state seventeen years later. Lexington is a wealthy town and so cultured is it's lifestyle; its nickname is the "Athens of the West." It is also geographically and strategically located, being within a day's drive to two-thirds of the population of the United States, which includes the eastern seaboard and upper mid-west. The weather is moderate in the summer, very seldom getting over eighty eight degrees. The winter is cool with a fluctuation between 23 and 54 degrees and it has four distinct seasons. Because of the many thoroughbred farms in the area, the competition for the dollar is severe and very cutthroat, culminating in different forms of corruption, on and off the track. This is where the Windsor family made their bones, years ago when the land was affordable and when owning a horse was a hobby, not a business.

"Peace on the farm"

Roberta and Kate had us entered in three races prior to the filly Triple Tiara races, one at Saratoga, one at Pimlico and one at Aqueduct. These races were to prepare me for the three big races which were to be held in the summer, each one being held at Belmont Park Race Track in New York. Roberta said I had the potential to be the horse of the decade, if not the horse of the century. I didn't quite know what she meant, but by the tone of her voice, I knew it was good. The three preparatory races had both fillies and colts entered in them, the first time I would race against colts, while the Triple Tiara at Belmont had fillies only and decided the best three year old filly in the world.

Lauren and I practiced daily and even managed to have some fun along the way. She would take Winnie and me for long walks in the woods and along one of the many winding streams that ran through our farm. She would stop under the shade of the large sycamores and take my saddle off and let me graze near the stream while she sat on the grassy bank watching over me. When Bryan was in town, he and Star would come along too. Winnie would be tied to a tree and be grazing near us, just being happy to be along. She was my bud and

I enjoyed her company. All of us had a lot of fun together, so much fun that I hated to practice on the track sometimes. It was a tranquil place to visit with the bubbling water passing by through the winding pebble bottomed stream. The tall sycamore trees had large umbrellas of big bright green leaves that towered up to the azure blue skies, where large white puffy clouds slowly passed by in the distance. The summer breezes would rustle the leaves of the trees and stir the flower's fragrant scents, making it an enjoyable experience. Occasionally, we would see deer drinking from the creek and rabbits and quail scurrying around in the brush as we passed by. There was always the sound of frogs croaking and woodpeckers pounding the trees above us. It was so clean and peaceful in the country and very different from the noisy traffic of the cities and loud roar of the racetracks we visited. It was a place where I was truly at peace with the world. Lauren thought we were just walking in the woods and enjoying the peace and serenity of it all, but to me, it was much more important than that; to me, we were making memories. Memories! Although I didn't know it at the time, memories that I would cling to forever.

We won all three of the preparatory races that spring and summer, beating both fillies and colts quite easily and now focused on the Triple Tiara at Belmont Park. The Triple Tiara consisted of three Stakes races, each to be run two weeks apart, the first one starting June 7th, and ending July 4th. The tight schedule not only tested your speed, but it tested your endurance, as each race was progressively longer and there was only a two week margin in between each race. If you took away the travelling time for each race and the time to adjust to the facility, it didn't leave much time for practice. The first race was 1 mile, the second was 1 1/4 miles, and the final race was 1 1/2 miles, each race being a quarter of a mile longer than the last, and the third race was at a distance none of us had ever run before; it was a distance reserved for champions. Belmont Park is the only race track in the country with a distance of 1 1/2 miles, and is the same place and distance that the last leg of the Triple Crown, the championship series for colts, is run. That extra distance separates the wheat from the chaff.

Angelo became extremely nervous as we approached these races and began to ramp up my practices even more. Roberta became more involved in my daily routines too, visiting me daily with her lawyer Kate and her secretary Pam. I really sensed the urgency in their voices and I wanted to please them all, but I knew I wasn't a hundred percent. Thank God I had Lauren to give me stability. Roberta said I was one of the greatest fillies that ever raced and was proud of Lauren for bringing me along so steadily, much to the chagrin of Angelo, who always winced and looked away when she would praise Lauren. My mom was very proud of me too, and one day my dad even came over to the fence that bordered our pasture and honored me by nuzzling me in strokes of praise and congratulations. He was very stoic, void of any emotion, but gave me some advice while we stood there.

"Summer, I'm pleased with your progress, but you must remember, every race is different and every horse comes with a new game; you mustn't get overconfident. You'll learn to read them and you'll see it in their eyes. One thing though, you should always break cleanly and grab the rail as fast as you could. You're fast and they'll try to box you in. You can't display your speed when you're boxed in and they know that. If you can't hold the rail, resist the temptation to pass in the turn until you get to the straightaway, when you're out of the turn and where it will be safer and easier to pass. Trying to pass in the turn not only burns up energy, but could be dangerous too, as your legs and hoofs can be dangerously close to the horse your trying to pass if she's pushing you out. I ran the same distances those three races have against colts when I won the Triple Crown. It is important to pace yourself during the race and save it for the finish. Each race gets progressively longer, so don't punch your ticket until the end."

I listened to him with complete reverence, not only because he was a champion, but because he was my dad too.

It was summer in Kentucky and the hills were a beautiful emerald green again. It was pleasantly warm and you could hear the bubbling stream, smell the aromatic flowers, and see the deer herds wading and drinking in the water. I looked at the beauty of it all and thought about how everything recycles every year, how nature takes care of itself and everybody in it and how we're reborn and revitalized every spring. The birds would sing their cheerful songs and you could see the quail families stir about as we walked through the paths that cut into the woods, sometimes twenty to thirty of them at a time. It evoked a calmness that was so different from the race tracks I visited and a serenity that I learned to love. We went for our daily walks through the woods and really enjoyed each other's company. If there was a day that Lauren didn't visit me, I felt let down and would brood. I would always let her know about it too. The next day I would nip at her long hair when she showed up. She'd laugh and would always say she was sorry, but I knew whenever she wasn't here, it must have been for a good reason, but even though she would have a good excuse, it didn't mean I had to like it. I also knew Bryan just graduated from college and they were spending more time together planning their wedding and perhaps I was a little jealous of that too. They were to be married in July, two weeks after the Triple Tiara was over and about seven weeks from now.

The simple pleasures and serenity of the summer would soon be forgotten, however. It was time for us to leave for New York and our first leg of the championship; it was time to go to work. The sky was sunny when we arrived, but you sure could tell that you weren't in the country any longer. It was noisy again and the air was dirty. Because it was so hot and humid, the air seemed even dirtier. The airport was close to the race track and the big jets would fly right over the race track and barns, taking off and landing, their exhaust burning my lungs even more. Although I had been here a few times, it still was hard to sleep at night. You could hear the planes, trains, trucks, taxis and sirens, all of them alternately blaring out their noise and disrupting the night. I realized you don't really appreciate quiet until it is taken away from you. Angelo said this is the city that never sleeps and I believed him now. Lauren and Winnie were very comforting, staying with me at night and I appreciated it very much, as I loved them dearly. Bryan fully understood Lauren's relationship with me and stayed in the plane with us on our way to New York, and much to my surprise, slept in the stall that first night too.

Angelo was his old crotchety self. He wanted these races badly. When Lauren wasn't around, he would give me a shot of "steroids." It now seemed I got one before every race. I was puzzled as to why he always did it when Lauren wasn't around and why he never mentioned it to her. But I kept winning, so I trusted him. I know one thing though; my mood would change dramatically after each shot and I would be full of energy for the race and hard to relax and sleep the night after the race. It made me edgy, but it was almost as if it made me mean and uncontrollable, very sensitive to everything around me. I also overheard him telling a fellow trainer that winning was important to him and would be a feather in his cap. It would also give him glory, making him more famous as a trainer, having trained a Triple Crown and Triple Tiara winner too; no one had ever done that. Roberta and Kate were busy entertaining my value and were planning out my life for me years in advance. I guess I had no say in my future. Lauren and Winnie were my friends and didn't make any demands on me. They just enjoyed being with me and I appreciated that.

The sun was shining brightly when we walked out on the track that Saturday, illuminating the large crowd in the stands. Roberta, Pam, Kate, Angelo and Bryan all sat together in the owner's box seats, which were located close to the start-finish line. Because of my stellar record, they had prime seats; close enough to the rail, but high enough to see the complete track. The crowd roared the loudest when they announced my name, but I was used to that by now. My mind was all business today and I was focused on winning, extremely focused. I strutted with my head and tail up high, just like my Arabian mom taught me; that was how she walked. No horse walks like an Arabian. The pride we have is exposed in our gait. I saw California Miss walking with her green and gold colors behind me, and knew she was the horse to beat. I had beaten all of these other horses before, including her, so I was heavily favored, going off at 3-5. But California Miss had just lost one race, the race I beat her on her home track and I knew she was good and wanted revenge. I saw it in her eyes. Perhaps she just had a bad day, I thought. Plus, because of the nagging pain in my leg, I knew I wasn't a hundred percent now. Because of that, I was worried, but I felt I was still good enough to beat her today. Before we entered the gate, I turned around and looked at her.

"You're not in California anymore; now you're racing on my turf," I said, stopping at the entrance of the gate.

She didn't say anything. She just stared at me. I saw in her eyes she was ready and wasn't intimidated; she was all business. I knew in my heart it wasn't going to be easy. The look in her eyes and the pain in my leg were telling me that.

After being escorted to our gate, Lauren sensed I was uptight and rubbed my neck and tried to calm me like she always did. While she leaned over me, she looked me in the eye. She didn't have to say anything, it was understood; we had been together too long. I knew what I had to do. I had the third hole today, while California Miss was right next to me, occupying the fourth hole. She was quiet and anxiously waiting for the gate to open. This meant we were going to break together, side by side, but I had a slight advantage as I was closer to the rail. Her jockey was talking smack to Lauren, but Lauren ignored him totally. She was ready too. I was very tense and ready to explode, but just then the gate loudly snapped open and we were off. As I ran, Miss tried to nudge me and push me off my line. I held her off and we both met at the rail again with California Miss even with me and to the right of me, with me holding the rail. We went into the first turn, still side by side and racing each other hard, and because of my advantage I tried to force her further outside like my dad told me. This would tire her, with her working harder as it was hard to pass me in the turn. Our legs were dangerously close as we bumped into each other and jostled for position. We then ran into the straight away nose to nose, with everyone else far behind, but I couldn't shake her this time. Lauren was talking to me and patting my neck as we ran, while California Miss was getting flogged with a whip right next to me. I could feel the rage building in her as she was being whipped. We continued to run in a dead heat throughout the race, as the crowd was roaring in excitement. But when we rounded the final turn and I saw the finish line ahead, I was still neck to neck with California Miss and running as hard as I could. Lauren whispered into my ear and tried to give me some encouragement. I heard her and then pulled away ever so gradually, ever so slightly, and won by half a length, but a full second and a half off my best time in the mile even though we had a fast track. I was totally exhausted when Lauren slowed me down.

My leg was aching badly as we slowly walked to the winners circle. There was a contingent of dignitaries assembled there with photographers from all over the world. Roberta reached up to me and gave me a big hug when we walked up to them, and although Angelo was beaming, you could tell in his eyes he was upset the race had been so close. His Crown Royal was catching up with him too, as his face was flushed and he had a grin on him from ear to ear. Bryan walked over to us and reached up and gave Lauren a kiss as she bent over my neck. He was very proud of her riding abilities. As they put the ring of Roses around my neck and proclaimed me the winner of the first leg of the Triple Tiara, I put my head down and picked up my leg and winced. I didn't know what to think, it was throbbing badly and more painful than ever. It was a deep burning pain that radiated up my leg. I felt afraid and wasn't sure of myself any longer. My confidence had reached its peak and was now waning. Doubts filled my mind because I knew I couldn't turn it on at the end like I always did. I seemed to have lost my "passing gear." After another sleepless and restless night, thanks to Angelo's "steroids," we boarded our plane for the flight to our farm the next morning. I was more than happy to get out of there. Something bothered me about New York, something I couldn't forget. Although I always won here, the aura of it all affected me deeply.

We had less than two weeks to prepare for the second leg of the Triple Tiara, and Angelo was wondering why the race was so close, being I had beaten her so handily at Santa Anita last year. I didn't favor my leg, so nobody knew I wasn't one hundred percent, not even Lauren; I had too much pride for that. I just walked slower than I ordinarily did, never letting on I was injured. We gradually increased my practice time on the oval at home, with less time to rest. Winnie sensed something was wrong and tried to comfort me when we were alone at night, bleating out to me in her soft tones, as the pain in my leg made me restless and difficult for me to sleep, difficult for everybody in my stall to sleep. I used to lie in my stall, looking at Winnie, and wondered what to do and wondered what's wrong with me. But, she and Lauren's love kept me going through all of this, as their love comforted me and took my mind off the throbbing soreness in my leg during the daylight hours. It was the night that wasn't my friend. It brought out the demons that haunted my mind.

In the darkness of my stall was when I felt the pain the most. It was when doubt clouded my mind and distorted reality. Fear of losing to inferior competition bothered me immensely and would keep me awake, lying there and staring at the cedar walls of my stall for what seemed like hours at a time. Scenarios would play out, me winning, me losing, and of course the worst scenario of all was me getting injured, falling to the turf like the great Ruffian. I wondered how to gather the strength I needed for my task at hand, knowing what was expected of me. Perhaps not meeting their expectations was my greatest fear. So after a torturing and tiring week and a half of practice, it was time to fly to New York again for the second leg of the series.

During our plane trip to New York, Lauren and I lay in the hay while she talked to me, and Winnie stood close by and listened. As Lauren lay there with her head on my neck, Bryan lay there with his head on Lauren's lap. So there we were, all four of us travelling together now. Lauren would stroke my head and look into my big black eyes as she talked. She told me she was so proud of me and that we wouldn't be doing this forever; that we would be resting soon and I would join my dad as one of the premier race horses in the world. I understood her, but didn't know if she knew I understood. I understood more than I let on. She and Bryan would hold hands and talk about their trip and the sights of New York they wanted to see while we were there, and I'd listen, being very happy for the two of them and happy we were together. Their relationship was great and I could see how much she loved him. She looked forward to their wedding next month and building their own house on the farm. She told me Bryan majored in business and economics, so he could take over his family's horse farm some day. And because Lauren was the only heir to Roberta, they also knew that Chestnut Mountain Farm would someday be theirs too.

When we landed at JFK, we had an official police escort to Belmont Park and then arrived at the track amidst flashbulbs from photographers and writers from all over the world. I was the only undefeated three year old filly in the world and everyone wanted a photograph of me and an interview from Roberta, Angelo, and Lauren. I was the star and I knew it. The weather was nice and not too warm. It was kind of balmy, actually, but the downside of it was that the overcast skies made the humid air seem heavier and dirtier than usual. But I was used to that now; I was back in the city again. Since each race was only two weeks apart, we only had three days to acclimate ourselves and prepare for the race when we arrived. The travelling time gave my leg a little rest, much more respite than I would have gotten back home. Angelo was his crabby and critical self, almost afraid of the upcoming race, while Roberta beamed in the limelight of my fame and reputation. It was Lauren's composure and calmness that brought stability to this travelling sideshow.

It was finally race day, and it didn't come too soon, as I anticipated it greatly. This race was called the Mother Goose Stakes, and was the second leg of our journey. After all of the photographs, the pre-race hoopla and the introductions that seemed to go on forever, we were finally escorted out onto the track. As I walked to the gate, I saw California Miss walking behind us with her jockey smiling at Lauren in a cocky sort of way.

"What a good omen," I thought; "She belongs behind me. I'll soon teach him not to smile like that."

I drew the two hole today, while California Miss got the eight hole; big advantage to me, putting me closer to the rail. I took my time walking to the gate, saving my leg for the race. Angelo had given me my "steroid shot" and I tried to control the nervousness that was consuming my body and brain. It was a nice warm day and the track was called "fast." After all the pre-race revelry and the long walk to the gate, it wasn't long and we were waiting for the gate to snap open. There wasn't any smack talking by me and Miss; we both were focused on the race. I broke cleanly with California Miss catching me at the rail again, with Miss' jockey talking smack to Lauren while he beat Miss with his whip. I held the rail as I maintained a nose lead on her around the track, all the while her jockey was beating her unmercifully as she raced next to me and making her aggressively bump into me occasionally. I heard the whip slapping on her thin skin and her jockey yelling at her and was glad Lauren didn't treat me like that. I remembered what my dad told me and paced myself, waiting for the final straightaway to let it go. But going into the straightaway, Miss surprised me by passing me slightly, with her now taking the lead by a nose. I just didn't have it today and I knew it. Even though I had my "steroid" shot, I didn't have anything left in my tank. Lauren whispered into my ear and I tried to turn it on, all the while my leg aching badly, making me grimace with each long stride I took. As we went into the stretch, I put my ears back and gritted my teeth and dug in hard. I gave it everything I had and barely caught her at the finish line, winning by a nose in a photo finish, and far less than the half a length I beat her by last time. Each race we ran, my winning distance over her shrunk considerably. For the first time in my career I didn't rear up after the race like I usually did, and Lauren immediately sensed something was wrong. She now knew something was bothering me and it wasn't a secret any longer.

"What's up, honey? What's the matter?" She asked, as she looked down at my legs. "Are you okay?"

I just turned my head and looked up at her and stared. My eyes were sad and I couldn't hide my feelings any longer; they spoke volumes. I felt downcast and subdued when I got to the winner's circle. The ring of flowers was put around my neck and as the flashbulbs popped, they blinded me momentarily. I then put my head down and stared at my throbbing leg as I heard Roberta tell Kate to set up a match race between me and the best three year old colt in the country.

"It's time to make some money," she said, as she turned to Kate. "You know Kate, you can watch her run and you can watch her win, but her story hasn't been written yet; she's that good. When her career is over, she might even be better than her dad, and that's saying a lot."

Kate smiled and agreed with her and then looked at Angelo. Angelo looked very worried and seemed not to be paying attention to them. Although he was with us, his mind was far away, as though he was preoccupied with something. He looked scared.

The match race would just be him and I, the best colt against the best filly, for one million dollars, winner take-all. All I had to do was win the last race of the Triple Tiara, just one more race and they would set up the match race. As I heard her talk, I stared at Roberta and Angelo and then put my head down and looked at my leg. I then shook my head, as my leg was throbbing in pain. I didn't want to be here at all. I wanted to lie down at home. I needed rest and solitude.

"How was I going to do this," I thought. "How can I muster up the energy and the will to overcome this injury in less than two weeks? How can I live up to Roberta's expectations? It seems like my leg's getting worse. I had to give it everything I had to win this time."

Doubts filled my head, because I knew what I went through to win today and the next race was going to be longer still. I didn't know where the speed and power they demanded from me would come from and honestly felt there was no way I could win that last race. I barely won this one. All I could do was keep my head up and pray that I got better. It seemed like it was out of my hands.

Everyone was happy and smiling but me and Angelo, but Angelo couldn't keep quiet any longer. While Roberta glowed in the limelight with the press, in a rude manner, Angelo unexpectedly grabbed Lauren by the arm.

"What happened out there? Her time was way off; why did she just barely win? What are you doing? Don't you realize how important these races are?"

"Take your hand off of me Angelo; I don't know what happened. I think something is bothering her. She didn't have passing gear today and she didn't want to rear up after the race like she usually does either. That's the first time she hasn't done it. It ain't me! She just didn't have it today!"

Roberta turned and saw the friction between them and immediately broke up their conversation. Angelo looked quite upset and wanted to question Lauren further, but realized this wasn't the time or the place. It was quite unusual for him to act like this in public. He looked really scared. I looked at the both of them arguing and looked down at my leg again. I couldn't believe Angelo was so upset at me for winning by a close margin. I mean I still won, didn't I? I gave it everything I had. Didn't he know that?

"I've got to talk to my dad. He'd surely know what I'm going through; he's been here before. Maybe he could help me," I thought.

THE TRIPLE TIARA

When we returned to Kentucky, Lauren insisted that I go through a battery of tests, as I wasn't eating like I ordinarily did, leaving quite a bit of my food untouched. Angelo was still fuming and asked Lauren again if she noticed anything unusual during the race.

"No, I always let her run her race, I never have to push her. You know she's too proud to fall behind, so I just let her go. I always let her run her own race, but today I had to encourage her at the end. And she didn't rear up after her victory like she always does! Something's wrong! Something's definitely wrong! I think she doesn't feel well. Look into her eyes. She's not eating either."

Angelo stared at me while she spoke and wondered if he had "over medicated" me. He took his hat off and leaned against the cedar wall of the stall.

"Well, let's keep an eye on her. Of all times for something like this to happen, right before the championship race; the timing is incredibly bad."

Angelo put his hat back on and then left feeling a little perturbed and went to the farms veterinarian and asked that she give me a checkup.

Lauren then slowly walked me down to the clinic and I was soon scanned by Loretta, the farm's veterinarian. Loretta was the farm's vet and had worked here for years. She knew me well and not only administered all of my shots when I was a youth, but she was the only vet I've known.

On our way to the clinic, Lauren filled me in on the vet's background. Loretta Ciapriano was about fifty years old and was the farm's vet for twelve years, having been the vet for my dad when he was young too. She was Italian and was brought up in south Philadelphia, having earned her degree at Temple University. She initially earned her stripes on the race tracks of New York and New Jersey, starting out as an assistant and worked her way up to Lead Veterinarian at a prestigious Equine clinic in upstate New York. Roberta had hired her after receiving a tip from Angelo that she was available and wanted to move down south. She was considered a progressive vet, having established herself along the way as someone who didn't believe in drugs, but instead believed in herbal remedies. Her expertise was race horses.

We then walked to the hospital area where Loretta did the yearly physicals and operations when needed. Loretta put a reassuring hand on my shoulder and listened to my heart with a stethoscope. She nodded her silver head in approval and then scanned my back with her rough hands. She then rubbed my legs with a firm hand and looked at Angelo.

"I think we should X-ray her leg; there appears to be something wrong. There's a small knot here and it is sore to the touch. I hope it's not what I think it is."

Angelo looked worried as she spoke.

"What do you think it is?" He asked.

Loretta didn't say anything. She then x-rayed my leg and after a short while, she came out of her office and studied the film on a mounted stainless steel light box and pointed to my knee on the x-ray with a pointer. She said I had an inflammation in my sesamoid bones in my right foreleg and she found an outbreak of hives on my skin. I heard the vet say that the sesamoid bones are some of the most important bones on a horse and said it looked like the tissues had been inflamed for quite a while and wondered why no one had ever noticed it, as the injury could have killed me or crippled me.

"Has anyone been injecting anything in her, steroids, amphetamines, herbal remedies, or anything else?" She said as she looked at Lauren and Angelo.

"No, she is kept under surveillance at all times," Angelo replied in a stunned manner. He looked at Lauren for affirmation. "Why do you ask?"

"This outbreak of hives could only stem from a reaction to injected amphetamines or even acepromazine. It looks like somebody got to her; someone gave her something. This is a typical reaction to an overdose."

Angelo looked at her and then looked at me, knowing I wasn't going to reply. "She's a tough filly and never showed any weakness at all. She hasn't lost a race. In fact, most of the time, she leads wire to wire. We didn't suspect nothin until she stopped eatin and these hives that just came on today."

Loretta looked at Lauren. "Lauren, this is very unusual here, but I've seen this before elsewhere. Has her disposition changed at all? Is she edgy or relaxed before or after a race? How does she sleep the night after the race? I have to know these things. Edginess can indicate growth hormones, steroid or amphetamine use, while calmness can indicate the use of acepromazine or herbal medication. Either drug will bring out speed in a horse, but acepromazine and growth hormones are undetectable in tests. I took blood and urine tests for amphetamines and am awaiting the results."

"Yes, now that you mention it, she has been edgier than usual and I've noticed that preceding each of the last few races, she has become harder to handle in the gate and it's taken her longer to unwind after each race. She also has been hyperactive the night after each race and hasn't had much of an appetite." Lauren said.

"This looks like a classic case of amphetamine use or growth hormones. Are you sure that no one has gotten to her? That no one shot her up just to win a race? Since you two know nothing about this, is it possible someone could have gotten to her at the stall at the track?"

Lauren and Angelo just looked at each other dumbfounded. Angelo then looked at me again and looked worried. Neither one said a word.

"Well, as of now, there is no structured testing for race horses and I'm sure that someday there will be. It appears that someone is altering the chemistry of this horse and that can be dangerous. You know, winning isn't everything, you could kill a magnificent animal like this. This could have led to a serious injury. I'm going to prescribe anti-inflammatory painkillers and herbal remedies and advise you to rest her."

"You sound like you're accusing one of us. How long do we rest her? We have an important race coming up." Angelo said in a panic.

"First of all, I'm not accusing either of you. And do you think I'm stupid? Everyone in the horse world knows about that race. What's more important Angelo, winning the race or killing this beautiful animal?" Loretta said.

Angelo scratched his head. "Of course the horse is more important, but we've come so far. It's just damn unlucky for this to happen now. It's the championship, for Christ's sake!"

Lauren looked at Angelo and then Loretta and spoke; "We know nothing about this, but it scares me to think that she is vulnerable when we are not around. Who would want to do this Angelo? Who do you think would want to gain from this?"

"I don't know. I'm shocked too. But I'll ask the stable hands if they've seen anything unusual around here and I'll keep an eye out too. How long will she have to rest? Will she be able to run this last leg of the championship?"

"Angelo, this didn't happen here; it happened at the track. It had to be administered there to be effective. It had to be given right before the race. Someone got to her there!"

Angelo seemed to ignore her and inquired again as he anxiously looked me in the eye and then scanned the hives on my back and my right leg again while he scratched his head again.

I heard all of this and wished I could let Loretta and Lauren know somehow what's been going on. They then taped my leg and short—splinted me and let me rest for a few days in my paddock. All the while I was taking herbal remedies, ice packs, and Loretta's prescriptions. My days consisted of just taking daily walks, with Lauren and Brock leading me and Winnie following close behind. I wasn't even allowed to go to the pasture to see my mom or dad. They didn't want me stressing my leg or running at all. It was great getting this needed rest, and after a few of days I was starting to feel stronger. I had forgotten how good it felt to feel good again.

Five days went by and they lifted some restrictions on me, allowing me to walk to the pasture. I saw my dad in his pasture and called him over to the fence that separated us so that we could talk. He slowly walked over to me, as this request was unusual. I was as tall as him now and I looked him dead in the eye.

"Dad, I have to talk to you. I injured my leg some time ago in a gate and never let anyone know. It progressively got worse and now I'm really worried because I can't kick it in like I'm used to doing. It's my front leg and I hurt it while thrashing about in a starting gate before a race. Has anything like this ever happened to you? Have you ever hurt your front leg?"

"No Summer, I've never hurt myself like that. Oh, I've had muscle cramps and strains, but not anything that didn't heal in a few days. Why didn't you let on you were hurt so they knew about it? Your wheels are important to you. I told you how important it was to compose yourself and stay in the moment while you were in the gate."

"I always felt on edge in the gate Dad, really tense. I heard what you said, but it was my pride Dad; I always won and I thought I was invincible. I didn't want to show any weakness anywhere. I wanted to be strong like you."

"How bad is it Summer?"

"It's bad Dad; it keeps me awake at night and it hurts bad when I'm racing; it takes all I got to stay focused. I have to run in pain. When I rest it, it feels better, but when I push myself it comes back and hurts more than ever, more than the previous time, like it's tearing or something. When I push it, it burns bad. It's not a sharp pain, but a deep burning pain that takes forever to go away."

"Pride can kill you Summer. If you don't want to let on that you're injured, just do the best you can, but don't overdo it or it will kill you. I can promise you that. I've seen some good horses put down with bad wheels. Some of them were my friends. You didn't know this, but you had a brother before you were born that had to be put down. He injured his leg too. It broke my heart!"

"I didn't know that. Was he fast? How old was he?"

"He was three years old Summer, and he was good. Not as good as you, but we all have different competition at different times. His times were very respectable."

"I'm sorry Dad. I hear your pain. But Dad, one more thing is really bothering me. Did Angelo ever give you a shot of "steroids" before a race?"

"Why do you ask Summer? Did he give you a shot?"

"Yes, it started at Santa Anita last Christmas when I raced that horse from California that was undefeated. Did you ever get a shot? I got to know!"

"He did Summer. It always seemed to come before an important race too. He called it a "steroid" shot and said it would help me with inflammation, so I trusted him. That is probably why you're tense in the gate. I remember being overly tense too. Oh, I also noticed whenever he did it, that he would be acting very nervous and coincidentally he would be visited after the race by the same two guys. It didn't matter where we were. They seemed to follow us around the country."

"I noticed that too. Did you ever feel weird after the shot and hard to relax at night?"

"I felt that way every time he gave me a shot. You know, after thinking about it; something stinks here. You really got me wondering because I never thought about it before. It seems like he's done the same thing to you as he did to me and I wonder if he shot up your brother too. If you don't want the shot, rear up and scare him if you can. Does Lauren know he shoots you up?"

"I know she doesn't know. He always does it when she's not around and he never mentions it to her and she never mentions it either. I'm beginning to think this is what got me injured."

"I think you're right Summer Storm. The ball's in your court now. But just remember what I said, bad wheels can not only kill you, but they can kill your jockey too. You've got to take care of yourself. People are really funny. If they get hurt, they go to a doctor; if we get hurt, they put us to sleep! It's like we're not worth anything."

I looked at him with fear in my eyes; "Would Lauren really allow that to happen," I asked myself?

I thanked him for his advice and slowly walked back to my paddock, staring at the bluegrass as I walked. After a couple of long and boring days in my paddock, I started eating again and I wanted to run, as I was getting edgy and temperamental in my paddock and I knew how important this third race was. The importance of the upcoming race consumed me and disturbed my reasoning. I wasn't used to being cooped up either and it only made me feel all the more tense. Although I was undefeated and entered in the final race of the trilogy, Loretta said they should exercise caution in my prerace training and not to push me too hard. I was glad to hear that, because I had no way of telling them how bad I hurt, and yet how bad I wanted to continue running and win the final race. It was a dual edged sword I faced. I wanted to win, but yet I was running on the edge because my health was at stake, and maybe my life. She said the Triple Tiara is a true test of strength because even though the three races are two weeks apart and each one progressively longer, the schedule is actually deceiving, as the three races are actually run in a span of four short weeks, with less time to rest and train because of the travelling involved.

TURMOIL ON THE FARM

It didn't take long for a full fledged investigation to begin. That very day, Lauren said she went straight to her mom, who immediately called Kate and Pam to her office. Lauren told Roberta exactly what the vet said and she immediately summoned her to the office too.

Before Loretta could sit down, Roberta spoke from her desk; "Loretta, Lauren tells me that you think Summer Storm was doped up, and you think it was done to increase her speed, basically to win races. Is that correct?"

"That's correct Roberta," Loretta said in an angry and self-righteous manner. "You know the shadow that hangs over this sport. Whenever there's money involved people get greedy and values and ethics fly out the window. There's no other reason to shoot up a horse. I've seen this many times in the past, but never on this farm since I've been here. I was quite surprised actually, but the blood work confirmed my suspicion. I know you run a class operation here and that is one of the reasons I wanted to work here in the first place, but this stuff happens quite a bit in this sport and hopefully some day there will be testing and regulations to prevent this. It is quite harmful to the horse and can be quite harmful to the rider too. Frankly, I was very surprised to see it happen here, especially on a horse of this caliber."

Roberta, surprised by her tone of voice, studied her face and then looked at Pam and Kate.

"First of all, I want to tell you I know nothing of this and would have never condoned it. I appreciate your compliment about wanting to work here, but you've been here for twelve years now. Is it possible that this has happened here before and you weren't aware of it? Have you ever detected anything unusual? I want to know if you think there's a history of this."

Loretta looked at her and spoke with a confident air in her voice.

"No, but of course anything is possible, as I mostly see horses when they are in trouble only. But, I haven't seen a horse with so much potential and spirit as this one has in a long time. This is a horse of championship caliber, a horse that doesn't come along every day. It appears to me that her future was so great, that someone wanted more out of her, more than she could give, or maybe someone was trying to control the outcome of a race and make money at the window for somebody, either for themselves or for someone else. It's a dual edged sword, however, it also can work the other way too. Drugs can control the loss as well as a win. Either way, somebody is making money off of her or this wouldn't be happening; that's my theory. It always comes down to money; follow the dollar is what I say. But no one seems to know anything here. Do you know of anyone who both would want to do this and has access to her too?"

Pam took notes while everyone talked and Kate surveyed her calendar and journal, trying to bring up past races and results for comparison sake.

Roberta remained silent as Kate then looked at Loretta and said; "How long do you think this has been going on?"

"From the X-rays and the inflammation and swelling on her leg, I could tell you her leg has been bothering her for quite a while, maybe months; it is very tender to the touch. This didn't just happen recently. I can't believe that she hid her injury from anyone that long, or perhaps someone knew of her injury and didn't tell anyone, perhaps trying to capitalize on it at the betting window. I can't believe no one brought this to my attention."

Roberta looked at her and replied to her assertion. "Loretta, are you accusing Angelo or Lauren? They're the only people who spend time with her. No one else would want to capitalize on it at the window like you said, especially my daughter."

"No, no, no! I'm not accusing anyone. Whoever is shooting her up is doing it before post-time. Someone is getting to her then, right before the race. Is she alone at any time before a race?"

Lauren thought about what she said and spoke. "I'm with her most of the time and I've never seen Angelo with her alone, so I don't know what to say."

"Looking at her races this year, she has been gradually posting a time that wasn't as fast as previously. In other words, her times are consecutively slower than distances previously raced and her margin of victory is less too. This has been happening for months. Why hasn't anyone noticed this?" Kate said. "She's gradually been getting weaker and weaker."

"I saw a difference in her performance, but I attributed some of it to weather and track conditions and the tribulations associated with travelling. We've had a lot of rain this year. But being a novice as a jockey and knowing her well, I didn't try to push her. I know she simply likes to run her own race and she doesn't like to be behind. In fact she hates being behind. I could tell by the tension in her neck as she runs. It's as though she has a soul. She rears up in pride after every race to show her dominance. I do know one thing though. Angelo has really been pushing her hard at our practice sessions. I could see her gradually tiring as the season progressed. Why isn't Angelo here Mom? I'm sure he could shed some insight into this matter."

"I wanted to talk to you people first," Roberta said. "Is there anything else that you could shed light on Loretta? Anything at all?"

"The fact that she just contracted hives, which is a direct response to the drug she was taking, tells me that her dosage was just increased lately and quite coincidentally it coincides with the occurrence of the running of the Triple Tiara. I'm positive now that she has had amphetamines pumped into her, and not acepromazine, by how Lauren describes her behavior preceding and during the race, plus the fact she takes a while to come down. She essentially stays aroused and uptight for a while without an appetite. Amphetamines have been detected in her bloodstream, but we have only taken one test. Acepromazine, on the other hand, is never detected in the bloodstream and her behavior would be totally different than amphetamine use. Acepromazine can help a horse win too, because it relaxes a horse and allows her to be more focused during the race, whereas you tell me she was always uptight. This behavior is magnified in a horse with this tenacity and disposition. Being she is high strung anyway, I would see why this behavior would be difficult to detect. With her tenacity and strength, it's a wonder she hasn't got hurt badly."

Roberta listened intently and stood up to face Loretta and reached her hand out.

"Thanks Loretta for your expertise on this matter. I want you to monitor her regularly and report back to me every morning. I want to know her food intake and whether the prescriptions you are giving her are having any effect, any effect at all. I also would appreciate you looking out for any kind of visitors or behavior on the farm that you feel is unusual. Lauren, I want you to observe her behavior closely and report back to me daily on her condition."

Loretta shook Roberta's hand; "You can count on me; I'm here to help. I'm just glad we caught this before a catastrophe occurred. At this time, I cannot say for sure if she will be ready at race time, but I will be treating her and monitoring her daily and reporting her progress back to you, just like you want."

"Thanks again Loretta, I know I can count on you. Do your best; this race is very important."

"I will. I'm totally aware of that."

They shook hands and when Loretta left the room, she immediately got on her two-way radio and contacted Angelo on their own frequency.

"Angelo, can you meet me in my office in ten minutes, it's important."

"Sure, what's up?"

"Just meet me there. We'll discuss it then."

Angelo then hastily left the practice oval and made a beeline to the clinic, where Loretta was waiting for him. She anxiously met him at the door.

"I came as soon as I could. What's up?"

"I was just called to a meeting in Roberta's office regarding Summer Storm. I told them I suspected she was drugged and it's been going on for quite a while. They're going to be monitoring her closely, as well as anybody who looks suspicious. I thought you should know."

"I appreciate you telling me, but why in the hell did you say you suspected her of being drugged?"

"I had to. The evidence was too great. I had no choice; I'm her vet for Christ's sake. She had amphetamines in her blood and she developed hives from a reaction to it."

Angelo, seemingly dismissing the gravity of the situation, said. "Do you think she'll be ready for the next race?"

"Right now, I don't know. She's strong; it's a 50/50 shot, a crapshoot."

Angelo looked at her and realized he forgot about the "cumulative effect," of how drugs remain in your system and creep up on you. He had simply given her too much, too often.

"Is there anything I can do to help her out, anything at all?"

"Just let her rest and let the herbal remedies take over. Don't give her anything and don't exercise her. I'll do my best to have her ready. I know how important this is to everybody."

While they spoke at Loretta's office, the meeting in Roberta's office continued. Kate and Lauren looked at Roberta.

"You know, I can't tell you how disgusted I am about this situation. My father always ran a tight ship here and I tried to carry on his legacy. I'm mad as hell and I'm terribly sad at the same time; it's a strange feeling. It's almost depressing, knowing this has been going on."

"Why isn't Angelo here Roberta?" Lauren asked.

Roberta looked at them, then looked down at her large mahogany desk and fiddled with her pen. She blinked, while holding back a tear, and then stared at a picture on the wall of her father. She recollected on how he ran the farm and his words of advice to her before he died. She then turned to Kate.

"Have any of you seen any difference in Angelo's behavior lately, or anything suspicious?"

Kate closed her journal and looked at Roberta, weighing her words; "I do remember he wanted to take complete control over Summer Storm, and was actually upset that she won her first race in the mud up there in New York. It was almost as if she took the wind out of his sails that day. I also noticed that he has been more uptight and drinking more lately too. Why, do you suspect him of doing this?"

"Since this incident has occurred Kate, I've thought about his behavior and I remembered how upset he got when I refused his numerous requests for a male jockey. I also noticed that he would break away from us at the race tracks, often being gone for extended periods of time. He also had the same two guys visiting him in the stands and it didn't matter what part of the country we were in; they were always there. I thought at first that they were other trainers, fellow colleagues, but I know most of them. It made me think about what my father told me before he died. These guys were dressed like gangsters, always dressed in a silk suit with a fedora, always smoking a stogie."

"Now that you mention it, I have seen them too, but I never thought anything about it. I also noticed that he has been tense and very excitable lately and I've had to admonish him about yelling at Summer Storm. But I thought it was just the booze talking. He even grabbed my arm real hard after the last race and asked me why she barely won. I had to tell him to let me go." Lauren said.

"I wish you would have let me know that. I saw you guys arguing but didn't know he grabbed your arm. Have you ever seen those two guys in the stables Lauren, or any other strangers around Summer?"

"No Mom, I can't say I have."

"Do any of you know Angelo's history?"

Kate looked at Lauren and Lauren shrugged her shoulders. Then Roberta spoke; "I've been in the business world many years, and I've always done things the clean way, the honorable way, trying to run this place the way my dad did. I've always had a code of ethics that I followed and tried to instill it in my family and employees. These days, everything has changed and the industry has gotten progressively corrupted."

"What I'm telling you is between us only and is not to leave the room. As you know, Angelo worked for my dad for years and I inherited him when I acquired the farm. Before my dad died, he took me aside and told me of Angelo's past history with the New York mob and the influence his friends had at the Mafia controlled tracks and told me to look out for him. He told me Angelo's racing career actually started with the help of a Brooklyn Mafia Don who was his godfather when he first entered the states in the thirties. Angelo actually came here in exile, as the Mafia in Sicily was trying to kill him. You see, Angelo's dad was a Mafia Don in Sicily and getting to Angelo was retaliation for another murder. My dad told me of two incidents that happened and that he thought Angelo was responsible both times, but he couldn't prove it."

"What kind of incidents?" Kate nervously asked.

"Have you ever heard of a "milk shake," and I don't mean the one at the malt shop?" Roberta said.

"No," Lauren and Kate replied, as they both looked at each other dumbfounded.

Roberta continued; "A "milk shake" is a virtually undetectable way to boost a horse's performance on the track. It can make an also ran run like a champion. It is simply a magic elixir that can make hooves fly. It works by stopping the release of toxin into the horse's bloodstream. First, a trainer or stable hand uses a garden hose to suck out the contents of a horse's stomach. A half an hour before the horse is to run its race, a mixture of baking soda, sugar and a sports drink is poured through the horse's nose and down its throat. This procedure removes and prevents the absence of toxin in the bloodstream and prevents the horse from tiring as he pounds his way down the track. Dad caught Angelo doing this before a race once and admonished him, with Angelo saying he was sorry and would never do it again. He said he was doing it for the farm so that my dad would make money on the race. Because Dad treated him like a son, he let it go. Dirty trainers are common in this sport, but their deeds are hard to prove. That horse was an underdog that day and won by a whopping four lengths. Being the concoction was virtually undetectable in urine tests, Dad didn't know how long this thing had been going on before he caught him. That same horse died suspiciously after a race just three months later, but Dad couldn't prove anything as nothing showed up in the horse's blood. The horse was only three years old and had never shown any kind of illness in the past. He asked Angelo about it, and Angelo didn't know anything. Another time Dad found amphetamine bottles and syringes hidden on a shelf in the back of a tack room, but no one knew anything about it, of course. He confronted Angelo, to which Angelo immediately fired a jockey and blamed it on him. Now I'm beginning to wonder if the firing was just a front to make himself look clean."

Kate kept her head down and nervously thumbed through her journal looking for past race statistics and then looked at Roberta and said; "What do you want to do?"

Roberta said; "What can we do? We have no proof; we're just going to have to watch that horse closely. My father took him on and treated him like the son he never had; they were very close. Because of that, Angelo always got the benefit of the doubt from him."

Roberta looked at Pam. "Pam, I want you to contact a security company and get cameras set up as soon as possible, not only in Summer Storm's stable, but every horse's stall that is currently racing. Eventually, I want them set up in every barn and corridor and I want someone hired to monitor them, 24/7. I also want them set up in Loretta's clinic; whoever is doing this is getting the drugs somewhere. This has to stop."

Lauren, surprised at her mother's words, looked at Kate, then at her Mom.

"Are you saying you suspect Loretta too?"

"I don't know what to think right now. I'm just trying to cover all bases, that's all. This whole incident reminds me of how much Angelo wanted me to hire Loretta years ago. I might be wrong and I hope I am. Either way, with a camera in her clinic we can see who is going in and out of there."

Kate rubbed her head with an eraser and gave it some thought, while she stared at Roberta.

"Why don't we hire a private investigator to keep an eye on Angelo, and Summer Storm too, not only here but at the track too.

And as a bonus, maybe we can find out more about his shady looking friends."

"Great idea! Kate, get a list of good PI's and let's get on it. I don't care what it costs. I want him followed and photographed everywhere. If he sneezes, I want to know if he uses a hanky. We have to get to the bottom of this. I want this done yesterday."

Meanwhile, while they were talking late that afternoon, Angelo came to the door and wanted to know the results of my tests, but mostly was there to "feel" things out, as he felt paranoid after his meeting with Loretta and thought they were onto him. Roberta came out on the porch and told him the lab work was sent into Lexington and she would have the results back tomorrow and she would notify him.

Angelo then left the farm and drove his old Buick down the winding and hilly road; the noise from the bad muffler and the smoke from the exhaust leaving behind a noisy blue trail. He led a life few knew about; some of which I heard about, and some he kept secret; he was a real loner. On the outskirts of town, he stopped at the local watering hole and ordered a boiler maker and got a roll of quarters. He downed his shot of whiskey and walked to the phone located on the wall in the rear of the bar next to the restrooms with a beer in his hands. He nervously called his contact in Brooklyn to give them a heads up; he had to tell them what was happening.

"Vinnie, it's Ange. How yo doin?"

"What do you mean, how yo doin? What's up? You never call me unless there's a fucking problem."

"Alright Vinnie, you know me too well. Yeah, we got problems!"

"What are ya talking 'bout? What kinda problems?"

"The horse is sick Vinnie. She's come down with hives and that woman vet discovered her front leg was lame too. And because of her obvious symptoms, she also suspected that the horse was doped up and I think they think I done it. I think they're suspecting me. I could tell by the way they look at me."

"Who's They? How in the fuck did this happen Ange? Will she be able to go next week? She's got to go Ange, we got a lot of dough riding on her fucking losing next week and California Miss winning; we'll have the odds at the track changed by then in our favor. We set her up to win every race but this one. Everybody and their fucking uncle's going to be betting on Summer Storm to win the crown. If she loses next week we make a ton!"

"Yeah, yeah, I know. She's got juiced up to now, but this week she won't get none Vinnie. Plus this race is longer and her leg is sore and that should slow her too. She barely won last week! I figure next time she can't win. It's a whole quarter of a mile longer and they're forecasting rain!"

"I know she barely won. You scared the shit outa me. Ange, I'm fucking asking you, how did this happen?"

"I guess I gave her too much fucking juice; she broke out in hives and because of that we were forced to have her seen by the vet on the farm. She's pretty sick now. She ain't eating and her leg is swollen."

"Jesus, Ange; of all times to fuck up! I can't believe you're so fucking dumb. How could you let this happen?"

Angelo felt the tension in Vinnie's voice and got worried bad; he didn't like the tone and he didn't like being called dumb. His stomach started to churn as he thought about the consequences.

"Don't worry 'bout it Vinnie; I can handle this! I can handle this! Tell Richie "Frog Eyes" not to worry either; it'll be alright. I'll fix it. I'll definitely make it good; you'll see. I got it under control."

"It's got to be alright. We pay you fucking well. Don't you disappoint me. You hear me Ange. Don't you fucking disappoint me."

"Yeah, yeah! I told you I got it under control. I'll see to it she'll be okay'd to go for the race and there's no way she's gonna win either; it's in the bank."

"Alright, keep me informed. I want good news next time, you hear me? Good fucking news!"

"You got it Vinnie. I'll call you when things change."

Angelo got off the phone and sat down at the bar with his face cupped in his hands; he knew what he was dealing with. Vinnie D was a "made" man and was the Don of one of the five New York families, a direct heir to the late Sammy Luccido. He was so cold, he could kill you and then sit down to a steak dinner with no remorse. In fact, Angelo once heard of a story where Vinnie D arranged a killing of a Capo that had crossed him; he had the man killed while the man sat across from him eating dinner with him. He had one of his "wiseguys" come up from behind with a garrote and choke him while he was eating, then dropped his lifeless face in his spaghetti dish when he was done. Vinnie D then finished his dinner and drank his glass of wine while he stared at the dead man from across the table; he was ruthless and had no conscience. His nickname was "The Grim Reaper," because he left death in his tracks.

Richie "Frog Eyes" was his "enforcer" and ran the gambling interests for him too; he essentially controlled the rackets in Brooklyn; the "bug", loan-sharking, shy locking, race tracks, sports betting, and off-track betting. Richie was an "off the hook" kind of guy with wild eyes and was real explosive, having spent time in the mental ward on Ryker's Island as a teenager. He too was a "made" man and the "underboss" to Vinnie, the direct heir to his power. To be a "made" man meant you killed someone for the mob and you not only were Italian, you can trace your roots back to Sicily. In other words, if you were Italian but you weren't Sicilian, you couldn't enter their private dens no matter how many men you killed. The mob simply figured if you weren't Sicilian, you couldn't be trusted.

Richie "Frog Eyes" made his bones when he and his gang brazenly hijacked one of the New York Dons and the Don's son outside an Italian Restaurant in Manhattan in the seventies. As Don Patty Mangiarelli and his son Vince were casually walking to their parked Cadillac after dinner, Richie and two wiseguys put a gun in their ribs and escorted them to their car. It was raining and the streets were lined with tourists at the time, which made it all the more brazen. When Don Patty opened the door of his car, he found his bodyguard lying on the floor of the back seat with a knife in his throat, his blood turning a gory black on the beige carpet. Don Patty and his son Vince were frisked for weapons and then forced to sit in the back seat with their feet on the dead bodyguard while they drove away. Richie and two of his henchmen then took them to a meat processing plant on the waterfront in Manhattan, where they brutalized and tortured them for hours. They tied up Patty and Vince and cut Vince's fingers off with bolt cutters while Richie lit a cigar and laughed while Vince's blood spurted on the floor, continuing to make him suffer. After he finished his cigar, and Vince was practically unconscious from the loss of blood, he stripped the dead bodyguard and Vince and threw them into a large commercial meat grinder while Vince was still alive. All the while Don Patty was tied to a chair and forced to watch the carnage, while his son was slowly sucked in, screaming in pain as he was slowly being chewed up by the giant grinder.

"My son, my son! You fucking pigs. I'm gonna kill you. I'm gonna fucking kill you." Don Patty cried as he struggled to get free.

Richie puffed on his cigar and laughed at him; "You ain't gonna fucking kill nobody anymore you slime ball. You're killing days are over you fucking prick."

When Richie talked, he just didn't blow smoke. He then sent one of his men to the meat rack and grabbed a side of beef and threw it into the grinder with the two shredded bodies. Then they mixed them all together in the automatic giant stainless steel grinder, making some "hamburgers." Then they cooked part of the mixture in front of the crying Don and made the Don eat it, forcibly shoving the meat down his throat. After Don Patty vomited from the taste of his son, they gave him the coup de grace with a bullet to the back of his head and left him hanging on a meat hook in the refrigerator next to a side of beef, with Vince's cut off fingers shoved in his mouth. Before walking out the door, Richie called Don Patty's crew and told them where he could find Don Patty and told them to come hungry. On the way home, in the back seat of his caddy, Richie laughed about it uncontrollably and said; "Someone's going to have some good fucking burgers tomorrow."

When there was a change of power in Rome, the populace would look to the window of the Vatican for white smoke. On the streets of New York, when there was a change of power, it was the blue smoke of a gun that ushered it in. Either way, the repercussions vibrated throughout the community and eventually were felt by all.

These guys meant business and didn't like to be crossed. Seeing Angelo looked worried, Billy Joe, the bartender, looked at him and asked him what was wrong.

Angelo came back to the moment and turned to Billy Joe, knowing he couldn't divulge anything and marinated the truth again. "Summer Storm is sick and I don't know if she can make it next week. Her whole career, and mine, rides on that race."

"What's wrong with her? I didn't know she was sick!"

"She ain't eating and is acting like she's sick. And this is just between you and me. You understand? Jesus Christ! This can't get out. You hear me?"

"Sure, sure, I hear you. She'll be okay Angelo. That's one hell of a horse. I've never seen anything like her. She looks fucking invincible."

Angelo shouldn't have been disclosing private information about the horse, but at this time he was drinking and didn't really care. Though his guard was down, he tried to contain his inner feelings. His mind was preoccupied with the mob and what they could do to him. He's known horse trainers in the past that have disappeared when the mob was "disappointed." He put his hands down and cupped his shot glass, all the while, staring at the empty glass. He remembered a friend of his, a trainer named Joey Pascarelli from Youngstown, and what happened to him. The first time Joey fucked up and let a horse win that wasn't supposed to, they broke his leg. The second time, they beat him unconscious one night in front of Angelo, and then drove him to a metal salvaging yard in the industrial section of Bensonhurst, in Brooklyn, and threw him in the trunk of an old rusty Chevy that had been sitting there for years. Then they picked up the car with a massive hydraulic claw bucket and dropped the car into a hydraulic metal compressor which squeezed that car into a steel cube three feet by three feet, while Joey was still alive. He heard the metal screech and the tires pop and saw Joey's blood and body fluids ooze out from the compressed steel and watched it instantly turn to a pink vapor from the heat and never forgot it. He knew the world he lived in. You knew the rules and you didn't ask questions.

Vinnie D then looked at Angelo and said; "There, let that be a lesson. If you're smart, you know better than to ever fucking cross me." He saw the fear in Angelo's eyes and put his arms around him and laughed; "Ange, don't worry, it's not personal. I like you. It's only business! You take care'a business, there's nothin to worry 'bout."

While Billy Joe stared at him, a tear streamed down Angelo's cheek. Billy Joe could tell he was far away and walked away, deciding it was best to leave him alone. Angelo then turned his head away and drifted off again, staring in the mirror opposite from him and wondered where the years have gone. The booze was getting to him now and he was turning melancholy. The devil was dancing in his head now and distorting his basic thoughts. He really didn't recognize the image staring back at him anymore. His hair was white and the years in the sun had left his face as jagged as a country road map. He used to be young and handsome, but now he looked like a hunch backed old man, even though he still felt young inside. He hated that mirror. It was like looking at a photograph of someone he didn't know and didn't want to know. He then turned his head to the end of the bar and stared at the lit Budweiser sign that hung over the pool table, studying the Clydesdale Horse team, which was enclosed in glass, and continued to reflect on his past. The melancholy tune, "He Stopped Loving Her Today" by George Jones, was playing on the fancy Werlitzer jukebox in the corner. As he rehashed his wretched past, the song that was playing made him become more and more somber, almost depressed. "They laid a wreath upon his chest . . . . And now they're carrying him away . . . . He stopped loving her today." Angelo was raised in New York and although this was "hillbilly" music to him, the words were hitting home hard, slamming against his brain. They were reaching his basic emotions now. Where was Bobby Darin when you needed him? While listening to the sad lyrics, with a tear running down his cheek, he thought of Morgan and how he had to leave Sicily years ago and then Apecchio. He reminisced about the long voyage to the states and wondered how different his life would be if he would have been nurtured in the Mafia and whether he would have liked "The Life."

"The Life!" "Ha," he thought. Yeah, there was good looking broads, big cars, jewelry, wads of cash, and no forty hour week like the regular stiffs, but what else would he have to contend with? Robbing, stealing, having to kill your best friend sometime, and constantly looking over your shoulder, sleeping with a gun, not to mention the constant threat of jail time if you got caught. It was the fast lane alright, but it didn't take a brain surgeon to figure out how it may have ended, he probably would have been dead by now or in prison. Nobody "retires" from the mob. If you're lucky, you go out in a box. If you're not so lucky, you're brutalized and they never find you. You either sleep with the fish, shredded to the chickens, or you're part of a concrete freeway.

He thought about his first menial job in America too, mucking the stables for a dollar a day, and strangely, how much happier he was then. Gas was fifteen cents a gallon and a loaf of bread was only a nickel. A studio apartment above an old ladies residence for forty dollars a month, ah, what simpler times they were. There wasn't the stress there is now days. Where has the time gone? It's amazing how soiled you can become once you dip your hands into the dirty pool of crime. The ripples that resonate outward touch your very soul and the fundamental values you once had, the values you selfishly tarnished

The Jagged Side of Midnight

and destroyed. But the ripples don't stop there. They continue to envelop and reach out; destroying everything you cherish as they monopolize every day you live.

Angelo then came back to reality. While staring at the hanging Budweiser Clydesdale sign; in a soft voice, downcast and almost apologetic, he emphatically waved his arms and spoke. "Billy Joe, have you ever been afraid? I mean really afraid, I mean afraid for your fucking life?"

"No, I can't say I have Angelo. Oh, I've had automobile accidents that happened quickly, but they occurred so fast I didn't have time for fear. Why? What are you afraid of?"

Angelo quickly gathered his senses and realized he couldn't answer the question with honesty and just shrugged his shoulders and looked down at his empty shot glass again. He knew Billy Joe led a sheltered life here in the hills of Kentucky and wouldn't understand what he was talking about or where he was even coming from. Angelo had been dancing with the devil for years and had friends that did things that Billy Joe couldn't even imagine, things you didn't even see in movies. He wanted to put cheese on the crackers, but he knew better than to disclose anything else. He tried to keep his mouth shut as his mind raced with fear.

The booze was getting to him now and he became more somber. After a couple minutes of silence, he looked up at Billy Joe with watery eyes; "Hey, I'm just like you and everybody else. My mind talks to me all the time, always thinking its right and what I do is wrong. Sometimes it gets you down, that's all! I don't know, I guess I'm just getting old. I guess I just fear death, that's all. I feel like it's just around the corner sometimes. I look at the obituary column everyday just to see if there were people younger than me who died. I find someone dying that was younger than me and say; "Hey, I won again." You're lucky, you're still young. You probably don't even know where in the hell I'm coming from."

129

"Hey, forget about it! Everything will be alright Angelo! Snap out of it. You're just feeling down right now. Here, can you handle another boilermaker? This one's on me."

Angelo grabbed the basket of peanuts on the bar, cracked opened a few and threw the shells on the wooden floor. He knew he needed some food in his stomach. He also knew he had drunk too much and was feeling woozy, but tonight he didn't care. He then nodded at Billy Joe, as if to agree with him, and downed his shot of Crown Royal and grabbed his Budweiser to wash it down. It was eight o'clock in the evening now and the Yankee game was just starting on the TV, which was suspended from the ceiling in the corner of the bar. Angelo turned on his stool and stared at it awhile, his elbow on the bar holding his head up. The vision of Yankee Stadium reminded him of his time in New York and how he never wanted to become involved in the mob.

"How did this happen. How did I get in so deep?" He thought, as his mind raced through his past.

Now he's their patsy, their flunky, making big money for them and from them, and then giving it all back when he gambled and lost. He didn't know what to do. He was trapped in their tangled web of crime and deceit and he knew it. He also knew he could be sent to the slammer for what he's done at the tracks if he got caught. He finished his beer and ordered another boiler maker and a meatball sandwich. He had to put some food in his stomach. The peanuts weren't cutting it.

After eating his sandwich, he went to the restroom and then walked over to the fireplace in the corner of the bar and sat down, sinking into the soft couch.

"Loneliness, what a bitch," he thought!

The hot embers of the fireplace glowed in front of him while he stared at the dancing flames. It was a peaceful sight that demanded recollection and reflection of the past. The third shot glass of Crown soothed the relentless feelings of solitude and isolation that suffocated each breath he took. Although he was staring at the glowing flames, his mind came alive with the lost feelings and the beautiful memories of yesteryear. The discreet passion of uninhibited youth with the invincibility that is recalled with each sip of whiskey gently danced through his head.

"Mom, Dad, Morgan, where has the time gone?" He asked himself. "Where have all of you gone?"

It was just yesterday that beautiful women, aged wines and beautiful rhapsodies played a fine balance his life. The glass needed filling again. What a sweet taste, sweet and yet bitter, biting at his stomach but numbing his brain. The glow of the amber liquid reflecting in the fire was mesmerizing and yet peaceful. He stared at the kaleidoscope of the gold tinted crystal and got hypnotized as it revealed his youthful memories.

He put the shot glass down and wondered; "Do I have to be alone, or am I just punishing myself again? It seems I do have a choice. I don't have to be alone tonight, but somehow, someway, I enjoy the solitude once in a while. Once in a while is the key. I do enjoy a lady's company and the niceties they bring with them; their smell, their touch, and the beauty they bring mesmerizes me. But women; can you trust any of them? I think some of them were born to lie. It's the exception to the rule when you meet one with the intelligence to maintain a relationship for what it is instead of what you can get out of it. It's the lying that disturbs me. When you promise your undying love and give from your heart, you expect the same in return. Is that asking too much? I've known some good decent women, but they are rare. I hope I can find another one before I die. Loneliness is such a bitch," he thought

He climbed out of his seat and walked to the bathroom again. Ah, the prostate; another reminder of his age! One shot of whiskey equals two trips to the head. It's like a math formula. He stares at the commode while he relieves himself and recalls different commodes in the past. Why? He doesn't know; it seems he's been here often, too often. A bar in Brooklyn and one in Santa Anita, the long line at

Yankee Stadium and the Super Bowl at half time, pay a Euro for a piss in Rome, Florence, Naples, and Pompeii; same feeling, same result. The pause that refreshes, that's what he calls it. They all look the same, white with a deodorizer that doesn't work, yellow stained cigarette butts soaked with piss, and if you're lucky, a handle that flushes. And the smell? Nothing like the odor of dried piss! But regardless of the displeasure they emanate; they all give the same comfortable result. It's the porcelain God staring up at him, the face looks the same everywhere.

He looks in the mirror while he washes his hands. "God, who is that stranger staring back at me? I don't recognize the face, although he has a sharp likeness to my father."

"Do we become our father," he thought, as he stared at the image.

He feels twenty years younger and can't identify with the image staring back at him. He simply can't identify with him at all. His face was ruddy, with a nose that was bulbous, a direct reaction to the booze he had consumed through the years. Deep lines now framed his eyes and ran across his forehead. His eyes were open and fixed, with drooping lids and dark shadows that showed the stress he's been under. His thin hair was snowy-white and grey stubbles monopolized his ruddy face.

"Look at those lines on my forehead. Look at those tired eyes. And the hair? When in the hell did it turn white? Where did he come from? How did he get here? Has life been that rough that I should have to look like this? I was a good looking guy once, almost handsome. Every woman I wanted, I got. I had muscles that ripped. Now look at me, recovering from a hip replacement and feeling debilitated. I can't look any longer, but damn it if he didn't follow me out of the room."

The couch at the fireplace awaits him as he sinks into the softness of the leather. He stares again at the glowing embers and ponders what he's just seen.

"I watched in the mirror as he followed me out of the restroom. Is he always following me? Always aging me as I go? I've come to the conclusion, after many years, that it's inevitable that I age and how I handle the change I experience is a reflection of the inner peace or turmoil that I am experiencing at the time. Good thoughts reflect positive attitudes and dark thoughts reflect gloom and negativity. For now, let me have these thoughts, damn it, all of them, perhaps I'll grow from them. Right now, they are dark and deep and I have miles to go before I sleep."

He reached over to the little table that sat between him and the fireplace and watched in a trance as his golden beer flowed into the curved glass, bubbling in the glow of the dancing flames. He was getting drunk and he knew it. He also didn't care. He was escaping the real world.

As he drowned his sorrows down the road that night, the gears of compliance were already in motion. Pam was making arrangements with a local security company for security cameras to be installed everywhere on the farm and Kate was setting up an appointment with a private investigator for the next morning. Roberta and Lauren were reviewing tapes of the past races and checking for any weakness or abnormality I may have had, any abnormalities at all. Richie "Frog Eyes" and Vinnie D were purchasing tickets for a flight to Lexington. In the meantime, I had around the clock care and surveillance. Angelo's world was getting squeezed fast.

The Race

Ten days went by and Loretta gave Roberta the green light for the race. The hives were gone and the swelling had gone down on my leg. She said I would be okay with some tape and a cortisone shot. Lauren spent a lot of time with me during that week and I didn't see much of Angelo. Cameras were installed everywhere and the newly hired gumshoe hovered around the farm, essentially impersonating a newly hired contractor and inadvertently kept an eye on Angelo and me. Angelo nervously snuck off to The Tack Room every other night and assured Richie and Vinnie that everything was "under control," as I often heard him talking to himself. He said that I would indeed be racing and that I would indeed lose; he'd make sure of that. That really confused me. "How would he make certain I lose, and why would he want me to lose? I don't get it."

During that hectic week and a half, Sportswriters from all over the world visited the farm while I recuperated and wondered why I wasn't training regularly. They were always told that I was done for the day and that I practiced on the oval very early, earlier than they were allowed on the farm. None of them were made aware of my injury.

"After all," Roberta said; "We want to keep her image as a "Super Horse," a horse that doesn't come along very often."

She knew that the idea of infallibility would only bring more dollars down the road in breeding fees. My unblemished record would be a huge plus in the breeding world of Horse Racing.

The final race of The Triple Tiara was scheduled for July 4th, which was on a Saturday, so we left for New York on the preceding Thursday, later than usual. This gave me more time to rest at home and less time to be scrutinized at the track. Roberta had the private investigator send one of his colleagues with them to the race track, as Angelo was familiar with the one who worked the farm as a "contractor." He traveled on a private airliner so Angelo wouldn't see him. I had gotten used to the original PI's presence, seeing him frequently around the farm and thought nothing of it. Angelo had noticed him too and asked Roberta who the stranger was, and he was told he was an Irrigation Consultant, someone to design a system to keep the bluegrass on the hills at their full potential, all year round. We arrived in New York before noon, which gave me another day to rest. On Friday morning, I was awakened by Bryan and Lauren and Angelo with his beloved timer. I hated that timer and paid no attention to it. I would run my own race. The combination of the herbal remedy I was taking and the fear of my injury not healing completely made me a little nervous. I couldn't understand why I was edgy now because I was coming down from amphetamines, as I hadn't been shot up in a while. I thought about his timer and the "steroid" shots he had given me in the past and got angry again.

"Why do they have to time me all the time?" I thought. "Don't they know I don't like to lose? Lauren says I'm the one who fights the bull and knows how to turn it on when I have to. They don't have to push me to win. I don't want to lose."

I knew more about me than they did. I spent the rest of the day relaxing in my paddock and going for a short walk around the complex with Bryan and Lauren leading me.

Saturday soon came and Winnie and I woke up to a loud thunderstorm about five o'clock in the morning, with lightning flashing all around us illuminating the stall and barn. This occurred in the dark before the sun came up. Little did I know that hell woke up with me this day and would not only monopolize today, but many more days to come. This Saturday was not to be my friend.

It wasn't dawn yet, so I paced the stall nervously while waiting out the storm. Winnie watched and tried to talk to me, bleating and bleating, not really knowing the pressure I was experiencing or what I was going through and what was expected of me in just a few short hours. California Miss was directly across the stall from me this time and I hated looking at her. She just made me feel all the more tense. I was forced to be in her presence with all the attention she was getting all week and I was glad we were going to race today; I was sick of it. I was glad we were finally going to get this over with. They made me feel like I was a has-been already, a dried up piece of toast. "I'd show them," I thought.

Bryan and Lauren came down to see me at seven o'clock in the morning and fed me a little. They were just about to leave when Angelo walked in. He wanted me to walk a little, warming my muscles, as my splint had been off for only three days now and I was just taped. It was pouring outside, but Lauren, Bryan and I walked anyway. It was July and the warm summer rain felt comforting on my skin, easing the tension that had been building in me. Our race was scheduled for three o'clock and the pomp and circumstances began around noon. I would have plenty of time to bathe and dry off and rest before the race. There were photographers and writers here from all over the world, all here to see me achieve my destiny, mainly because there hadn't been a Triple Tiara winner since the great Ruffian. Roberta was in her glory, all dressed up, smiling and talking to the writers. After a couple of drinks and being under the spotlight and microphones for an hour, she mistakenly told them all about my nagging injury, but said I was okay and ready to go. After her comments, the word spread like wild fire through the track and for the first time since my race at Santa Anita last year, I overheard I was a slight underdog in Vegas with California Miss listed as the favorite. This only made me more edgy and irritable because this was my most important race of my career. I was also angry about not being favored, as I was the only horse in the race still undefeated. I don't understand humans. I figured someone had to beat me first for me to be an underdog.

Lauren and Bryan left around ten and said they'd be back around noon. Angelo than showed up with the same two guys I saw in California, Chicago and New York. He was giving them a tour of the stables, but all they were interested in was me and my leg. Angelo told them not to worry as they surveyed me closely; "I have to give her her "vitamins" yet," he said. He then made a quick motion with his hand and injected me and left. It was done so quickly, I couldn't rear up or do anything about it. I didn't see it in his hand and I didn't even see it coming. The three of them quickly left and I walked over to the opening in the door of my stall and looked down the corridor that separated the barn from the other side. As I stood waiting at the opening of the stall watching them walk through the barn, California Miss came to the opening in her door and gazed at me from her stall.

"So you're injured, huh? Well, I guess your reign is over. I'm favored today, and today I'm going to make sure you go down. I owe you big time!"

"Don't get so happy about yourself. I was injured the last two times I beat you and I still beat you. You're just not good enough. All I have to do is keep pace with you and turn it up a notch at the end. It's that simple; been there, done that. After today, they'll never hear of you again. You'll be going back to California with your head between your legs and you'll be racing nags from now on. When this race is over, you'll have lost to me four times and they'll never put you up against me or anybody else that's good again."

Then out of nowhere, Lauren surprised me by abruptly rushing in my stall with tears running down her face. She grabbed a brush and talked while she groomed me and told me that she and Bryan just had a fight and that she didn't know what to do. She was beside herself. Apparently Bryan just told her that when he graduated in June last month, he accepted a job as a Business Consultant at an internet company in Seattle and they would have to move there when they got married. She had just received the news and she was completely blind-sided by this, as they had planned to build a house on the farm and Bryan was supposed to take over his family business. She told him that she didn't want to leave me behind and that I would never be allowed to go with them, as I was part of her mom's business. She sobbed while she held my head, making me feel very confused. I was psyched up to run this race in pain, a race that I prepared so long for, and now I was getting bombarded with emotions that was draining me, both hers and mine. I couldn't do anything but stand there and let her go on and on, letting her emotions spill, hoping that she would feel better soon. As for me, I would deal with this later. I had bigger fish to fry, like that damn horse across the barn staring at me and talking smack. There were only four hours to the start of the race and we had to get our act together. Angelo then returned by himself, and upon seeing him, Lauren quickly turned her back on him and dried her eyes.

"Is anything wrong?" He said, while studying her motions, thinking perhaps Lauren might have suspected something.

Lauren didn't want to divulge her personal life to him, so she turned to him and said; "No, I was just thinking how proud I was of our progress and how far we've come. Today is her day. I'm so proud of her. She's an amazing animal. I can't tell you how much I love her."

Angelo, relieved to hear Lauren wasn't suspicious of anything, said; "Good, let's get ready, we have an important day ahead of us. We have history to make. The world is waiting for a new champion." He then left the barn, relieved of any paranoia he may have had.

I knew this was my big day and wanted to get it on. I wanted this over with. After finally getting calmed down, Lauren saddled me and held my head again while she talked to me, looking in my eyes. She looked so pretty today with her new blue and white riding suit and shiny black boots on. The days and months preceding the race made me on edge as I knew the importance of this race, but this recent turn of events only made me more anxious and tense. She then led me out to the paddocks, which was a very large enclosed circular opening surrounded by applauding fans and photographers. My eyes were wide open and my ears erect as the flashbulbs popped all around me. I was the star of the day and I knew it, even though I was an underdog. But I felt really weird inside from the shot I had, different from the previous shots. My head was starting to relax but my legs and hind muscles were twitching uncontrollably. I should have been used to these pre-race jitters, but because of my injury, I was afraid for the first time in my life. I had always been in control, but I felt something else was controlling me now and I wondered what Angelo had given me, knowing he wasn't supposed to be giving me anything.

Each horse entered in the race had to pass this area on the way to the track, as we were escorted in a line separated by twenty yards or so. We'd walk the perimeter of the big circle of the enclosed paddock where the gamblers were waiting to survey the horses, always looking for a weakness they might exploit before they ran to the window at the last minute to bet on the race. Because of my now known and exposed injury, I had a larger crowd than usual studying me and my gait. My leg was taped and it seemed like everyone was pointing at it. The skies were a dreary dark purple and looked terribly ominous, but the cool wet drizzle actually made me feel good. It made me feel alive. I was starting to relax. My reins had to be held by Angelo while Lauren dismounted me and sat with the other jockeys and got their official instructions for the race. When Lauren was finished, she walked over and reached up and gave me a kiss and then mounted me as we posed for the photographers and media again for the last time.

"Let's do it baby," she said, as she patted my neck.

After all the commotion, she then slowly rode me through a dark tunnel under the grandstands that led us to the track; each horse would walk through this tunnel, each separated by twenty yards or so, so that each can receive their own applause when they came out onto the track from the tunnel. The tunnel was about one hundred feet long and dark inside but as you walked through it you could see the track exposed, and daylight, which was visible at the end of the tunnel. This long walk through the dark tunnel, void of light and noise, gave me time to reflect on the task at hand and what I had to do today.

"Just one more race; I could do this. I just have to turn it on one more time," I thought, as I saw the rain dancing on the puddles on the track in the distance.

All the while, Lauren was comforting me by rubbing my neck and caressing my mane as I felt the adrenaline being pumped into my blood stream. I could sense the tension in her voice and in her fingers and legs and knew this race meant a lot to her too. The bugles blared out our entrance from the tunnel and the crowd roared as we took the field in a pouring rain and driving wind. My head lifted back and my nostrils flared as we left the tunnel and walked onto the bright and noisy wet infield. "New York, New York," by Frank Sinatra, was playing loudly on the speakers and drowning out the crowd. I could smell the rain in the air and I could smell the competition. I was absorbing everything, the wet and slimy mud I walked in, the falling rain, the cool and windy air, the noise of the crowd, the television cameras and banners everywhere, the blimp flying overhead, the flashbulbs going off, the gelding escorting me, and most of all the competition. This was my moment to shine. This is what I was bred for. Today was my day. I was ready to rock. Little did I know that in a few short minutes, destiny waited for me around the corner and would not only change my life, but everybody else's life forever.

I turned around and locked eyes with California Miss while we were escorted to the starting gate by a steward on a gelding. She was about forty yards behind me and looked confident as she walked. Geldings were always used for escorts to the starting gate because they were infertile and their scent didn't excite the stallions or fillies. My post position was the two hole today with California Miss drawing the four hole, meaning I was closest to the rail, advantage to me again. She knew she was favored today and she pranced around like she was going to beat me, like I was going down. I had beaten her the only three times we raced, with the last two races being very close. But this time they figured the distance was greater and my health wasn't a hundred percent. It was a long mile and a half race and my leg was sore. I was worried about the extra quarter mile distance we had to travel and hoped I could hold up. It was also a wet track, which would make the weight of the mud tougher on my leg. The bookies figured if I were to lose, that today would be the day; so the odds were 8-5 against me. But even though I was listed as the underdog, Angelo said everyone wanted me to win, everyone would be betting on me. He said everybody loved me. And though, after everything that seemed to be against me; that was all the motivation I needed. I had long strong legs, a long fluid stride, and when I flared my nostrils and pinned my ears back, an energy would overtake me that was incredibly powerful and hard to describe. No one was going to beat me today; no one was ever going to beat me. As my pride and confidence returned, I knew I simply wouldn't allow it. Lauren leaned over and patted and rubbed my neck as we slowly walked to the gate and then she whispered in my ear.

"Look around baby. Look at all of the people who came to see you today. You're the reason they're here in this weather. You're the best one here Summer Storm. Today is your day baby. You've already beaten everyone here and today we'll do it again. We just need one more win. We just need one more win to make history."

As she talked, I turned my head around again and saw California Miss' jockey staring at us with complete impudence and audacity, like he had already won the race. He was rudely smiling at us with a total lack of respect. It just made me all the more eager to put them down. I wanted to win for Lauren and I wanted to win for my mom and dad back in Kentucky. I already knew I was the best horse here and I wanted Lauren to be just as famous as a woman jockey. My dad achieved this kind of glory before, winning the Triple Crown against three year old colts on the same track we were racing on today and I also wanted him to be proud of me. But inside I had doubts for the first time in my career. I just wished it wasn't raining and I had a few more days of rest. This was going to be a long and muddy race, the longest race I've ever run.

I looked down at the slop I was walking in and realized it was a rainy quagmire the first time that I raced here too. That was last year and the track was a mess. Today the track had turned to soup! Because I got a slow start out of the gate last year, Lauren and I were covered with thick mud and slime from the horses running in front of us. I vowed that day that I would never let that happen again and it never did. I surely wasn't going to let that happen today. There were only eleven horses entered in today's race, with the media advertising this race as the best filly from the east coast vs. the best filly from the west coast, and disregarding the rest of the field. Lauren's friend

Tisha was here today too, making two female jockeys in the race. She was riding Destiny's Child, a horse from down the road from us in Lexington, and she was a 3-1 underdog. The race was scheduled for one and a half miles, the longest distance run in all of horse racing and a distance that neither one of us had ever been tested on before. Being there was a wind driven rain and the track was muddy, some people figured anyone could win today. The time went by as if we were in slow motion and it seemed like forever until we got to the starting gate. But the long walk only warmed my leg and increased the adrenaline that flowed in me.

It was the kind of a day when fans sought cover anywhere they could while waiting for our race, the race of the year. They had hooded ponchos on and huddled together under overhangs and wherever else they could find shelter. The concession stands were out of the weather and very busy. The wind was brisk and affected everyone, but to me it was invigorating. Lauren searched the crowd as we walked and found Bryan and threw him a kiss. I saw him too and looked at him with anger and disgust, as I didn't understand why he had to upset her on a day as important as today. I also saw Roberta, Pam, and Kate in their box, but I didn't see Angelo with them. Then I looked to my right and took one last look at California Miss in her gate and knew I had the advantage getting to the rail today, only because I was closest to it; I knew I had to give it all I had. I knew she would be right there today; I saw it in her eyes. The last two years of hard work all came down to this one last race. In a little more than two minutes, it would all be over and I would be crowned Champion.

Lauren continued to rub my neck while we were in the gate. The delay seemed like forever. Being I had the two hole, I was second entering the gate and had to wait while the gates were filled, one by one, by each horse walking slowly to her spot. I could hear some of the other horses nervously banging around in their gate, but I was unusually calm and focused this time, calm but waiting to explode. Above all the noise and clamor in the gates, I then heard California Miss' jockey yell out to Lauren.

"You shouldn't be here today Lauren. This is the boy's club. Today you and her are going down! No woman wins a championship."

I then turned and looked at him with fear in my eyes and nervously pawed at the wet ground as I stood there waiting to explode. That's what the colt said to me in my dream, damn it! "Is this déjà vu or what," I thought, as goose bumps quickly ran through my body. I was highly excitable now and wanted to run. I wanted to run now. I'd show him. I'll shut his big mouth.

As he continued to trash talk, the gate slammed opened with a loud bang and we were off. Tisha's horse, Destiny's Child, slipped in the mud upon leaving her gate and almost took her down, but she recovered nicely. I quickly forgot what Miss' jockey said when I heard and saw the gate slam open and concentrated on the task at hand. I got off good and jumped to the rail immediately with California Miss coming up by my side, just like I figured. We ran neck to neck and side by side, in a blazing pace for the wet track conditions, leaving the others behind.

"Slow down a little baby, this race is long and the mud is heavy. Let's save ourselves for a big finish. Just pace yourself honey and save it for the end. I don't want you to hurt yourself. Just pace yourself," said Lauren.

I heard her, but thought I knew better. I don't like hanging back. That's not my style. I had too much pride for that. While running through the turn, I tried to push Miss outward from the rail, making her work harder in the turn like my dad told me to do. But as we got to the straightaway and the half mile point I was behind by a neck. I was doing my best, but my leg was hurting badly and I was trying to run through it, trying to forget the pain, trying to stay focused and keep going. But now I was in a panic, the pain was burning and radiating up my leg for the first time, starting to hurt my right side with every stride. I had never lost a race and I didn't want to lose now, not in a race with so much importance attached to it. Frankly, I couldn't imagine losing under any condition, yet today. At the three fourths of a mile pole, I was keeping pace and was still behind by a neck, with Destiny's Child making a move on the outside of Miss. I was keeping pace with Miss, but I just couldn't go any faster. California Miss slowly continued to gradually outpace me, lengthening the lead at the one mile pole, all the while Miss' jockey was talking smack to Lauren and angering me further. Lauren thought I was being smart, hanging back and pacing myself, but I was really trying as hard as I could; I just didn't have it in me today.

With only a 1/4 mile left and Miss eventually leading me by 3/4 a length; Lauren then whispered into my ear; "Come on baby, you can do this, you can do this; you're the best horse here, you're the best filly there ever was. Let's turn it on. It's time to go baby. It's time to plug it in."

I heard her, and for the first time in my career I couldn't respond. My tank was empty and my leg was killing me. As we closed in on the finish line, the three of us were side by side and Lauren hit me with the whip. I couldn't believe it. It shocked and stunned me. She had never hit me before in my life. I didn't know what to feel, but at first I felt insulted because all this time I thought I was special. I wasn't whipped like the others. I was good; I didn't have to be whipped. I was angry now, and as I got filled with adrenaline, the pain in my leg subsided. I gritted my teeth and pinned my ears back. My nostrils flared as I slowly increased my gait. I can't say if it was anger I was feeling, or the great desire to perform for Lauren, but I started to catch up to California Miss ever so gradually. Through the wind, rain and mud we ran, side by side. I heard the crowd roaring loudly in the background and knew this was special. First by a neck Miss led, then by a nose, then me ahead by a nose. I glanced over at her and her jockey, and I glanced over at Destiny's Child. I knew I had them both and dug in hard and continued to outpace both of them as we closed in on the finish line.

"It's Summer Storm by a nose. It's Summer Storm coming on strong now. It's Summer Storm by half a length. Oh my! Summer Storm comes from behind in the rain and wins The Triple Tiara. What a horse," is what I heard over the loudspeaker as I fell and crashed down hard while crossing the finish line. My front leg had snapped and went out from under me in great pain. It hurt so bad, I thought

I was shot as I had no control over it or my body. As it snapped, I instantly tripped and rolled head first to the ground, throwing Lauren to the turf with me rolling on top of her very hard. As noisy as the crowd and loud speakers were, a gasp suddenly came over the crowd and it instantly became eerily quiet.

The loudspeaker blared to a stunned and hushed crowd; "Ladies and Gentlemen, we have witnessed a horrible event. Summer Storm and her jockey Lauren Windsor are down. Please bear with us and pray with us until we can give you more information. Emergency personnel are enroute to the track, please bear with us."

After we fell, Lauren was then immediately run over by the horses running closely in back of us and thrown up in the air like a rag doll. I witnessed this while lying on the ground too, while a horse tripped on me too, sending her to the turf, but not causing any injuries. I then struggled mightily to get to my feet. Lauren was motionless, lying there face down in the mud about fifteen feet away from me, her new pretty blue and white silk suit hardly recognizable. We were alone on the track now and I was very scared. I tried to walk over to her, but I couldn't. I just stood there on three legs, writhing in agony, and found it hard to even move. In tremendous pain, I then gathered all the strength I could muster and slowly limped over to her, hobbling on my limp and bloody front leg as I slowly waded through the wet and sloppy track. The rain was dripping down from my head onto her as I looked over her lying there motionless. In sorrow, I put my head down and gently nudged her shoulder with my nose, but she didn't move. I nudged her again, hoping she would respond. Nothing! I looked around and everybody was gone from the track. Even though we were directly in front of the grandstand, I was all alone as I looked up to the rainy dark sky and then looked around again at the hushed crowd.

"Lauren, Lauren. Somebody please help. Where is everybody?"

Forgetting about my injury, I turned and searched furtively for help. The horses had all left the infield and the track was consumed with an eerie silence. I then heard a siren, and as I turned I saw the lights of an ambulance coming towards us in the foggy rain with the stewards rushing towards us on foot.

"Please get up Lauren, please get up," I thought, as I nudged her again with my nose, with fear and panic overtaking me. Please?"

While I stood there in the cold and soupy mud, Bryan jumped the railing and ran out to her before the ambulance arrived. He got on his knees and was crying as he pulled her up from the mud. Then he held her bloody and limp body in his arms, trying to comfort her, trying to get any kind of a response. But she just laid there, her eyes closed and her head limp on her shoulder, without a reaction of any kind. He then carefully took her muddy helmet off and cried while he hugged her and kissed her cold and wet muddy face. It continued to rain unmercifully on us as the ambulance came out, but the cold rain comforted me in a strange way as I stood above them watching. Maybe I was in shock, I thought, as numbness filled my body, tingling my nerves, as my pain subsided. The track was a muddy quagmire and the ambulance had trouble getting to us, taking much longer than it should have. They circled us first while I stood there with Angelo holding my reins. He ran out to grab me, getting there after Bryan. Although I was standing, I was in great pain and bleeding badly and could only stand on three legs. I watched Lauren being carried into the ambulance and I put my head down and cried inside as I watched the ambulance drive away with her and Bryan, still confused as to what happened. I never saw her open her eyes or move at all. Her last words she said to me kept repeating like an echo in my mind; "Come on baby, you can do it, you can do it; you're the best horse here," before my wheels went out from under me and I fell in a thundering crash. The crowd had an eerie silence as they watched horror stricken. All you could hear was the engine on the ambulance idling and the wind driven rain hitting the wet, quiet puddles on the ground. I picked my head up and looked into the gray rainy sky and wondered what was happening. "Why was this happening to me?" "What will happen to me?" It had all happened so fast.

The blinking lights from the ambulance were flashing an eerie red on the blood spurting down from my bleeding leg. When I hung my head in the rain and looked down at it, I instantly thought about what my dad told me; "I've seen a lot of good horses put down after their wheels went out from under them," and wondered if that was my fate today too. I looked around and wondered if this was it for me, if this was my last view on earth.

Angelo then helped the track attendants walk me into my ambulance and then rode with me to the infield Veterinary Hospital where Kate and Loretta were waiting. Roberta, Bryan and Pam were at the infield hospital with Lauren. I always sensed I hated New York Even though I hoped for the best. Little did I know that I would never see Lauren again. She broke her neck and died that day, with most of me dying with her. My best friend was gone and her smile and kindness was to be missed. As for me, I would never smile again, and now I knew why. This is where I was first injured last year and this is where my career would end. But most of all, this is where I would lose Lauren, my best friend. I recounted that damn dream again and again and now knew that it wasn't a dream, it was a premonition. I also remembered the funny feeling I got whenever I got to this town and now I knew why, it was my sixth sense talking to me. It was warning me, but I was too proud and too stupid to realize it. I heard my mom's words echo through my mind again; "Don't go there, you'll never be the same." And Lauren telling me; "You're a big girl now," and "There will come a time when I won't be with you any longer." "Wow," I thought, as I got the chills thinking about it. "Why didn't I pay more attention to it? Could I have changed the outcome? Could I have changed anything?" Although hindsight is 20-20, I think I could have, but I thought I could do anything. If only I wasn't so proud and competitive. After being sedated, I slowly lost the thought and stared at the gray walls and bleak surroundings of the hospital that confined me.

I didn't know how to process what had happened, although I tried mightily. Crazy thoughts ran through my mind as well as thoughts of morose and regret.

"Why did this happen? Are they going to put me down," I thought as I watched them closely? "Will I ever see Lauren again?"

Then I saw the vet's assembling and conversing with Kate, Loretta, and Angelo, and wondered what my fate was. Dad had always told me that going through life was like walking a tightrope, but today I had lost my safety net. My support system was gone and I felt terribly alone. I knew the severity of the accident and I felt like I was ready to die if I had to; the medication, the pain, and the loneliness were consuming me. I didn't care about anything anymore.

But thankfully, and after much deliberation, they decided to spare my life. However, this day would be a rainy, muddy nightmare that would change my life from this day forward. In my confined state at the hospital, I had plenty of time to recall my competitive races with California Miss and how Angelo constantly warned me of her, even before I met her. California Miss wasn't her name, I thought. Her name was death and hell followed with her.

LIFE WITHOUT LAUREN

After being anesthetized and examined, they found out my sesamoid bones were shattered in my right front leg and I had to be either put down or operated on immediately, with a very little chance of success. I overheard the vet's say they wanted to euthanize me, saying I'd never be able to race again, as I was too high strung and I'd only reinjure myself after surgery and bleed to death. They said it was humane to put me to sleep. I felt a cringe in my stomach, because that's what my dad warned me of. But Roberta didn't want any part of it. Even though I was insured for five million dollars, losing Lauren was more than she could take in one day. Besides, Kate said I could make a fortune breeding and this could have been the main reason they spared my life.

After more X-Rays and a blood and urine test I was in surgery for over four hours and was tended to by the best veterinarians in the country. Because Angelo had injected me with acepromazine, instead of amphetamines, no drugs were found in my system. When I came out of anesthesia I was suspended in warm water in a "recovery pool." The recovery pool was a very large stainless steel tank of temperature controlled warm water with a crane like device suspending me in the water with straps around my belly to support me. It was a new invention to the sport and probably saved my life, as this helped me from thrashing about and reinjuring myself. It also kept my weight off my leg and the warm whirlpool not only felt good, it offered circulation and resistance. As I hung suspended in the recovery pool late that night, all alone except for two vets monitoring me from an office with a glass window, the large room seemed awful empty, bleak and cold. It had a concrete floor with a large drain for bodily fluids.

The walls were made of gray cement block and adorned with stainless steel cabinets around the walls. It had a huge stainless steel operating table with a crane overhead, surrounded by neon lights on the ceiling. There was also a large window in front of me about ten feet away from where I was suspended.

The rain had finally stopped and explosions were taking place everywhere. The skies of New York were filled with bright colors illuminating the clouds in the night sky and the outline of the tall buildings in Manhattan, while flashing intermittingly in my room. It was the fourth of July and it was the first time I had ever seen and heard fireworks. I was very uncomfortable and nauseated from the anesthesia, but at least my leg was numb. I was suspended in a tank of water and hanging my head, wondering what in the hell I was doing here all alone. I could see flashes from the fireworks out the large window in front of me and smell the smoke through the air conditioners, as the wind must have been blowing in my direction. Although I was in a drug induced stupor, it gave me plenty of time to think about my circumstances and what had happened today. How was Lauren, I thought? Nobody informed me of her condition. Was she okay? Was she in better shape than I imagined? My dad said that sometimes life throws you a curve ball, but what happened today was more than a curve ball, it was a shutout. The noise of the city only made me feel worse. The fireworks sounded like gun shots going off and made it difficult, if not impossible to relax, as Lauren wasn't there to comfort me anymore. I wanted to run away and escape. This seemed like a nightmare I was living through and I wanted to wake up, but I couldn't even move.

"Maybe I'm dreaming again," I thought, as I prayed to wake up. I kept thinking Lauren would come through the door and tell me everything was going to be alright. Because of the medication I was taking, I felt very sad and confused as I hung there, my legs suspended in the water.

The next day I was placed on more sedatives and corticosteroids and after twelve long and lonely weeks of rest and therapy in New York I was sent back home to Kentucky, all splinted up. Although I had suspected it, it was here on the plane that I was told Lauren was gone. After all, twelve weeks had gone by and she never visited me and I had only saw Roberta once in a while. All the hope I had anticipated came crashing down and I took the news real hard, blaming myself, thinking it was I who killed her. I traveled with Winnie and a groomer from the farm this time; my best friend was gone and my heart felt like it was shattered and fragmented into little pieces. I hung my head and visualized Lauren again on the muddy turf, as I was broken inside and wanted to die. I felt terribly responsible and badly wanted to be with her. Throughout the pain of this terrible nightmare Winnie was a good friend, giving me love by leaning up against me and talking to me as I lied in the straw on the flight home. She had missed me as much as I missed her. But I was so broken inside that I couldn't respond to her kindness. I felt her presence, but just lying there and staring at the walls of the airplane was all I could do. I had made a huge mistake; I had surrendered my sense of reason for the passion of winning and caused an accident that was irreversible and non-rescinding, leaving me with nothing but pain and the terrible feeling of loneliness. There was no going back now. I had a deep scar in my soul that bled with a variety of emotions, emotions that I didn't even know existed. It was a life learning lesson that stayed with me and reminded me continuously of that dreadful and eventful moment when I hit the track in a violent thunder with Lauren pinned beneath me, crying out in pain. My days would be long and my nights would be longer still.

When I returned home, I stood in my stall with Winnie and thought of the events that preceded the race and the nightmare my mother had a while ago on that stormy night and her words that echoed in my mind again.

"Don't go there. Listen to your heart. Your brain will fool you . . . You'll never be the same," . . . and but sadly, "this will only be the beginning."

The weird feeling when I was in New York, the thunder and lightning, the muddy track, Tisha falling with her horse dying, Lauren's muddy blue and white silk suit, her neck brace, the weird messages from Mom, Roberta, Lauren, and the jockey; sadly, it all made sense now.

After a long and uncomfortable couple of months, I was allowed to leave my stall for the first time, so I slowly walked the long white rail fence that led to the pasture with my head down; the fence seemed to go on forever today. Although I was glad to be home, it just wasn't the same. As I walked, my mom and her friends soon surrounded me in the pasture and rubbed their heads on my neck, talking to me and trying to lift my spirits. My mom whispered comforting words in my ear and my brothers and sister cautiously came up to me and gave me some loving words. They had always been jealous of my relationship with Lauren and the success we had, but today they were there for me. We were family and they comforted me too. I had a huge support system if I could recognize it, but I felt dead inside. My emotions overtook me and I couldn't see their kindness or the brightness of the day. Bryan and his sisters, Tawnee and Gina, came around to see me once in a while, but as time went by, I saw Bryan less and less, as he had moved to Seattle and started his new job. I guess the farm just brought back memories of Lauren that he wanted to forget as his eyes would well up with tears when he would visit me and hug my head. Bryan, on one visit, after sensing I was despondent, held me by my neck and told me he didn't hold me responsible for Lauren's death.

"I grew up around the horse racing business and I know that these things happen sometimes. Lauren knew the risks that were involved with riding the fastest race horse in the world, but she met the challenge head on. That was one facet of her personality that I loved, but unfortunately the quality I loved also took her away from me. This wasn't your fault Summer and it wasn't Lauren's fault. If anyone is to blame, it's Roberta and Loretta. That's one of the reasons Roberta is taking it so hard; the decision was ultimately hers. I could tell that you're lonely. Let it go baby! Just let it go!"

I heard him and though I couldn't respond, I appreciated his words of kindness. I had always loved Bryan, and although I heard his reasoning, I couldn't help but think that the argument they had in the morning of the race had something to do with it. After all, this was the first time Lauren had ever used her whip on me, which made me mad and pushed me to my limit. But of course, this was also the first time I had ever been behind at the end of a race too. I didn't know what to think.

Some things on the farm changed and some remained the same. Princess had another litter of kittens while I was gone, so she spent more time in the stable mothering her babies, who joyfully ran and played all over the stable. She would take off every once in a while and would then return with a mouse or a mole for her young. Sometimes the mole would still be alive and she would toss it in the air trying to teach her young about the circle of life. It was also refreshing to watch the little kittens run and play. If they weren't playing, they'd be wrapped in a furry ball, snuggled next to their mother. I used to stare at them and drift away, as they brought back memories of when I was young and had that much energy and vitality. Winnie tried to lift my spirits too, but I couldn't see the beauty in the farm anymore. While my world was gray and void of color, my thoughts were a dark blue and clouded with remorse and sorrow. When my leg finally healed and I was able to walk to the long white rail fence that separated us from the stallions; my dad saw me and slowly walked over. He then nuzzled me and told me that he was very proud of me and that in time I would be okay, as time heals all wounds.

"I heard what happened to Lauren, Summer. I know you were close; I liked her too. I watched her grow from a little girl to a young lady. But don't beat yourself up. It was a terrible accident and you could have died too. You're a champion now so hold your head up high. Of all the colts and fillies that I ever sired, you are the greatest. You've made me very proud. The apple didn't fall far from the tree when I made you."

And although I heard him, I couldn't acknowledge him, as I was empty inside. I was just happy to be with him. As he talked, I just nodded and put my head over the fence that separated us and laid it on his shoulder and sighed.

"Dad, I'm to blame for all of this, me and my stupid pride. I just didn't know how to turn it off; I couldn't quit."

Although I was now the best filly in America and had won "The Triple Tiara," which was the most celebrated award for fillies, it meant nothing to me without Lauren there to share it with me. It didn't belong to me, it belonged to the both of us. I felt awfully alone and tremendously guilty. I picked up my head and looked him in the eye.

My dad looked at me and spoke; "Pride can be a dangerous thing and is to be treated with a double edged sword Summer. It is good to be strong and proud, but you have to be smart too. You have to be in control of what's happening around you and be aware of the circumstances that can sometimes develop with vanity. Vanity is a sin that can consume and destroy you."

I looked at him and nodded, not knowing how to respond or what to say, but I knew he was right. All I felt now was guilt for the loss of Lauren. He then reached over the fence and lovingly put his head next to my ear and whispered in his low voice.

"Summer, you have to remember that this was a horrendous accident. You didn't plan it; it just happened. She knew what she was doing when she mounted you for the first time and the risk she was taking every race she ran. It ain't yours to carry. I've never seen you like this. You've got to let this go or it will kill you."

"I hear you Dad, but I don't know what to say or where to start because I feel so guilty. I knew I wasn't a hundred percent that day, but my stubbornness and heart wouldn't let me quit. You've always given me good advice and I listened to most of it, but wish I would have listened to all of it. I feel like my heart has a hole in it now."

"Summer, I know you feel bad, but from my experience, guilt and depression are best overcome by anger. Anger will conquer your guilt and make you forget your depression. You have to get mad at somebody or something. But you must be very careful though, because anger directed inward will make you more depressed, and that will kill you. You must get angry at somebody or something and let it go, let it out. The way I see it is you are walking the line right now. You're on the jagged edge of midnight. You have to snap out of it and you have to snap out of it soon."

He put his head down and then lifted it again. Then looked me in the eye again and lovingly said; "Look, I know you're hurting, but just remember I'm here for you kid. I'll always be here for you; you're my baby. I can help you through this, but you're going to have to let me. Don't isolate yourself in your stall. Get out and smell the fresh air. Take in the wonders of nature; they're all around you. This is a beautiful place to live."

In anguish I looked at him; "I hear you Dad, but don't leave me now Dad; don't walk away." I said; "Please spend some time with me today. I need some comfort more than ever. I feel terrible."

"I'm here for you Summer, I'm here for you. I'll stay here with you as long as you want."

As we quietly stood there, with our heads across from the fence and our heads on each other's shoulder, a green 4x4 John Deere Gator slowly and noisily came up the hill carrying Roberta and Loretta and stopped about ten feet away.

"Wow, a picture's worth a thousand words! Isn't that a sight, maybe the greatest two horses that ever lived standing next to each other like that," Roberta said. "It's simply beautiful. I wish I had a camera with me."

"Yes, they sure are beautiful together. She is so much like her father. Are you going to breed her?"

"Oh yeah! But you're going to have to tell me when she's healthy enough. We already have offers on the table lined up from the best stallions all over the world, even some Arabian stallions from the Middle East. But, you know Loretta, I'm really curious. The blood and urine results came back negative after her injury, not detecting amphetamines at all. But she ran a hell of a race, considering the track conditions and her previous injury. The private investigator I hired gave me photos of Angelo with his shady friends before and after the race, even pictures of them entering her stable, but no sign of any drugs administered. Even though she won, they didn't look too happy afterwards. I don't know what to think. She didn't have any drugs in her and she still won. What a heart she has!"

Loretta couldn't hold in the feeling she was surprised when she heard a P.I. was hired. "I didn't know you hired a PI. When did you do that?"

Roberta, realizing that she had a slip of the tongue again, said; "Oh, it was done after your discovery of her injury and just before her last race. From what you told me, I figured it was the right thing to do. It appeared somebody was getting to her, just like you said."

"Did you find out anything?" She nervously asked.

Roberta, sensing the tension in her voice, said; "No, just pictures of Angelo and his friends at the track, but nothing at the farm. I couldn't find any impropriety here. Why, did you suspect somebody?"

"No, but I'm glad you didn't find any improprieties on the farm. I'd like to think we're a family here. Getting back to your question, if you want my professional opinion, she could have been given acepromazine to her sometime before the race, because she was calmer than usual. Acepromazine isn't detectable in the blood or urine and allows the horse to relax and focus on the race, which I think she did. But since your PI didn't find anything wrong, I can't explain it. Was she under surveillance at all times?"

Roberta, noticing her anxiety, studied her eyes while she spoke. "She had a camera on her at all times Loretta, except for inside her stall at the track, but I had a P.I. hovering around there. He recorded Angelo and his friends visiting her momentarily, but Lauren arrived seconds later and didn't see any unusual behavior with Summer Storm."

Loretta nodded and said; "It sounds like somebody got to her, but I can't prove it though. But I really think it was the big heart she had that brought her down; she simply refused to lose. She's an alpha female, the best of the best. Lauren always said she didn't like to be behind."

"Yes, I can't help but think what Angelo requested so many times. He wanted to put a male jockey on her. Now I wish I would have done it. Lauren would still be here and maybe this wouldn't have happened."

"Don't beat yourself up. Summer Storm simply refused to lose that day."

I heard them talk and knew what happened more than anyone. I couldn't even acknowledge their presence, I felt so low. I just felt the comfort of my dad and stared straight ahead at the hazy forest over his shoulder. I was in a zone; I didn't even see the pasture in front of me. After a while, they just drove away, the noisy drone and smell of their Gator's diesel engine getting quieter and fainter as they went over the hill, gradually disappearing into the hazy fog.

We stood there leaning on each other for what I felt was the longest time. We didn't speak, we just stood there. My brain felt calm and at ease for the first time in months, as Dad's presence comforted me. All I could hear now was the wind whistling through the tall trees that surrounded us and the leaves swirling around on the ground.

The day slowly passed by and the sun began to set in the hillside, casting dark shadows from the hill covered with giant sycamores in the distance and cooling the air. I then thanked him and asked him if he could meet me again tomorrow. Then I walked slowly back to my paddock, sadly dragging my hoofs and staring at the ground as I walked, thinking about my future, but not knowing what it may bring. When I reached my paddock, Winnie was happy to see me, as I was gone all day. We both nuzzled each other in a greeting and lay down in the stall and tried to go to sleep. A flake of alfalfa was left for me at the door, but I ignored it. I couldn't eat if I wanted to. We quietly leaned against each other as we lay there in the cedar chips, each trying to seek solitude and peace from the recent events. I solemnly stared at the redwood lined wall of my stall while we lay there and tried to rehash the events again that led up to the fall and thought about what I may have done to change the outcome. I came to the conclusion that all of it was my fault because I couldn't lose to Miss; I would have never let that happen. Dad was right, it was my pride that caused this. I couldn't let it go, though, and I didn't know how to let it go. I knew who to get angry at, but I didn't even know how to get angry. I was a train wreck waiting to happen.

Debts Due and Payable

It was winter now and darkness came early to the rolling hills of Kentucky. For weeks the cold rain came and went, always leaving a blanket of fog that hung over the valley between the hills. The dense fog, draining the hills of their color with its suffocating gray and silver mist, seemed impregnable at times. Snow in the higher elevations was also visible when the wind would blow, and a cold dampness would envelope that would chill you to the very bone. The air took on the smell of saturated earth, for the fallen leaves were decomposing amongst the small streams, and puddles dotted the countryside everywhere. Because the wet winter seemed longer than usual, work on the farm had slowed to a crawl.

The bright green neon sign was blinking slowly and methodically outside when Angelo cautiously pulled up to the Tack Room. He slowly scanned the parking lot and the thick woods that surrounded the bar before getting out of his car. There were only two cars in the parking lot, the bartender's car and a customer's, a car he had never seen before. He pulled out his snub-nose revolver from his jacket, opened the chamber to confirm it was loaded, spun the chamber and closed it, and then put it under his seat. He has been very suspicious lately of everything and everybody, almost paranoid. He knew he was a marked man; he knew the rules. It was just a matter of time. He got out of his car and took a long deep breath of the cool night air while he carefully scanned the thick woods again that were mired in fog and enveloping the parking lot. Their wall of darkness, comprised of groves of thick birches, maples, dogwoods, and sycamores seemed eerie tonight, darker than usual. Then he slowly walked into the dimly lit bar and sat on a stool at the curve of the horseshoe shaped bar where he always sits. The bar was dimly lit and quiet, except for the clicking noise of the pool balls on the table in back of him.

He took off his wet hat, and dried the water from his glasses. In a gruff manner, he yelled at the bartender who was busy stocking the cooler; "Hey Billy Joe, get me my usual and make me one of those Italian sausage sandwiches with onions and green peppers on a hard roll. And put some of them pepperoncini's on the side!"

After Angelo downed his shot of whiskey, he turned around and saw two men shooting pool that he'd never seen before. His mind was racing now and because he needed a drink so bad when he walked in, he didn't notice them earlier. There were no other customers in the joint except for him and them. The pool tables were near him at the corner of the bar, about six feet away, so he turned his back to them with his elbows on the bar and had no choice but to listen to them talk while he drank his beer and they played pool. After a couple of minutes, he stopped drinking; his eyes opened wide and his ears felt like they were on fire. He knew they were from out of town by their eastern-Italian accent. They were dead ringers for city guys. He was having a drink in the hills of Kentucky and these guys sounded like they were from the east coast. They sounded and talked like "wise guys." After nervously listening to them for a while, he picked up his beer and casually walked down to the other end of the horseshoe shaped bar and sat down on another stool. He was facing them now, his silhouette obscured in the shadows and dimly lit by the Budweiser sign which was flashing in the window in back of him. He had become extremely apprehensive and he wanted to observe them closely. Their accent and voice brought him to life. As he watched them, sweat began to accumulate on his brow and he could feel his heart thumping against his shirt. He put his hand in his shirt pocket and pulled out his pack of Lucky's and lit one up. It was the last ticket in the book, so he crunched it in his hands and threw the empty pack down on the bar.

He motioned Billy Joe over and quietly asked him; "Hey, have you seen these guys before?"

"Oh yeah," Billy Joe said, as he turned around to look at them. He then leaned on the bar and quietly spoke.

"They've been coming in regularly every night for about three days now. They seem like nice guys. They said they have business here in town with an old friend. They said they owe him a favor."

"They owe him a favor? What kind of business they talking 'bout?"

"I don't know; I didn't ask them!"

"How long they been in town?"

"About three days I told you. Why?"

Angelo had a lot to fear and he felt the muscles in his stomach tightening. Summer Storm was supposed to lose her last race, but she won it and this cost Vinnie D and Richie "Frog Eyes" a ton of money. He wasn't worried about the acepromazine he gave Summer Storm because he knew it would never be detected by the vets. Nobody saw him give it to her, so the suspicion and the bullshit on the farm didn't bother him at all. Nobody could prove anything; he was smarter than that. He had bigger fish to fry. One of the five Mafia families from New York was pissed off and he hadn't been able to get in touch with Vinnie D or Richie since Vinnie asked for a "meeting" and he didn't show up. Angelo knew the rules. If you don't show up, you're a dead man, but after watching Joey Pascarelli show up for his "meeting" years ago, he wanted no part of it. He figured he was a dead man either way. Showing up for a "meeting" is no different than entering a lion's den; you were in there territory. Now they simply don't answer their phone when he calls. Is it possible these guys are here for him, he thought, as he stared at their pool table? He quickly thought of Joey Pascarelli's fate and started to sweat bullets. He needed to talk to somebody bad. He wanted to talk raw meat to Billy Joe, but knew he'd better marinade it. He didn't want to arouse any suspicions. After thinking about it for a few moments, he spoke.

"I don't know. You usually don't see strangers in these parts, especially in a country bar like this. Give me some quarters will ya? I gotta make a call. Hey, where's that sandwich?"

"It's coming, it's coming! You wanted those onions and peppers fried, didn't you? That's why it's taking so long!"

Angelo then grabbed the roll of quarters and picked up his beer and cigarette. While his head was spinning with fear, he walked over to the cigarette vending machine, put two quarters in, and bought a pack of Lucky's. He looked down to the other end of the bar again and stared at the two men shooting pool. He knew he had to walk past them on the way to the phone and would have a better chance to look them over. As he approached their pool table, he studied the men carefully and in detail. They had their backs to him while he approached, so he eyeballed them closely. They looked like they were both in their thirties and were dressed casually and inconspicuously in local attire, jeans and a tee shirt, trying to blend in. They had dark hair, brown eyes, and a dark complexion; they were Italian all right. The thing that really set them off, though, was they had pointed stilettos on, the shoes of a "wise guy," not the shoes of a local. But most telling were their "Pinky" rings. They couldn't go anywhere without those; they stood out like a neon sign. As he passed the pool table, one of the strangers turned and cockily nodded at him, as if to say hello, to which Angelo stared at him and cautiously nodded back. He then walked over to the phone, dropped a buck in, and nervously called New York while he leaned over the phone with one hand on the wall. He stood there at the wall phone smoking, less than ten feet away, with his eyes glued on them and watched while they talked. All the while, the phone rang and rang in his ear. No answer again, damn it! He then slammed the phone down, swore out loud, grabbed his quarters, and walked past them to his dimly lit seat at the other end of the bar. When he slammed the phone down, they both started to laugh. This made him feel all the more paranoid. He could feel their eyes penetrating his back as he walked back to his stool. He wanted to leave, but he knew he had to be cool. He needed more information.

He sat down and quietly called Billy Joe over again. "Hey Billy Joe, do you know what these guys are driving?"

"Yeah, they told me they got a rental car, a little white Chevy Chevette. They laughed about it because they said they're not used to that fucking roller skate. They said they're used to driving a big ass Caddy. They're flashing a fist full of C-notes too."

"Do you know where they're staying?"

"No. Angelo, I didn't ask them and they didn't tell me. Why are you so interested in these guys anyway? What's up? Do you know anything about them?"

"Hey get me another boilermaker, will ya? I got no interest! They just look out of place, that's all. When's the last time you seen guys in here with Pinky rings with a fist full of C-Notes? Can't a guy ask a fuckin' question around here?"

Billy Joe just looked at him and shook his head while he walked away; "Angelo. I've never seen you act so weird!"

After Angelo downed another shot of Crown Royal, Billy Joe brought him his sandwich. Angelo felt terribly jittery and compulsively ripped the label off his Budweiser bottle as he talked to him. He stared at his sandwich for the longest time and knew he'd better shut up, but he wanted another shot; he needed it now. He wasn't hungry anymore either. Fear was gripping him and his stomach was tightening up. He looked up at the two men at the pool table again and felt pressure on his chest, like an elephant was sitting on it. In pain, he grabbed his chest and took a deep breath. Then he turned to his right and stared at the mirror behind the bar, looking at the glistening bottles of booze on the shelf and knew he had to get out of town quick or he was a dead man. These guys are here for him and he knew it. His sixth sense told him that.

Seeing Angelo grab his chest, Billy Joe walked up to him.

"Are you okay Angelo? You don't look well!"

"Yeah, yeah, I'm okay. Heartburn, that's all, must be all this booze on an empty stomach!"

Angelo nervously dismissed him and continued to stare at the two men shooting pool, all the while thinking about the predicament he was in. He knew the routine of hit men all too well. They would go to the town of their mark seven to ten days earlier to check everything out. They'd steal local license plates and change the plates on their cars, not only in the state they had the hit, but every state on their way home too. Most people are creatures of habit, and they would know everything about the man they had to hit and all his habits before they struck.

"Hell, they probably knew what time I take a shit and how I fold the paper," he thought.

He then stared across the bar at the two men again. The more he thought about it, the more scared he became.

After mulling over his thoughts for a while, he then ordered another Crown Royal and threw it down and abruptly walked outside, leaving his sandwich on the bar untouched. The paranoia and shots of Crown were ravaging his brain now, leaving him scared and confused. He didn't know what to do, but he knew he had to get out of there. When he got outside he saw the Chevy Chevette parked in the gravel parking lot and recognized it, instantly confirming his feelings. He realized now he had seen it lately near the farm on at least two occasions. It was an inconspicuous model and he forgave himself for not examining it further when he drove up. He stopped and took a deep breath of the clean, cool mountain air and looked around, trying to relax but checking everything out. It was cold and misty with no moonlight, and dark and very quiet, except for the feint noise of the juke box playing inside the old wooden building and the cold wind whistling through the tall trees in the woods that surrounded the bar. Although he had downed several boilermakers in a short amount of time, the cold night mountain air and rain invigorated his senses, which were acutely aware of everything now. He knew the drivers of the Chevette were shooting pool, so he cautiously walked up to the Chevette and tried to look into the wet and water dropped windows. The car was small with a large windshield and a large rear window; it seemed to be all glass. There wasn't much light in the parking lot, so he pulled out his Zippo lighter and placed it near the window with his hand cupped over it, trying to illuminate the inside of the car. He saw a black overnight bag on the front seat that was partially open. As he tried to get a better look inside the bag through the locked door, he saw a reflection of light in the bag that startled him; it looked like the barrel of a gun. He snapped shut his Zippo and put it back in his pocket. He then looked back at The Tack Room's blinking neon sign and the front door again. It was quiet, way too quiet, except for the rain dripping off the roof into puddles that surrounded the building. Frightened by the sight of the gun, he figured he better get the hell out of there and quick, before the door to the bar opened.

Then a loud bam, bam, bam went off, making him duck in fear, and sending him down to one knee. Filled with a sudden rush of adrenaline, an immense fear ripped through his body, instantly giving him goose bumps that made him shudder. Angelo quickly turned his head to see a semi coming down the hill, its engine back-firing with the jake brake in use. The truck engine's loud backfiring sounded like a gun going off, and though he was relieved he wasn't shot at, it scared the hell out of him and brought him to his senses immediately. He took a deep breath of relief and hurriedly walked to his car. When he got inside, he reached under his seat and picked up his .38 and looked at it for a long time, spinning the loaded chamber, and kicked around the thought of killing both of them right now. He stared at the bar's front door, he stared at his gun, he stared at their car; then he stared at the front door again. Should he ambush them when they leave the bar or just run and leave town without doing anything? He thought of every situation that may develop if he confronted them. Shooting them would end it, he thought, or would it? His mind was racing with questions. The parking lot was practically empty and he had enough whiskey in him to alter his better judgment, actually making him braver than he usually was. He knew they weren't packing heat by the way they were dressed. Besides, he saw a shiny gun barrel in the open bag on their front seat. Their guns had to be in the bag, or did they have another bag on their table he didn't see? Was it possible they had a small heater in their jackets? He should have looked more closely. Questions, questions! The more he thought about killing them, the more fear he had. Although he led a life of lying and cheating, killing was new to him. He had heard stories and knew about "The Life," but now he was totally immersed in it, in further than he wanted to be.

After searching his soul, he started his car and slowly drove across the street with his lights off. He crossed the two-lane highway and parked it in the dark woods under a group of trees, facing the bar, and stared at the bar and the dimly lit parking lot. He was about fifty yards away now and could see the dim neon light blinking off of the wet Chevette and trees that surrounded the parking lot. He could see everything clearly, even in the mist. While he stared across the street, he took off his glasses and wiped the moisture off of them. He picked up his gun and opened the chamber, nervously spun it again, and made sure it was loaded. It was. It had five bullets, all hollow points. He always carried hollow points for self defense. They enter a body with a hole about the size of a dime and come out the other side with a hole as big as an orange. And because they were hollow points, you couldn't trace the bullets; he heard the stories. That's what the mob used. The only difference was the mob rubbed garlic on the bullets to cause blood poisoning if the initial impact didn't do their job. Either way, you were dead. Besides, after hearing that Semi back-fire coming down the hill, he was confident that the gunshots could easily be mistaken for another truck and not alarm anyone inside. He knew he was taking a huge risk here and it somehow made him feel more alive, more powerful. Angelo was a gambler, and this was a huge adrenaline rush to him. However, it wasn't money he was gambling with this time, it was his life. It was the ultimate wager. The "juice" didn't get any stronger.

Although it was cold, windy and raining outside, his hands were shaking and his face was perspiring now with sweat dripping off his heavy brow. He had gathered his senses and had a plan now, though rash and ill conceived; it was a plan that would radically alter his life from this day forward. He reached in the backseat and grabbed a hooded navy blue sweatshirt that had been lying there for a while; he had used it on the cool mornings he trained the horses. He felt more secure, knowing his clothes were dark. Then he got out of his car and walked across the quiet, wet and dark highway, crossed the dimly lit gravel parking lot of The Tack Room and waited in the shadows of the thick woods in front of the white Chevy Chevette. While he stood there behind a tree, lying in wait about five feet in front of the car, his mind raced with thoughts from his overactive conscience. He reflected on the upbringing he received from his mother and how she wanted so much for him to lead a life different than his father's. He had never killed anyone before and knew she would be terribly disappointed in him. But just because Angelo had a different zip code now didn't mean he forgot his roots. His father was a seasoned killer and the apple didn't fall too far from the tree. It was hidden in his genes and its fury was about to be released. This was different though, he thought, as he rationalized it out. They were here to kill him. He had to do it. He had no other choice. He had to defend himself. He looked to the heavens and made the sign of the cross. Why? He didn't really know. Was it his altar boy upbringing? Was he praying it went well? It was almost as though he wanted forgiveness for what he was about to do. This was a mortal sin and he knew he would go to hell for this. His stomach grew nauseous as he waited in the cold winter air; the bar's green neon sign blinking slowly and methodically in the shadows, flashing on the parking lot and woods like a camera going off every three seconds, one snapshot in time after another. His heart was ticking slowly now, ready to ignite the time bomb within. He was ready.

"Where are they? Damn it, let's get this over with," he thought, as he anticipated the opening of the front door with every second, each second seeming to drag on forever. It is amazing how fast your brain can ramble when frightened, he thought.

It was extremely dark now, with the clouds and sleet obliterating the moon and stars. The cold wind was beginning to blow hard too, blowing a winter front in, howling in the tall trees above him, singing its winter song and blowing leaves across the parking lot. This made the wait all the more longer, as it got colder and windier with every minute that passed. Just then, another car pulled into the parking lot, its headlights momentarily flashing across the wooded area he stood in. He ducked and receded into the trees and stood there watching until his heart stopped banging. As he watched a couple exit the car and walk into the bar, a bone jarring shiver rattled through his body. While his hood was soaking wet and dripped cold water on his face; he wished he had a bottle of Crown Royal with him. He had shivers and didn't know if they were from the cold and rainy night wind or the fear that gripped him thinking about his task at hand. He grabbed his glasses again and tried to dry them off on the inside of his hoodie.

"What if something went wrong," he thought again?

The different scenarios played out in his mind. He had to shoot straight and make it quick; he wasn't allowed to miss. He didn't want them to reach the gun inside their car and he didn't want to give them the opportunity to shoot back if they had a gun in their jacket. He was confident his gun wouldn't misfire because it wasn't a Saturday night special; it was a reliable Smith and Wesson, one of the best revolvers ever made. He knew his load was powerful too; he hand-loaded them himself. Even a misplaced shot would leave a lot of damage.

Again he questioned himself. "What if he missed and they were able to reach their guns? What if they were packing heat? Did they have a bag near their table he didn't see? Did they have a gun in their jackets?"

All of these thoughts just kept reoccurring and made him sick to his stomach, but he had made the decision to do them in and he had to go for it. The envelope had been sealed, their fate and his was decided. His heart was in his throat; he had butterflies now and he had them bad.

"Where are they? Damn it, why aren't they coming out?"

He was smart enough to know that killing them wouldn't end it though. He knew Richie would really be pissed and send others. Maybe he would even be mad enough to come himself. But, regardless, he knew he was a dead man, doing this just bought him some time to get out of town and he knew it.

He looked at his watch. He had been standing outside in the cold rain now for two hours and he had to piss bad, real bad. Just as he was about to unzip his fly and relieve himself on a tree, the feint juke box music suddenly got louder as the front door of the bar opened with them coming out, zipping up their jackets and slowly walking to their car, their hands in their pockets and their heads staring at the ground as they talked.

"This is it," he thought, as he crouched down in the bushes, being careful not to snap any twigs or make any noise. His fear was reaching a crescendo now. He could feel his heart beating in his throat as he watched every step they took. He looked at his gun again, reassuring himself he was ready. He noticed everything; the blinking light, the cold vapor coming from their breath, the cold wind, and the crunching of the gravel as they got closer and closer. He was sweating profusely in the cold night air as everything was happening in slow motion. He felt relieved they weren't carrying a bag. That meant they probably weren't armed, but he wasn't sure.

"Do they have a snub-nose in their jacket?" He thought.

With each second that passed, another step closer they came. They were completely oblivious to him as they approached their car, talking to each other and laughing. He was inside their heads now, anticipating every word and every movement, everything was happening very slowly and deliberately. He took off his wet glasses and quietly put them in his side pocket, ensuring there would be no light reflection off of them. He slowly and quietly cocked the trigger, pulling the hammer back with his thumb. For some reason, his hands suddenly stopped shaking. His genetic makeup had come into play. He had come full circle. He had found himself and gone somewhere he never went before and he liked the feeling that overcame him.

Larry Maro and Tony Ciccolilli were both "made men," having earned their stripes on the streets of Cleveland and Youngstown in the Mafia wars that ravaged those towns in the sixties and seventies. Larry took down Joey Galliano, a big player in Youngstown, gunning him down on the front porch of his girlfriend's house, and Tony was recognized for the efficient assassination of Charlie Carrabelli, a mob boss in Cleveland who was blown in two when he started his car. Angelo was half right. They were Italian all right, but they weren't from Jersey or New York; these guys were hired assassins, brought in from out of town to keep Richie and Vinnie's nose "clean" up in Brooklyn. The Commission had connections everywhere. It just took a phone call to get who you wanted and what you wanted. There was a "specialist" for every crime you wanted to commit.

"Did you see how nervous that sucker was when he saw us?" Larry said, as he laughed again and cleared his throat, spitting on the wet gravel. "I think he's onto us!"

"Yeah, if that poor mother fucker only knew he had one more day to live, he'd still be in there drinking. Let's hit him tomorrow man, just like we planned. I'm anxious to blow this hick town. It's colder than hell here too. It's done nothing but rain since we've been here. I think we have all we need to know about him. He's a simple bastard. He doesn't go anywhere but here and his girlfriend's house. Blowing up that piece of shit car of his would be doing him a favor too."

"Yeah Tony; but Vinnie wants us to kill him in front of that horse. We can't blow up the car. He wants that fucking horse to be the last thing he sees before he hits the ground."

"Are we supposed to kill the horse too?"

"Vinnie's really pissed at this guy; big time! He called him in for a "sit-down" and he never showed. He's a degenerate gambler and owes his shylock fifty large, not counting the vig. Plus he cost Vinnie and Richie over a mill on that last race just at the track, not to mention the side bets at the bars. Richie said the horse got to go too; we ain't got a choice. We have to make a statement here. I think we're going to have to use a sawed off shotgun on her and split fast. I don't want to get hurt. I hear she likes to rear up and kick her legs out."

They were only about fifteen feet from Angelo now and he overheard every word, as sound travels well at night. He was hiding behind a tree in the dark, thick woods, now only three feet in front of their car, and was close enough to see the neon light blinking off their eyes. The night was cold, wet, and windy, except for dripping sleet and the faint sound of the juke box playing and their footsteps getting closer on the wet gravel. As Larry fumbled with his keys and turned to unlock the door, a cold and calculating Angelo stood up in the shadows in front of their car and fired two shots, hitting him in the shoulder and chest. As Larry fell to the ground, Tony yelled out in fear and instantly started running across the parking lot. Angelo, anticipating this, put his glasses back on, and quickly ran to the back of the car. He methodically got down on one knee and fired two more shots, hitting him in the back and watching him fall on his face in a thud on the wet gravel. He heard a moan from the driver of the car in back of him and slowly walked over to him, firing his last shot, putting a bullet in the back of his head, execution style. It was a gruesome sight because of the ammo he used. Larry's brains were scattered in the gravel. The hollow points did their job well. He felt weird, but at the same time he felt in control and terribly powerful. He felt stronger and empowered somehow and for the first time in his life, more in charge of the lonely shell he occupied. He had been a lapdog that had broken his chain and proved he could live as a predator. He then, swiftly and quietly, slid back into the woods and hurriedly crossed the empty highway and jumped in his car and sped away. Luckily, nobody came out from the bar and nobody saw him. He had done it. It was over now. He lit a Lucky and glanced at the bar while he drove away, his windows down for fresh air.

He wasted no time as he hastily sped down the country road to Chestnut Mountain Farms, his windshield wipers beating time to the music on the radio. "Proud Mary," by Creedence Clearwater was playing, and he turned the sound up loud, tapping on the steering wheel to the music. He felt alive now. As he entered the long and winding driveway that led to his room, he looked up to the big house on the hill and saw the lights were still on. The farm was quiet this time of night, as it was late and most of the farm hands were probably sleeping. It looked like Roberta was still awake though; smoke was coming from the chimney and the lights in the big house were still on. He parked in front of his little house near the barn and left his engine running. He then ran into his room and reached into a slit in his mattress and grabbed his stash he had been saving up for years and counted it; it was all there, fifteen grand in C-notes. Angelo had lived through the depression and was from the old country and didn't trust banks. After taking his cold wet clothes off and throwing them on the floor, he took a quick hot shower. He was shivering badly from the exposure and sat on the floor in the shower for what seemed like a half an hour, absorbing the heat and trying to sober up. While he sat in the shower, with the hot water pouring down his head, he thought about what he had just done. He thought about a get-away plan, and he thought about his future. It didn't look so bright anymore. He shut the water off, dried himself off, and got dressed. He then packed an overnight bag as quickly as he could, trying to remember the essentials. After all, he was going to be gone awhile, how long he didn't know. He saw his wet clothes on the floor and figured he better throw them in his car too. Somebody might come to the room. He might be a suspect, he thought. He was still nauseous from the shooting and went to the toilet to throw up. The vomiting made him feel much better, but left a terrible taste in his mouth. He grabbed his bottle of Crown and chugged on it, trying to rid himself of the taste of vomit and hoped it would numb his brain. It still felt like it was going a hundred miles an hour. The bravado was now gone and the realization of the killings was sinking in, making him feel scared again. He then walked over to the refrigerator and held it open, leaning on the door. Four bottles of Budweiser stared at him with a few eggs on the door. There was a partially eaten sandwich sitting on a paper plate on the top shelf, a memory of last night. He knew he needed food, he knew he was drunk. The booze had caught up with him. He stared at the drawer marked Crisper. The letters were mesmerizing him, getting larger and then smaller, as if he was in a trance . . . c..r..i..s..p..e..r . . . C..R..I..S..P..E..R. c..r..i..s..p..e..r. He tried to breathe slowly, knowing he had to relax, but he was consumed with fear. He held onto the refrigerator door, feeling like he had to faint. The booze had fucked him up good.

"When will Ritchie get the news? What will he do when he finds out? How much time do I have, damn it?" Questions, questions, questions!

He grabbed the stale sandwich and slammed the refrigerator door and closed the bedroom light, leaving him in the dark. He walked over to the window that overlooked the farm and gazed out the dark water spotted window of his bedroom. As he looked out at the large pasture above him, he sadly reminisced for a couple of minutes while he ate and drank another beer. He fondly remembered when the trees were young and much smaller. John Windsor had given him a good job, years ago, and now he fucked it up big time. He had let his past and his all too cancerous greed catch up with him, each year and each transaction getting him involved deeper and deeper. He didn't know where he would go because the Mafia had their tentacles everywhere. But first he had to go to the big house on the hill. He had to talk to Roberta. He didn't want to look conspicuous by his immediate and unexpected absence and he didn't want to burn any bridges. And for some reason, he felt like he wanted to come back someday. He became melancholy. After all, this was the only home in America he'd ever known. He would be leaving his comfort zone and was ambivalent. Although the booze was managing his emotions in his head and scrambling his better judgment, he knew he had to have a plan. He had to get out of there.

He reloaded his revolver, grabbed his cash, and put some clothes and ammo in his bag. He then walked out to his old Buick, which was nice and warm from running for a while, and drove to the big house on the hill. Getting out of his car, he put his hands in his pants pockets and approached the porch. His head was down, and all the while he was thinking about what he was going to tell Roberta. As he stood on the veranda and waited for Roberta to come to the door, he leaned on the wooden railing and looked out over the beautiful farm again and thought of the good times he had here and the home he was leaving behind. Tears formed in his eyes as he became melancholy. The moon was hidden by the cold clouds blowing in, but it still looked like a postcard with the white fence bordering the dark pastures. He didn't know where he would end up or if he would ever return. He knew this could be the last time he saw the farm and, in a sad, heartfelt and bittersweet way, he absorbed it completely.

After waiting a couple of minutes, Roberta's nurse came to the door and turned the porch light on, the bright harsh light making him wince. She opened the door.

"Can I please speak to Roberta? I'm an employee of hers; my name is Angelo."

The nurse replied;" I'll have to ask her. Can you please wait a minute? I'll be right back."

Angelo slowly paced the porch back and forth while he waited. After a couple of minutes, the nurse returned and asked Angelo to please come in. He cleaned his wet shoes on the rug, and as he followed her into the dimly lit house, he noticed a large Trophy Room they had to pass to get to the Den. He saw pictures of Bold Czar and Summer Storm, father and daughter, side by side; they were his two biggest claims to fame. There was a picture of Lauren and Summer Storm when Summer Storm was a foal and another of Lauren mounting her at the Triple Tiara, the last picture of Lauren taken alive. There were also pictures of him when he was younger and worked for Roberta's father, John. A Gold Cup from the Derby, Silver Trophies, Blue Ribbons, and photographs filled the house. It was like a horse racing museum. She then led him down the dimly lit hall, the old wooden floors creaking as he walked, and opened the door to the bright den where Roberta was sitting under a crocheted blanket near a warm and glowing fireplace.

"Angelo. What a surprise! Are you okay; you look pale?"

"Roberta, I'm sorry to bother you at this hour, but could I talk to you?"

"Sure, come on in. Is something wrong? My God, I can smell the whiskey on your breath from here! What's going on? You look really pale. Are you sick? You never visit me!"

"No, no, I'm good. I just want to talk to you. I just have a request and I hope I'm not disturbing you."

"Not at all! I was just reading a book. Please come in and have a seat!"

Angelo sat down on the sofa and faced her from across the room. He leaned forward with his hands on his knees and looked her in the eye.

"Roberta, I'd like some time off. It's winter and we don't have much going on right now and I'd like to see some family back in the old country. I haven't been there in years. I was wondering if you'd give me two or three months off?"

Roberta, sensing the urgency in his voice and the apprehension in his eyes, said; "Why sure Angelo, I know the farm hasn't been the same lately. You take as much time as you need. Are you sure you're okay? You're beginning to look flushed. Do you want some coffee? When will you be back?"

"Yes, yes, I'm fine; but thank you! I don't really know when I'll be back. I just need some time off. I've felt awfully depressed since the accident. Thank you very much. I'll be leaving tonight. I'll get in touch with you when I land in Rome."

He stood up and nodded at Roberta, putting his fedora back on. Roberta watched Angelo rise from the couch and abruptly walk out the door, as if he was in quite a hurry. She felt that it was all so strange and abrupt and wondered what really was going on because he had never visited her in the evening before. After twenty years of knowing him, this was a complete change of behavior and it all happened so suddenly.

Angelo's hasty decision in the woods left him without much of a game plan, not knowing what lay before him. He knew if anyone came looking for him, he said he was going to Italy to see family. That was a good cover and in the opposite direction from where he was really heading. But before he left the farm, he was compelled to stop by the barn to visit me. It seemed he had developed a melancholy relationship with me since Laurens' death. I could always hear his old Buick when he drove up to the barn. It was loud and in need of a muffler. He had turned somber and subdued after the accident and didn't nag like he used to. I saw a different side of him, which was more gentle and caring. He walked up to my door and petted and hugged me and gave me a handful of carrots and rolled oats. I wasn't in the mood for them and wondered why he was here at this hour. The smell of alcohol on his breath was bad; I could tell he had been drinking again.

He then opened the half-door and walked into my stall, held my head and said; "Look, I know you miss Lauren, Summer Storm; we all miss her, but I got to talk to you. I got something to say to you before I leave. I only wish I didn't work you so hard and gave you more time to rest between your races. I also feel very responsible for you getting hurt and Lauren's death, but I didn't know when you got hurt. I was looking at the plums in the tree, and not the roots. You should have been brought along more carefully, more slowly. I know that. I was terribly greedy. I was looking at the rewards and didn't care about the nurturing. I thought you were invincible. I know you don't understand me, but I had a lot of pressure on me, damn it."

He rambled for the longest time, telling me about the events that transpired tonight. His booze and guilty conscience were talking now. "There were people who would have killed me if I didn't bring you along the way I did. I feel bad about all this. If I would have detected your injury sooner, maybe this all could have been avoided. If only you would have let me know somehow."

I looked down at him with disgust and disdain, because I did understand him and remembered all the times he shot me up with something and how it always affected me. I also remembered what Dad said and knew he did the same thing to him too, and perhaps it was the shots he gave to me were the same that killed her brother and caused this dreadful accident. He then cried uncontrollably on my shoulder while he talked and reminisced about Lauren for what seemed like a half an hour. It was comforting to see this side of him, but it was too late. I felt responsible too because I never let on I was injured. I also knew it was just the alcohol talking. He was so pathetic, I felt like I should be comforting him, but I couldn't even comfort myself. My dad said to get mad at someone and if anyone needed someone angry at them, it was Angelo. But I was so depressed I couldn't even get angry anymore.

"I'm going away for awhile. I'm going to miss you, you're one hell of a horse," he said. "But, I do want to tell you I just bought you some time. The people who wanted to kill me wanted you dead too." With a tear in his eye, he hugged me around my neck and left.

It seemed like he was here one moment and then gone the next. I didn't exactly know what he meant and felt very confused. He had never visited me at this hour and I tried in vain to understand what was happening.

"Why would anyone want to kill me? I didn't do anything to anyone. What is he talking about?" I thought.

Angelo got in his car and stared across the pasture at the little house next to the clinic that Loretta occupied on the farm. He thought deeply about saying goodbye to her too, as they had been close through the years. But after searching his soul, he realized that the less people he contacted, the better; plus if she was pressured, she might give him up. He then left the farm and drove in the opposite direction from where he told Roberta. He said he was going to Italy, but he was really going to Mexico. Angelo was the kind of guy that would be hard to follow. Because of his history in Sicily, he was always suspicious and constantly looked at his shadows. No one would ever creep up on him. There was also a dark side to Angelo, a side of him that very few knew, a side he inherited from his Mafioso dad. Angelo was a lone wolf with very few friends. He would survive in Mexico by himself just fine, but since he didn't have a backup plan, the chameleon was going to have to reinvent himself again. He was going to have to disguise himself and stay away from the track and the bookies, even though that was the only thing he knew; he'd have to change his habits. The Buick would have to go too. It would be his calling card. He didn't want to drive it across the border and he didn't want to leave it in Laredo, because they would have known he went to Mexico when they found it. It would stick out like a sore thumb. The best thing to do was to leave it at the airport in Cincinnati and make it look like he caught a flight there. Then he would take the old grey dog south to the border town of Laredo. He thought it out very meticulously as he started the drive to Cincinnati.

When reaching Laredo, he would walk across the bridge at the border, and then throw his overnight bag with his money and gun in it across the Rio Grande and pick it up after he crossed. This would have to be done at night, so he wasn't seen. It would be a long bus ride to Texas, but he could buy a fake ID in Laredo and get a visitors pass to cross the border and never return. He figured he could blend into the population down in Mexico City very easily, because the people were fairer there, of mainly Spanish descent, with blue eyes, not like the dark people with brown eyes of Indian descent around the border towns. The layers of the onion were starting to unravel, exposing the side of Angelo that had been hidden for too many years. Curiously, all of this became very natural to him and he began to like the adrenaline rush.

CLOSE CALL

While Angelo rehashed his getaway plan over and over in his mind, it had begun to snow; the wet and heavy snow rapidly obliterating the highway. He had to be careful, but his thoughts were scrambled from the terrible deed he had just committed and from the booze that was numbing his brain. As his old Buick ambled its way down the country road, he had no choice but to drive past The Tack Room on the way to the freeway, as it was the only way out of town. As he got closer, he saw it swarming with cops, their red, blue, and white blinking lights barely visible from miles away, shimmering in the white background in the valley below. For some reason, it felt good revisiting the scene of the crime again. Because of the heavy snow fall, the lights in the distance were soon obliterated, his headlights and heavy snow creating a "whiteout" effect. The cold wind that blew in the winter storm was also covering his tracks. Mentally, it all seemed so peaceful; he felt like the falling blanket of snow was also erasing the murders in his mind.

"Damn, I'm lucky it wasn't snowing when I shot them," he said to himself. "There would have been foot prints and tire tracks left all over the fucking place."

Then a momentary break in the clouds allowed him to see down the hill. Butterflies filled his stomach again as he slowly came down the hill and got closer to the procession of cars that were passing The Tack Room, their headlights lined up for at least a quarter of a mile.

"Damn looky-loos," he thought. "Get out of my way! I got to get out of here," he frantically thought as he lit another cigarette.

Coming down the long winding hill, with the lights at the bar being about a half mile away now, the unthinkable happened; a buck and a doe suddenly stepped in front of his car and froze in his headlights. Angelo, seeing them standing on the snow covered highway, quickly reacted and swerved suddenly to his right and hit his brakes hard. He began to slide off the road, sideways, hitting and throwing the buck, sending his car bouncing and careening off the snow covered gravel shoulder. Down into the drainage ditch he slid, roughly bounced down and then up the hill, coming to a stop and facing a large sycamore overlooking the highway.

During the bumpy ride through the ditch, Angelo had hit his head on the Buick's big steering wheel and was knocked out. His lifeless body lay slumped over the steering wheel with the horn blowing loudly in the cold darkness. After a couple of minutes had gone by, a good samaritan saw the lights shining off the side of the road and stopped and ran across the ditch and opened his car door, shaking him and waking him. The engine to his Buick was still running and his lights were on, illuminating the tree in front of him and the white wooded hills with the snow falling all around him.

When Angelo came to, he grabbed his steering wheel and felt dazed and a little groggy, but he instantly realized he had to get out of there. Even though he was dazed, fear of getting caught mobilized him. He put the transmission in reverse and then drive, rocking the car back and forth. He tried in vain to drive out of the ditch, but to no avail, as the wheels just spun and spun, sinking his tires into the wet ground deeper and deeper. The newly fallen snow and the mud underneath it from the weeks of rain had made the ground a quagmire and had probably saved his life, allowing the car to slow down faster before he hit the tree. The adrenaline that was being pumped into his body, the fight or flight response, brought him to his senses and made him think of everything. He knew he had been drinking and the Sheriff would be along soon to investigate the accident. He quickly lit a cigarette, thinking and hoping the smoke would disguise the alcohol on his breath. He looked at his bag, which had been thrown to the floor from the accident, and saw his .38 and rolls of cash on the floor mat, as they were thrown out of the bag. He put the bag on the seat and pulled the small box of ammunition out and put the .38 and the ammo in his jacket pocket. Then he collected the cash and stuffed them into some clothes in the bag. He then got out of the car and waited there alone for help, as the good samaritan had left to call for a tow truck. The air in the cool mountains was sweet at night, bringing out the fresh smell of the wet woods, and slowly bringing him to his senses.

He looked over to the highway and saw the deer sitting there on the side of the road, a beautiful buck with four or five points on each antler. The deer just sat there with glazed eyes looking into the woods, as if in shock and preparing himself to die. It appeared he had broken legs, as one of them was bent precariously and unnaturally to the side. A broken leg was a death sentence for such a proud animal that lived in the wild. Angelo walked up to him with remorse that touched his very soul. Although he had just committed a callous act an hour or two ago, the compassionate side of him came into play. Watching the proud animal just sitting there in the snow, just staring back at him, brought tears to his eyes. He wanted to kill him, to put him out of his misery, to end his pain, but was afraid to do so, as he knew a cop would be coming back soon to investigate his accident and didn't want to acknowledge he had a gun.

Angelo, realizing the Sheriff would be along soon, grabbed the .38 and ammo out of his pocket, wrapped them in a white sock from his bag and walked away from the deer, placing them under a rock close to a nearby tree. He stood there, puffing on his cigarette, and saw the red, white, and blue blinking lights of a squad car slowly approach him. His mind raced with fear, as he felt the warm blood dripping down on his face from the bump on his forehead. He wiped it away and thought of the murder, less than a half mile away, and the fact he was in the bar before they were killed. Because of his car's location in the ditch and distance up the road, it wasn't visible from the bar, so he knew Billy Joe wouldn't see it and say something regarding it. Nevertheless, he was afraid that they might be looking for him and his car, as he had asked too many questions. While he stood on the snowy bank, the Sheriff's white patrol car stopped at the road and the officer got out and shined a flashlight on the deer. Then he pointed it at him on the bank, blinding him momentarily.

"Are you alright over there?" He asked.

Angelo, shaking from fear and the cold wind that was blowing heavy snow, replied nonchalantly; "Yeah, I'm alright, just a bump on my head."

"What happened here?"

Angelo turned away and pointed at the buck, not wanting to breathe in his face. "I was coming down the hill, when a buck and doe jumped out in front of me. I tried to avoid them, but I hit the buck and skidded off the fucking road. There should still be some tracks on the road where my skid marks are, probably theirs too."

The officer, listening intently, but being cautious and vigilant, stared and studied Angelo while he spoke.

"Can I see your license and registration please?"

"Sure, let me get them for you, they're in the car."

Angelo walked over to the car and reached in his glove compartment; all the while the cop's flashlight shining on him, and hastily grabbed the registration. Then he took his wallet out of his rear pocket, producing his license. With shaking hands, he then handed them over to the officer.

"Have you been drinking sir?"

"Yeah, I had a couple before I left the house. I'm okay though!"

The Sheriff looked at his license; "You live at Chestnut Mountain Farms?"

"Yeah, I'm the trainer there. Been there for years; more than I can remember."

"You work for the Windsor's?"

"Yeah, I used to work for the old man years ago. Now I work for Roberta, his daughter; been there for years, like I said!"

"Are you Summer Storm's trainer?"

"Yeah, I'm her trainer."

"Here, follow me. I have a first-aid kit in my cruiser. Let's clean up that wound on your head. By the way, how is everything there? That was a real tragedy what happened. I watched it live on TV and couldn't believe it. Like losing someone you know, being they're from our hometown and all. A real tragedy!"

Angelo, sensing the cop wasn't looking for him, momentarily felt relieved. He then grabbed the gauze and cleaned the cut on his forehead and held it there, putting down pressure to stop the bleeding. "Doing the best we can. Losing Lauren was a real loss, and the horse's injury was heart breaking too. Hey man, can you shoot that buck over there and put him out of his misery; I feel really bad about it!"

"I can't do that. But I will call the proper agency to come over and pick him up. When they kill him the meat will be fresh and they'll bring it to the prison outside of Lexington. Inmates are fed with road kill all the time."

"Okay. I guess you run into this all the time. I just didn't want to see him suffer."

The officer, ignoring the comment, looked him in the eye. "Look Angelo, I'm going to let you go, but I want you to go home tonight. The road is getting worse and I know you've been drinking. Out of respect to you and your boss, I'm going to let you go home instead of hauling you in. I'll call for a tow truck. He'll take you and your car home."

Angelo, feeling at ease because he wasn't going to get arrested for drunk driving, stuck his shaking hand out to thank him.

"Thank you man; I appreciate it."

"Where were you heading anyway, on a night like this?"

"I was actually headed to the airport. Work has been slow lately and my heart just hasn't been in it. I was going on a long planned vacation."

"Well, look, I want you to be careful. Do you hear me? The only reason I'm letting you go is because of the Windsor's."

"Yes sir, I will. And thank you again."

As they spoke, a tow truck's blinking lights slowly approached them.

"I'll tell the driver to take you home. I have to get going. We had a shooting right down the road, at The Tack Room. You'll be running into a lot of traffic going in that direction. Good luck!"

"A shooting? Is Billy Joe alright? The bartender?"

"Oh yeah, he's okay. Someone shot two men in the parking lot. It sounds like it was orchestrated. I don't know. I was just on my way there."

"What do you mean orchestrated?"

"You know, like an assassination. Real clean like, up close and personal. Got to go!"

"Okay, thanks again."

Angelo watched him drive away in the driving snow and anxiously watched the tow truck get into position to get his car on the road again. While the tow truck driver was busy attaching chains to the underbody of his car, Angelo walked over to the rock he hid the gun under and quietly retrieved it. The sock was muddy and soaking wet. He removed the gun and ammo, dried them off, and put them in his jacket's pocket, throwing the sock away. Then he picked up a handful of snow and held it to his head, trying to reduce the pounding he felt. With the snow held to his head, he walked up to the buck and stared at him again. It just sat there, proud but pathetic, as if it was waiting to die, as if he knew it was eminent, as if he knew his life was over. The cold and heavy snow had covered his fur in a blanket of white, as if it was erasing his life. His black shiny eyes continued to stare at the woods. Angelo then turned his head in the direction the deer was looking and saw a doe in the thicket staring back. Emotions flooded his brain. His killing, the buck hit on the road, the doe left without a mate, his eminent escape. It was too much to bear. Sadly and reluctantly, Angelo walked away, his mind drifting away to the cop's comments, yet still trying to forget about the hapless deer on the side of the road.

"Real clean like, huh? What the fuck does that mean? What and who do they suspect?" He thought as he looked at the glowing flares and activity in the distance, the cops blinking lights illuminating the newly fallen snow.

After speaking to the tow truck driver, he watched and hoped his undercarriage wasn't damaged going through the drainage ditch, either getting there or being towed out of there, as he had many miles to go to get to the Cincinnati airport. After about twenty long and agonizing minutes of watching his car being pulled out of the ditch, his car was on the highway again, with a line of cars waiting for him. They had to stop while the tow truck was in position and weren't too happy about it. He told the tow truck driver he was fine to drive and didn't need a ride, slipping him ten bucks on the side. He then paid the tow truck driver for the tow, started his car, turned on his wipers, and stared at the deer and the woods again, seeing the doe still there. Shaking his head in disgust and apathy, he got out of his car and walked up to the deer and looked him in the eye. With tears forming, he reluctantly pulled the gun out of his pocket and shot the buck in the head, sending him to the frozen ground, his head falling hard with a spray of red blood shattering the white and calm snow, but relieving him of the pain he was in. The deer just lay there, with the headlights from the line of cars that were stopped, shining on him. He looked to the thicket and the doe was gone, leaving perhaps she knew her mate was gone, or perhaps leaving from the sound of the loud gun, he didn't know. But he knew it was final.

"Sorry buddy. Sorry we had to meet this way."

Then he put the gun back in his pocket and got in his car and proceeded to go down the hill, following a snow removal truck, which just passed by and was thankfully clearing the road for him. He was happy the car was running again, and though he felt sad, he was relieved that the buck was put out of his misery. He knew he had to get out of there.

As he approached The Tack Room, the snow was still heavy and was pounding on his windshield under a heavy wind. The wipers were in bad shape and just streaked and scratched the windshield as they scraped back and forth, leaving his view of the road hazy, to say the least. As he passed the bar, the crime scene looked almost surreal with the police car's blinking lights reflecting off the newly fallen snow in the parking lot and surrounding woods. He knew he acted weird at the bar and asked too many questions. Would Billy Joe suspect him and say something? Would someone recognize his car in the line of slow traffic that he was in? After all, it was only a two lane country road.

As the line of cars he was in slowly drove by The Tack Room, he rolled down his window and saw the two men lying on the ground, just where he left them, the area surrounded by yellow tape. Cops were milling around, talking to each other and trying to photograph the area.

"Damn, I'm lucky it started to snow. It's covering up everything." He thought again.

Yellow tape was strung around the perimeter of the parking lot and news trucks from Lexington were there already, their telescopic lights illuminating the woods. He saw the white Chevette, still parked where he saw it last. He wondered if Roberta would suspect him when she heard the news. Probably, he thought. He should have kept his mouth shut in the bar, but when he was in the bar he had no idea he was going to shoot them that night. It was a spontaneous decision made in his parked car, a decision he was going to have to live with, but at least he was going to live. He planned on coming back some day, mainly because this was the only home he ever had in America and he felt bad about leaving it, but he had to lay low for a while. He had to get out of here and wait for the heat to die down. And believe it or not, he also had a conscience and felt bad because he felt he betrayed the Windsor family with Lauren's death. But he also felt he was a victim of circumstances too, because he only gave Summer Storm the acepromazine to relax her and prevent her from getting hurt, never figuring she could win a race of that distance with her injured leg on a muddy track. And unfortunately for him and everyone else, it all backfired on him as he underestimated her heart entirely.

As he left the hills of Kentucky, going into the Ohio valley, the blinding snow gradually turned to a heavy rain. The white lines on the road clicked by ever so fast, each one leaving his past further and further behind. Angelo didn't see the white lines though. His mind was racing too. And so began the intrigue, the game of cat and mouse that would go on for the next three years from Kentucky to Mexico, a game that would transform him and his life dramatically. It would whither what was left of his life away and leave him in ruins, both physically and mentally.

ACTIONS HAVE CONSEQUENCES

Tawnee and Gina started to come by more often to spend time with me, as they knew how close Lauren and I were and they knew I was lonely. They used to lead me out of the pasture and down the path that led to the woods where Lauren enjoyed walking me, but it wasn't the same anymore. The woods were empty and silent now. I began looking at life through a different lens; a lens clouded with misery and didn't see the beauty in anything. I didn't hear the robins sing or see the rabbits stir. I knew they tried hard to comfort me and I appreciated it, but my heart wasn't there. This wasn't enjoyable any longer. I felt like I was just being dragged through a long dark tunnel, a time warp that brought me back onto the race track on that fateful day, a memory that kept repeating itself with subtle overtones which were completely sad and incomprehensible at times. Like a drop of water that falls into a quiet and calm pond, the accident had a ripple effect that carried over to this day and touched everything I saw and felt.

Although my good friend Winnie tried to help me, the days went by ever so slowly, each one seemed longer and longer, and then the days turned into months, each one more increasingly difficult to endure. My eating and sleeping habits were all awry; I was a mess. Roberta wanted me to try to run again, thinking it would lift my spirits and get me in shape for breeding, but no matter how much the jockey whipped me while we practiced, I just didn't care anymore. I didn't want any part of it. My times at the oval were way off my winning times and my heart wasn't in it. Lauren was the only rider I ever had and no one else could bring out my fervor for winning with her gone. It was amazing that I could even run again anyway, because my injury was so severe. No horse ever raced again after this type of injury, yet was lucky enough to be alive. The only thing that saved me was my big heart and modern medicine. Kate also felt if I got hurt again, I would probably be euthanized, therefore erasing my breeding fees. So she suggested they stopped trying to train me.

Next they wanted to breed me, but much to their dismay, and after numerous tests, they found out I was infertile, another collateral effect from the drugging I endured. I wasn't that walking pot of gold they thought they had and they both were severely disappointed, as they had breeding stallions lined up from all over the world for the next eight years. I was just a handicap now, someone they had to take care of daily, at least that's the way my depression made me feel. My drive was gone, my heart was empty, and I didn't care much about anything. The rich bluegrass that encompassed our farm didn't even taste good. I wish I would have died with Lauren on that cold and rainy day in New York, mainly because I felt so responsible for her death. Who knows? Maybe we'd still be together.

I kept replaying the accident in my mind over and over again like a sad movie. In the movie, I used to see Lauren getting up out of the mud and walking over to me, wiping the mud off of her and hugging me, both of us uninjured. She would then mount me and we'd walk over to the winners circle and she'd look down at me and smile and caress my neck, and I'd be happy again. The rain would be coming down hard on us, but we would both be looking into each other's eyes with a calmness on our face that was serene and tranquil. The cold rain would be dripping from our face as flashbulbs went off all around us and we'd be oblivious to everything and everybody. We had done it! We had won the championship together and would be looking forward to her marriage. I tried to replay that movie over and over, but eventually I couldn't anymore as I realized it was just a fantasy and it became very painful recounting the shocking and horrifying event that left her dead and left me so sad and lonely.

The cool crisp air of winter soon came to the farm again and with it came the depression and sickness of Roberta, who was now bed-ridden most of the time. All of the status and wealth she had couldn't stop the heartbreak and pain she felt by losing her only daughter. The farm had been in her family for almost one hundred and fifty years and now there was no family member to leave it to; the circle had been broken. Because of that, I rarely saw her anymore. I don't know if she had a broken heart like me or if she was physically sick. Lauren was our life, and Lauren was Roberta's only child and she took it hard. There were rumors she wanted to sell the farm, but her family's roots kept her here. There was also a Mausoleum built on the property which housed her grandparents, parents, Lauren, and a place reserved for her, which made it doubly tough to leave. She was raised old school with an appreciation for what her father had built and accomplished and she felt selling the farm would have let him down, but unfortunately, she knew she'd have to do it someday. She just kept putting it off. Everyone said she wanted to be buried here, next to her daughter, therefore relieving herself of the guilt of having to sell.

I then wallowed around for almost two years in the abyss of my soul, much of it a blur with huge vacant gaps, when much to my surprise Angelo stunned us all by coming back. And though he had been gone for only three years, I hardly recognized him. He was gaunt and tanned with deep lines in his face and had grown a full beard, a disguise I guess. Roberta had a ton of questions for him and Angelo lied his eyes out. He said he was surprised to hear about the killings. The fact they occurred on the night he left were just a coincidence, he said, because he had never been violent in his life. He had also planned his trip to Sicily for months in advance and after finally setting up an itinerary, it was time to go. And so Roberta took him back. Maybe she felt sorry for him or maybe she was sick and just didn't care anymore. After all, she had her own suspicions, and after three years of thinking about it her mind had been made up, no matter what he said. After the murders at The Tack Room, Angelo knew everyone would be extensively interviewed, but eventually the local authorities gave up on the case, figuring it was a mob hit after getting the victim's identities and rap sheets. After searching their car, finding their guns and stolen license plates, and discovering they had rap sheets a mile long, they knew they had spent time in an Ohio prison and were "connected" to the New York mob. What they couldn't figure out was why they were killed at a country bar outside of Lexington and what were they doing here?

Angelo didn't do very much on the farm when he returned, as it was winter and he didn't look very healthy; he was just happy to be home, happy to be in his own bed once again. He told me he used to lay on his back and stare at the ceiling and reminisce about his past, but each day he got more depressed too. Deep down inside, he knew he was still a marked man. He came to my stall to visit me often and would tell me about his trip to Mexico and where he had stayed. He told me he didn't stay in one place too long and found it hard to find a job at his age, hard to support himself. He understood the language because it was close to Italian, but didn't like his time in Mexico at all. When he ran out of money, he came back to the only home he knew. He started spending most of his nights at The Tack Room when he returned, down the road from the farm, drinking his life away. I think he felt a calmness revisiting the scene of the crime and knowing he got away with murder. Perhaps he had forgotten the mob wanted him and perhaps he forgot the mob never forgot a double-cross, or perhaps he just didn't care anymore either. But then again, maybe he knew all of that and got tired of running, perhaps just coming home to die. He always said this was the only home he ever had. He said Billy Joe didn't tend bar there any longer, so he didn't have to face the barrage of questions he may have had. He could just sit there at the horseshoe shaped bar, on his favorite bar stool, eating peanuts and enjoying the boilermakers that numbed his brain and ravaged his liver.

But Angelo wasn't completely out of the woods yet and he knew it. His past would soon catch up to him and rear its ugly head again. On a cold and snowy night that winter, I was awakened by two men in a black ski mask and black clothes, who barged into my stall, dragging a weak and fighting Angelo behind them. Winnie backed herself into a corner and I backed up away from them too, not knowing what to do. Because of the failed attempt on his life earlier, Richie sent some "wiseguys" down from Philly this time to finish the job. Because of their preparatory reconnaissance, they were aware of the surveillance cameras on the farm and the room that monitored them. I overheard them mention that the first thing they did was disarm the guard that observed the cameras and then tied him up with duct tape.

Salvador Di Matteo and Patsy Conti were seasoned hit-men, earning their stripes on the mean streets of Brooklyn and South Philly in the late sixties and early seventies. Angelo's hands, feet, eyes, and mouth were taped with duct tape and he was bleeding profusely from his swollen nose and ears, making it very difficult for him to breathe. They cut the duct tape off his wrists and propped him up at the wall in front of me and then pounded a six inch long railroad spike into his wrist with a sledge hammer, attaching him to the cedar wall. Then they spread his arms out and pounded another stake into his other wrist, hanging him on the wall. Angelo was too skinny and too weak to fight back, and because of the duct tape on his mouth, Angelo couldn't even cry out in pain. His head just hung there, passed out from the pain and slumped on his chest, while blood spurted out of his wrists, dripping on the wall and the straw below him.

He was still gasping for air when Patsy grabbed Angelo's head and ripped off the duct tape from his eyes, while Sal peeked his head out of the stall, making sure they were alone in the barn. Patsy then grabbed Angelo by his throat and lifted his head, holding his chin in his hand. He slapped his face and threw some of the water from my trough on him to bring him back.

"Open your eyes asshole, I got something for you."

Angelo slowly opened his eyes and hung there, nearly dead from the loss of blood and cringed in fear. He looked Patsy in the eye and knew his life was over. It was time to meet his maker. Unable to speak, he closed his eyes again.

Patsy, lighting a stogie, looked at Angelo. "You're pathetic! Here's a message from Richie, asshole. He wanted to make sure the horse was the last thing you see."

He then pulled a .357 out of his shoulder gun holster and pushed it through the tape around Angelo's mouth, shoving his head against the wall.

Patsy, getting angry now, said; "Remember the hollow points you used on Larry and Tony? Larry was my cousin. Take a good look at the chamber asshole; we have some for you too."

Angelo's blue eyes were as big as silver dollars now as he saw the hollow tips of the bullets in the gun's chamber. He tried to turn his head, but Patsy pushed Angelo's head against the wall with his gun, the gun forcibly cutting into the duct tape in his mouth. Patsy pulled the trigger. Click, no bullet. Angelo blinked with the click of the gun and pissed his pants. Patsy smiled and puffed on his cigar, blowing the smoke in his face. He pulled the trigger again. Click, no bullet again.

"Hey Sally, how many bullets did we put in this damn gun?" He said, as he looked at his revolver and spun the chamber.

Sal laughed, while he leaned up against the wall, watching Angelo suffer.

"I don't remember Patsy. Try again. There's got to be some in there."

"Yeah, you're right man. The third time's the charm. What do you think Ange?"

Patsy blew some more smoke in Angelo's face and stared at his gun for a minute, creating a tense moment. Then he put the gun to Angelo's mouth again, forcing his head against the wall, while Angelo looked at him, now sweating profusely. Patsy puffed on his cigar and then blew it into his face again.

"Goodbye asshole. It's time to punch your ticket. I'm not going to fuck with you anymore. We got paid good money to torture you. Richie wanted it this way."

He pulled the trigger again. Bang! The gun went off. It was finally over. Patsy pulled the gun away and let Angelo's limp head fall to his chest. The blood poured from the hole in the duct tape wrapped around his mouth onto his slumped over body, the large hole in the back of his head visible now with his brains and blood splattered on the cedar wall behind him. Patsy didn't get sprayed with blood because the duct tape on his mouth prevented the recoil. Angelo's story had ended where it began, born into a life of crime and dying in a life of crime. It had gone full circle.

"Fuck Sal! I guess I'm getting old. I don't like torturing like I used to. I'd rather just kill and leave, real clean like, like a surgeon. But this is the way Richie wanted it done. What the fuck? Did you bring the gasoline in from the car? Let's get this fucking thing over with and get out of here."

When the gun went off and Angelo's head slumped forward; I instantly got afraid and stepped back and reared up at them, scaring them and backing them against the stall door.

Patsy looked at me with his gun in his hand and said; "Let's get the fuck out of here before that horse tries to kill us! I got other plans for her. Bring that can in here! We're going to make a real fucking statement here; we're going to leave our signature here."

Winnie and I were petrified as we looked at Angelo's slumped over body, the blood pouring down profusely from his head. We then watched them hurriedly run out of the stall and down the corridor of the barn. As they ran, they threw gasoline on everything. I didn't understand what was happening, but I sensed it wasn't good. I walked over and tried to arouse him with my nose by nudging him. Unfortunately, it reminded me of when Lauren lay lifeless on the track. I then paced my stall, not knowing what to do, and wondered why this was happening here in my stall. "Why was this happening to me," I thought? After about ten minutes had gone by I started to smell smoke, which scared me. I had smelled smoke when travelling through the streets of New York, but never here. I didn't know what it was at first, because I had never seen or experienced a fire before. The smell of smoke and unbearable heat began to consume the air and the sound of my friends and family calling out and thrashing in pain was dreadful and frightening. It was a tragedy that was terribly horrific and hit me like a ton of bricks, briefly awakening me from my long bout of depression. The fire first broke out in our barn and rapidly spread to the other barns, causing great carnage to our stables. Our barns were huge, each capable of holding 48 horses, with their stalls and tack rooms. As the fire raged on, I heard my mom yelling out to me in the heated inferno. She was across the stable from me but closer to the middle of the huge barn we occupied. I was located near the front of the barn and away from the fire when it first started. I reared up, kicking my legs, and tried to get to her, but I couldn't break out, no matter how hard I kicked. As time quickly passed by, the crying in the barn gradually stopped and all you could hear was the fire roaring and the wood crackling and falling to the ground. I called out to Mom one last time, but I didn't hear her anymore and knew in my heart she was consumed too. Princess and her brand new litter of babies were eventually killed after being overcome with smoke in our stall and Winnie got killed by a falling fiery beam as she tried to escape, trying to leap over the opening in the top of the stall's half-door. It happened right in front of me, and as it crushed her, it thoroughly crushed my heart. Winnie was my bud and I couldn't help her. All I could do was watch her suffer right in front of me with the fiery beam on top of her crushing her to death. It was so traumatic, it seemed like minutes went by before she stopped thrashing about and calling out to me, all the while the fire getting hotter and hotter. My hide was singed and my lungs were seared as I violently thrashed about in my stall, rearing up and kicking and trying to break down the wooden door. It then became hard to breathe for me too, as the fire raged on and the heat only intensified.

As the flames made their dance of death through the stables, I lay down in the burning straw as my lungs were burning and my front leg hurt bad. I was getting weak and tiring and I felt my drive disappearing. I looked around and all I could see and smell through the smoke was death. Angelo's body had fallen to the ground from the burning wall, and Winnie, Princess and her babies; they all were gone too. My brain and body finally conceded the battle and I lied there and succumbed to my fate. The great heart in me, the competitor that wouldn't quit, was finally giving up. I stared at the burning wall and ceiling above me and laid there panting as the walls turned a glowing orange and the straw burned around me, catching my coat on fire too. I felt anger at first and then as I lied their waiting to die, I felt weak and really afraid for the first time in my life. I knew I was dying, I knew it was over.

"Why is life taken away so quickly and without notice? Where does it go?" I thought as I lay on the floor and tried to breathe the hot gassy air while the fire raged through the barn, knowing it killed my mom and all my friends.

As I closed my eyes and was about to take my last breath, just then a miracle happened as I felt a divine intervention. Suddenly, a farm hand wrapped in a wet blanket came out of the smoke and fire, miraculously running into my stall and putting the fire out on my coat. He then put a rope around my neck and encouraged me to get up, and then led me out of the glowing inferno. Diego and I had to sadly step over Angelo and Winnie and the beam that fell on her on my way out the door. After I was led outside, my coat was burnt and the blanket that covered Diego was in flames too. He then threw it on the ground and picked up some snow and rubbed it on my smoldering hair. The air was cool again and each breath I took was painful, but at least I was breathing clean air again. I stood there in the snow, in great pain, with my head down, gasping for air, with Diego holding the rope, while we watched the fire destroy everything. I looked down at my burnt legs and shook my head. It had all happened so fast. I then looked up to the sky. The glow from the barns lit up the snowy countryside with an eerie red color and the fireman were running around frantically trying to save anything they could. My home and everything I knew was gone.

As the fire raged, Roberta was awoken and came rushing down to the flaming barns in her Jaguar. She had her pajamas and a robe on when she saw me and came rushing over in tears, hugging me and yelling for a vet. I was happy to see her, as she was my only link to Lauren and I hadn't seen her in a while and I was very happy to be alive. I was weak and lied down on the frozen snowy pasture I was led to, as I was overcome with pain and emotions too. The snow I laid in cooled the burns on my coat, but my lungs were in pain and burning with every breath I took. I looked at my singed coat and felt the pain from the burns; the adrenalin was wearing off, making the pain all the more intense. Roberta immediately took charge and gave orders for the other survivors from the other barns and I to be gathered together in a distant pasture, away from the activity, until the vet was able to attend to us. We just stood there together in the snow, sad and confused, and watched the barns go up in flames, containing our homes and friends and families and knew not what tomorrow may bring. We watched the firemen work valiantly, trying to save both horses and property, but it was too late; the fire went off very fast. There wasn't very many of us who were saved that night, but coincidentally, most of the fastest horses were spared, about fifteen out of eighty. I met my dad in the pasture as he was saved too. He and I were the only ones left in my family, but he was in much better condition than me. I guess it wasn't my time to go, but it made me wonder why I was saved and what lied in store for me.

When daybreak came, we stood and looked at the smoldering ruins. It was an eerie sight. What once were three big beautiful barns was now black and charred wooden remains standing like toothpicks against the white and snowy background. It looked like a war scene with the feint hint of smoke and destruction everywhere, but the fact that it was our home made it all the more sad. The air smelled of smoke and burnt flesh, nauseating to say the least, for we all knew of whom the flesh belonged to.

As twilight came and illuminated the ghastly surroundings, Roberta and Kate were surveying the grounds with insurance men and police investigators, while contractors were removing the burnt debris. The police were here taking pictures and sequestering certain areas for investigative purposes, as there were tracks left in the snow from the arsonists feet and from their vehicle, along with two empty cans of gas that were left behind. There was a contingent of vet's on the property and they were attending to each of us. Large temporary tents were being erected for temporary housing for the few horses that survived, while plans were already in motion for reconstruction. I was sent to an Equine Hospital in Lexington and was treated for burns and smoke inhalation. Roberta, in all of her depression, was still very organized.

THE INVESTIGATION

Roberta came down to my stall early one morning to observe me with the farm's new vet. As the groomer carefully brushed me, they talked. It was found, after a lengthy investigation into the fire by local and federal officials, that the fire was started intentionally with an accelerant. Traces of gasoline were found in the charred remains and two gasoline cans were found at the source, partially melted in the nearby snow. They gave that as the reason the fire raced through the barns so fast. They also found Angelo's charred body in my stall, confirming the fact with his dental records. After an extensive autopsy, they discovered he had been shot in the head and had been dead before the fire began and probably tortured there by whoever set the fire, as there was remains of duct tape on his body and the six inch long spikes were still imbedded in Angelo's wrist bones. There was also no smoke in his lungs, which only thickened the plot. The security guard who was hired to monitor the video cameras was also found in the rubble of his building, with all security tapes destroyed. Since there was snow on the ground that night, they found the perpetuators foot prints and tire tracks where they left the scene. They knew what kind and size shoes they wore and what brand of tires were on their car. Their shoes were Italian and were bought in Manhattan, while the license plates were stolen in Lexington. The tires were also traced to a rental car company in Lexington, at the airport, where the car was rented to a "John Smith." There was a cornucopia of evidence, but it all led out of town.

The private investigator that Roberta originally hired had numerous photographs of Angelo with known Mafia members, not only at the race track in New York, but photographs of them entering my stable at that location too. Most damaging, however, were photographs of envelopes of cash changing hands between them and Angelo after the first and second race of the Triple Tiara. But since there was no physical evidence of drugs in my system, I overheard Roberta say he must have had a bad gambling problem and must have owed the mob a ton of money for them to cause such destruction. There were also photographs of Angelo with some gangsters before the big race at the watering hole down the road from the farm. It seemed Angelo did have a bad gambling habit and was fixing races to pay off his debts to the mob. It was either silver or lead all over again. They kept you in their pocket until they needed you. He had become Vinnie's boot-licking lackey and would have done anything to support his gambling vice.

After further investigation, it was then decided by the authorities that all the evidence led to the mob starting the fire and using it as a cover for the murder of Angelo and payback for me winning my last race. It was a revenge killing, up close and personal, with all the earmarks of being done by the mob, being done to send a message. And most fortunate for the authorities, a small gun safe was found in Angelo's room, which contained many old leather bound diaries and a copy of his memoirs that he'd been working on for years. This sealed the deal. It seems he kept a diary of all his transactions, both on the track and off, one for each of the last twenty years. These included every bet he made, how much he bet, who took the bet, and what the vig was. Which races were fixed and what horses involved were also outlined in detail. It told what he owed and who he owed it to. It was a wealth of evidence for investigators, the cherry on the sundae. The Feds went back to the records at the track for the last race and saw how the odds shifted dramatically before post time and how much negative payout there was when I unexpectedly won. They saw the mob took a big hit that day and after reading Angelo's memoirs, they saw how fearful he was and how much he feared retribution. Much to their surprise, Angelo outlined in detail the killing at The Tack Room years ago and his life on the lam. It was a mea culpa, saying he had done it in self defense. It all came together now. There was also a short discussion to whether the fire was caused for insurance purposes, as Roberta was tired of running the farm and only the best horses were saved. But that was quickly discounted because Angelo had a bullet in his head and me and my dad were insured for five million dollars each and we both were saved.

But most shocking and disturbing to Roberta was the finding of Loretta's charred body in the farm's clinic, next to the main barn, which was also burned down. She had been bound with leather reins around her wrists and feet and she too had been tortured and shot before the fire started, as there wasn't any smoke in her lungs too. They found three sets of footprints in the mud, all leaving the scene, of which one set was Angelo's. It was assumed she was tortured in front of Angelo before she was given the coup de grace. It was just another way of inflicting pain on Angelo before he died. According to Angelo's memoirs, she and Angelo had been seeing each other romantically for years, which explained why he was instrumental in her being hired in the first place. Not only were they an item, but they both had ties to the New York mob, with Loretta actually being the facilitator for the ordering of all drugs used, both legal and illegal, with Angelo being the transporter and dispenser. They were indeed a team, with Loretta having been planted here by the mob, operating under the guise of professionalism on the ranch and lying to Roberta on a daily basis.

According to his diary and memoirs, they had been doctoring the metabolism of the farm's race horses for years, outlining the amount of drugs given and the results of said drugs, even going back to when my dad raced. Experimental results were also explained, detailing how much was given to each horse per pound of horse. They basically controlled the outcome of many races up and down the coast for the mob, with Loretta having access to ordering the drugs and Angelo transporting them to the tracks on weekends, thus earning them both extra income and favors. Angelo's friends at the other farm's weren't left unscathed either. He threw them under the bus by not only recounting all of their dealings in his book, but he described all of their dirty details and all the participants involved. This information was the tongue on the envelope. It sealed the deal.

Coincidentally, years before the fire and discovery of the bodies and after the Triple Tiara, the Feds had systematically set up wire tapping on all the phones at the farm because they suspected someone was involved with illegal betting or doping for financial gain. They knew the farm had a history of success and the web was intricate and not only spread across the country, but it seemed to originate at Chestnut Mountain Farm. They knew of Angelo and Loretta's dealings and, interestingly, they found that Kate had been bought off by the mob too, with her making frequent phone calls to Vinnie and scheduling most races at their controlled tracks for years. As for the gumshoe Kate hired for Roberta; the photographs and information he acquired were "edited" by Kate before they were turned over to Roberta and meant to show that Angelo had a gambling problem only. She hid the fact that "doping" and rigging races were actually taking place. Kate's business transactions were between her and Vinnie only and no one else on the farm knew of them, not even Angelo. And although Kate was smart enough to be indiscreet in this dealing, it wasn't enough when they bugged the farm. This turned out to be a treasure trove to the feds, for it led to the core of doping and race track betting, both on and off the track, and straight to the big players. This ultimately led to the arrests of many trainers and jockeys nationwide and many "wiseguys" under the RICO Act. Down went the gambling bosses in New York, New Jersey, Philadelphia, Chicago, and Miami, ultimately jailing both Vinnie and Richie on racketeering and income tax evasion and thus disabling their gambling interests nationwide.

Roberta was aghast when she was informed of Kate's dealings. To say she was surprised is an understatement. It was one revelation after another that not only disgusted her, but made her physically ill. It was an intense and disturbing bit of information that rattled her to her very core, as she had trusted Kate implicitly with all matters, both financially and professionally. As for Kate, after being threatened with a long jail sentence, she flipped and fully cooperated with the authorities and got off easy, essentially throwing everyone under the bus. She lost her license to practice law and served one year in prison and then went into the Witness Protection Program, never to be seen or heard from again. Some say she moved to the countryside of Italy and some thought she was last seen in the affluent and scenic hills of western Ventura County, California.

After many heads fell, the federal government then scrutinized the racing industry and changed laws regarding drugging and betting procedures, subsequently making great reforms in the sport. Whoever started the fire thought Loretta and Angelo's body would be burned beyond recognition and didn't care that their death wouldn't look like an accident. But the biggest blunder the mob made was not realizing Angelo had a stockpile of information stored in his room that would bring everyone down. His diary was the gavel on the bench. It turned out the death of Loretta wasn't just an aside. She was tortured and killed in front of Angelo purposely. She was also punished for not being aware of my injury sooner, plus because of her involvement with Angelo and the drug distribution, they knew it was better this way. She not only knew too much but they knew dead witnesses don't tell tales, so her lips were sealed forever.

Even though many heads fell, no one was charged with the murders and arson fire of the farm, mainly because the lips of a dead man don't utter anything. There was no one to interview, so the police couldn't use the "ladder" of bargaining chips and pardons to get to the higher-ups, mainly because the men who perpetuated the crime had simply vanished.

I overheard that within a couple of months of the fire, Patsy Conti and Sal Di Mattio, the men who killed Angelo and started the fire, literally disappeared off the face of the earth. There were rumors that they were both killed by "friends" of theirs outside a Mafia controlled bar on Robinson Road in Campbell, Ohio, and then taken to a blast furnace at a steel mill in Youngstown, Ohio. The only blast furnace around was located under the Center Street Bridge, next to the Mahoning River. Their slain bodies were dumped into a large empty slag pot, about ten feet round in diameter, and were sent to the foot of the blast furnace on rails, where white hot molten steel was poured onto them from the furnace above it, the 3,600 degree Fahrenheit temperature vaporizing them and their clothes instantly. To say that batch of steel was "tainted" would be an understatement. Everyone knew these were mob hits, but as is the nature of mob hits, there wasn't any evidence to trace it to anyone, although everyone knew who orchestrated it. There was also an unwritten creed followed by law enforcement; if mobsters kept the killing amongst themselves, they didn't care and they didn't intervene. They figured they were just doing themselves a favor by not interfering with their internal crimes and letting them kill each other was a favor to the public. It was only when "civilians" were harmed that public outcry forced police to get involved, as most of the police were "bought off" by the mob anyway.

And because of all of this, after it was all said and done, after all the crime and heartache, all of Roberta's thoughts and fears of Angelo were finally realized. She had been right all along; the devil was in the details. Suspicion had occupied her thoughts and brewed in her heart for too long. She was terribly tormented by the fact she didn't heed her father's advice and didn't fire him years ago and wondered what other atrocities he had committed while he was here. Her loyalty had simply been stretched too far. With all the experience she had had in the business world, it bothered her immensely that all of this went on under her nose and she had been used as a patsy, thus only depressing her further. Between Kate, Loretta, and Angelo, the mob had its' fingers in every operation of her farm and controlled the lives and futures of each successful horse that raced. They basically controlled everything and everyone under her nose, except for Lauren and her personal secretary Pam. She felt that the legacy that she and her father had built was all a sham, a sham created by Angelo and Loretta doping her horses and Kate orchestrating their schedules.

Because of Angelo's life on the lam, he had no money when he died, so Roberta had what was left of him cremated and spread at the oval. That's the place he liked best. The bells tolled slowly for Angelo that day, echoing through the wooded hills and pastures of the countryside, reverberating another loss for me. Roberta was extremely hurt by the set of events that transpired, but no matter how much acrimony and animosity she felt, the ethics that were deeply ingrained in her soul made her do the right thing. The funeral service was small with only people from the farm attending. Angelo's status as a lone wolf left him with no friends and his gambling habit and his time on the run left him with no money. He had lived a lonely existence, a lone wolf in love with the greed and adrenaline of the mob and their way of life. The double life he led and the ill will he created had erased any good he had done through the years. Perhaps it was in his genes, predestined to commit these atrocities. His deceased father would have been proud of the legacy he left behind and his mother would have rolled over in her grave.

Ten years earlier, no one would have surmised that the most famous Thoroughbred farm in America would have been on a path to destruction with its fate doomed. It seemed to be a calmer, happier, more serene time, unsoiled by recent events. Lauren was in grade school and excelling in 4-H. Her future seemed bright and had great promise, guided by the money and power of the riches of Chestnut Farms. Angelo was immersed in training Bold Czar for the Triple Crown and was doing an exemplary job in his field, seemingly trusted by everyone. Loretta apparently was quietly doing a stellar job tending to the needs of the colts, fillies, studs, and mares of the farm. Kate was completely trusted and depended on by Roberta and appeared to be Roberta's right arm, her "voice" in the racing world. Roberta was learning the business and was excited by her new found fame, fortune, and status at the cocktail parties she attended in Lexington.

As for me; I was but a gleam in my dad's eye at the time, with years to go before I would be born. Now, everything has gone one hundred and eighty degrees. Lauren, Angelo and Loretta are dead, Kate has disappeared and the once stellar reputation of the farm that John and Roberta Windsor built was gone, having been disintegrated with the heat and smoke of the fire and the obscure corruption that brought it down. It left Roberta in a hapless depressed state, almost exhausted from the shock of ingenuous mistrust. And me, well only God knows what's in store for me. What once held promise here at Chestnut Farms has turned to ruins. The famous quote; "Power corrupts; absolute power corrupts absolutely," sure applied here in a magnanimous way.

OHIO

This turn of events unfortunately started a new life for me, a life that continued to spiral downhill from this day forward. After a couple of months of inhalation and burn therapy, the few remaining horses and I were then put up for auction, as Roberta decided to rid herself of me and the memories of the farm. Somehow I always felt that she blamed me for Lauren's death, but of course that was my own paranoia talking. My mom, Winnie, and Princess and her young family were all killed in that horrible fire, along with my brothers and sister and many of my close friends. The depression and disingenuous acts of deceit were too much for Roberta and she ultimately gave up and unfortunately died a few weeks later on Christmas day, the day before I was sold. This was more than I could take and only saddened me more.

Her funeral was large, as she had a lot of friends, not only in the horse racing business, but in government too. I had never seen so many cars, people, and activity as on the day of her funeral. Cars and Limos lined the mile long driveway that led to the house on the hill, with small buses making round trips to the cemetery area on the property. There were dignitaries there from Washington and notables from the world of horse racing, all here to pay their respects. Even the national press was here filming the whole thing with helicopters flying overhead. There was a family mausoleum on the property where her great grandparents, grandparents, parents, and Lauren were kept and Roberta was placed next to them, nearest to her daughter. The circle had been broken; the Windsor family line was finished. The future of the farm was up in the air too, as there were no dependants or relatives designated as heirs. Many people who knew the family speculated that her personal secretary would walk away with the farm, as she was the most loyal employee left, and probably the only one capable of running it.

After Roberta's death, I bided my time in my stall and empty pastures of the farm, trying to digest the changes that were going on. Although three barns had burned down, only two were reconstructed, and none of the horses that died were replaced, leaving the farm and pastures quite empty, a reflection of the pain and depression we all experienced. Bryan's family considered buying me because Tawnee and Gina knew what I meant to Lauren, but the deal was never consummated. I had hoped they would buy me, but they didn't, and unfortunately I was sold at an auction several months later, on July 4th, exactly three years to the date after my tragic accident, an accident that gave me world renowned fame and a heartbreak that continued to this day. Little did I know that that one single act, the act of not going to a good family that knew me, to Laurens friends, would change my life from that day forward.

My dad was subsequently sold to a farm down the road and continued to sire championship colts and fillies. He was still in his prime and was used for stud and was still siring winners, but none ever as good as me. I had gone from the fame of being the best female horse in the world to losing my health, my home, and all of my family, in less than four short years. I went from being on the very top of the world, to wallowing in the shadows of depression with memories of death and despair, and then going away to a strange home with complete strangers.

I was trailered to an airport the day I left the farm. When we were leaving the farm, I looked out my little window and saw the bronze statue of my dad rearing up in pride. I instantly thought of Lauren and the day she pointed him out to me and told me a statue of me would be there someday. It all seemed so long ago. Long ago and in another world, a world comprised of joy and happiness. As I looked to tomorrow, I didn't know when I would leave the dark tunnel that I occupied and whether I would ever see the sun shine again.

My new owner was a businessman from Ohio passing through Kentucky on his way home. He wanted to display me in different areas of the country at horse shows and county fairs. I was to be a one horse attraction, a draw to make money, like a carnival attraction. "Come see the greatest Filly that ever lived," was how it read. It seemed making money is all people wanted out of me. Nobody wanted me for me. My new home was Hubbard, Ohio, located in northeastern Ohio, fifty miles from Lake Erie and three miles from the Pennsylvania border. I had a nice barn with good facilities, but I hated it there and I hated the weather, humid in the summer and blistering cold in the winter. It was only four hundred miles north from my home in Kentucky, but the winter weather was quite different when it blew in off of Lake Erie. The locals called it "lake effect snow." The cold fronts that came down from Canada would heat up and pick up moisture when crossing the warm waters of the Great Lakes and dump large amounts of snow on the first fifty miles of land it crossed, which encompassed the area I now lived. I also hated our time travelling to all the exhibits my new owner set up. One week we'd be in Los Angeles, then the next week in San Francisco, then Denver, Phoenix, San Antonio and then God knows where. Although I was treated well, I missed Lauren and Winnie immensely. They had always traveled with me and comforted me on the plane, and now there was none of that; I was with a groomer and nervous all the time. I wished I hadn't fallen and broken my leg, as none of this would be happening to me now. I'm to blame for all of this, I thought. I created my own destiny.

Patrick, my new owner, was involved in the landscaping and grading engineering business, contracting out work to the major theme parks and golf courses in the country, and because of that he traveled a lot and was often gone leaving me alone with his family and his farm hands. Between his contracting responsibilities and my exhibits, it left him very little free time with his family. They had a big farm with other horses they rode for recreation and a large pasture where they raised Herefords and Angus for sale. They also had a dairy cow which they raised for their own use. His wife Anicia, and their young son Blayden, used to visit me often in my barn and were very nice to me. Sometimes Anicia would walk me on the farm and sometimes she would take me down to the banks of the green and slow flowing

Shenango River and let me graze on the sloping banks of tall green grass. Because they knew of my former injuries, Patrick and Anicia never rode me. But Blayden was only three years old at the time and she would often put him on my back while we walked. Blayden and I both enjoyed that a lot. He was a beautiful child and a real dare devil, though, and would try to stand on my back when we walked. His mom would be in front leading us and didn't always see his brave antics.

I was enjoying the new relationship's I developed, but after a few years, the economy turned sour, as well as Patrick's business. He was then forced to sell me, along with his farm and landscaping company, as they were moving out of state and "downsizing," as they called it. Unfortunately I had to adjust to a new life again. Patrick was forced to take a job at a large grading and engineering firm in southern California, running the grading and excavation dept., and I never saw him, Anicia or Blayden again. The day they left was a sad day for me and made me think about my Karma. It seemed every time I got close to someone, they disappeared. It seemed to me I wasn't wanted to be loved. It seemed people only wanted me to make money for them. Because of this, I also somehow felt like I was still being punished again for my accident that killed Lauren, Karma if you will, making me feel like I wasn't ever going to experience happiness again, that I had to pay for it somehow. It was a black cloud that hovered over me and engulfed me on that rainy day at Belmont Park and it never left. But the pain only intensified. It only got darker and the cut gouged deeper into my soul with every discouraging occurrence. It seemed there was always a new dark cloud coming over the horizon I had to deal with.

Every Tuesday and Saturday I was brought to an auction yard in New Castle, about twenty miles from our farm. I would be led into a large barn, with stadium seating, and led in a circle. Potential bidders, who would bid on the animal they wanted, sat there and scrutinized each of us. They used to open my mouth and look at my teeth, trying to figure out how old I was. Then they'd run their rough hands along my body and my legs. When they would get around to my right knee, they would stop, stare, and then rub their heads in confusion. "Her teeth say's she's young, but her knee is in bad shape," they used to say, and then walk away.

"The Amish auction"

In addition to horses, there were sheep, cattle, chickens, and pigs auctioned off too. Because the economy was so bad, no one wanted to buy a horse they couldn't ride. I was just pretty to look at, or I used to be, anyway. I had scars on me from the fire and I lost some weight after Patrick left me; so as a last resort I was then placed in a horse shelter and put up for adoption. Not only did I suffer from depression, my lungs were seared in that barn fire and I never fully recovered from the fire and my leg injury. I got winded early, had bare patches on my back, and wasn't good for much anymore.

The horse shelter in western Pennsylvania was the pits for me. It was located in the rolling hills and farm country between Hubbard, Ohio and New Castle, Pennsylvania, just outside of New Wilmington on the State line, a farming area that was occupied by a large contingent of Amish families. I had always been fed the best food available and lived in the best barns and paddocks that money could buy, and now I even hated walking to her trough. And when I did have an appetite, I had to compete for the food with the other horses, all 30 of them. We were all fed together, all at the same time, all inferior food.

So there I stood, in a new place again. I put my nose to the wind, my nostrils flaring, looking for what I don't know. My ears were erect and I felt alert again. I didn't detect danger, but I did detect sadness. It was all around me. It looked like a place you come to die.

Get in line Summer Storm; your glory days are over," I thought as I looked at my surroundings. Although I was extremely depressed, I still appreciated the green and wooded hills of the rural countryside, but hated the frequent thunder storms that rolled through the area. It looked like none of us were really healthy. Some of the other horses here were very old with sway backs, having spent most of their life pulling plows and wagons, and some could hardly walk. All of them kept their heads down and were sad, looking like they were just waiting to die. This was a farm filled with sorrow and gloom. Every one of us had a heartbreaking story, everyone had an unhappy past, but I think none as miserable as mine. I found it was getting more and more difficult to hold onto the good times because the unhappiness in my life was consuming me.

As I walked the bare grounds and looked out over the barbed wire fence that surrounded me, I often wondered; "How did I end up here? How long will I be here? Where will I go? Can I ever achieve happiness again? What will it take to get out of this funk? Why did this happen to me?" Questions that only gave me more fear and apprehension flooded my brain. I wanted to run away from it all. I wanted to jump the fence, but that was my mind talking. My body was telling me I didn't have the strength or desire to jump that fence, nor would I know where to go if I did.

Everyday an Amish family or two would pull up in a horse drawn buggy to study and scan the horses, always looking for a horse to pull their carriages around town or pull their plows through their fields. It was the same routine again, teeth and legs; that's what they looked at.

They all dressed the same too. The men wore a dark blue wide brimmed hat or a straw hat, a long sleeved light blue shirt with blue denim coveralls and work boots, and they'd tug at their beard and rub their chin while they perused us. The women always wore a light blue dress, with white socks, black shoes, and a white cloth on their heads. I was in fear every time they came, mainly because I didn't want to be pulling a buggy in the traffic or pull a plow in a field. Frankly, I didn't want to pull anything. And I simply couldn't if I wanted to. I had trouble breathing and my leg would never be one hundred percent again.

So here I stood now, a white tag on my bridle with a number attached to it. As they stared at me, I thought; "I'm a race horse, not a farm animal. Didn't they know that? Can't they tell by looking at me? I was an athlete!" I prayed that I could get out of there, that someone would rescue me, but rescue me where? And to what?

"How could this happen to me? Was I living a nightmare? Would I wake up and everything would be okay again? How could the greatest three year old race horse in the world go from unprecedented fame to the fear of being a farm animal in the hills of Ohio and Pennsylvania in eight short years? Will I wake up from this depressing dream, or will it kill me?"

I guess I still had that pride in me, and though my dad said pride can be harmful, this time I think it was pride that kept me alive, or maybe it was heart, I don't know. I had a lot of both. I had also heard horrible stories from the other horses that the Amish killed their old or sick horses for food sometimes and this really frightened and disturbed me, as I wasn't exactly healthy. Sometimes when things were bad, I was told, they would even pick up a horse at the shelter just to slaughter it.

STALLION SPRINGS

As the hot and humid summer slowly passed, I walked the fields thinking of my fate. Many people looked at me, but soon left, all of them leaving me behind. However, a stroke of luck finally befell me in the end of July, or so I thought. An elderly elementary school teacher from California was passing through Ohio in her motor home by herself. She was on her summer vacation and instantly fell in love with me, visiting me daily and spending time with me. Her name was Sherrie and I heard her say she lived by herself in a small rural town at the tip of the southern Sierra Nevada Mountain range. After talking to the man who ran the shelter, she immediately went to the airlines and got a price for shipping me to California, where she lived. She made arrangements at the shelter for shipping me and it wasn't long and I was on a plane in nearby Pittsburgh, Pennsylvania, heading for the long flight to Los Angeles, via Chicago. It wasn't a private plane, like I was used to, so I had to ride in a crate the whole distance. After an all day flight, she then picked me up with an old borrowed horse trailer at LAX and took me on a three and a half hour trip to her mountain home in Stallion Springs. We had to first traverse the busy freeways of Los Angeles on our way out of town, which scared me to death, because I had always lived in the country and wasn't used to this kind of traffic and I wasn't used to so much smog in the air. It was even worse than New York. After leaving Los Angeles we then drove north through the arid countryside of the Mojave Desert and saw the mountains that surrounded Tehachapi in the distance. I felt funny as we traveled through the Mojave Desert and the city of Lancaster, the same feeling I used to get when I visited New York years ago, and wondered what it all meant. I now knew why I hated New York, so this déjà vu feeling worried me. We continued our trip north and passed the wind mill farms that enveloped the hills of Tehachapi and then drove through the apple farms and vineyards as we climbed the mountain even further to Stallion Springs. Tehachapi was a small rural mountain community and covered a large geographic area, broken up into about seven little towns or boroughs with a total population of about 20,000 people. It was a long journey that exhausted me. First a trailer ride to the airport in Pittsburgh, then seven and a half hours in two planes and then three and a half hours in a trailer again, not to mention the wait everywhere and the three hour time zone change. It was a very long day for me, met with great apprehension, for I didn't know what to expect when I got there.

It was a hot August evening when I finally arrived in Stallion Springs, an affluent and quiet suburb of Tehachapi. Sherrie lived in a quaint little house near the top of a mountain with a fifty mile view of the valley floor beneath it. The house was old and very small but comfortable for her, as she lived alone. My living area consisted of a very small pasture in front of her house, with an electrical wire fence surrounding it. My paddock in Kentucky was bigger than the pasture I now occupied and our farm was bigger than Stallion Springs. I was also surrounded by scraggly oak trees and dry brown hills, as far as the eye could see, which was much different than the beautiful green hills of Kentucky, Ohio, and Pennsylvania I left behind.

"Could you imagine, I thought, a horse of my fame and stature surrounded by barbed wire? Is this my new home?" I couldn't believe my fate, but my foolish pride was showing again. "Damn that pride," I thought. "Why can't I accept things as they are? It could have been worse; I could be pulling a buggy through snow, a plow through fields, or God forbid, perhaps dinner if I had been left behind."

I knew in my heart that I would never have what I once had, but I also had no barn, no paddocks and no stalls here. I didn't even have a lean-to for protection; all I had was a huge oak tree looming over me for shelter; that was it!

"Why did she want me," I thought, as I stared at her house? I can't make money for her, and because of my leg, I surely can't even give her a ride anymore." Her property wasn't equipped for a horse either. It was very small and had inadequate fencing with no shelter.

I quickly forgot the negativistic thoughts I had as I realized she wanted me just for me. She was a good person and thought she was rescuing me and was the first owner in my life that didn't want to make money off me. For this reason alone, I garnished respect for her. After all, I was truly rescued this time, because she could have rescued a horse anywhere, she didn't have to pay for my flight from Pennsylvania. She could have rescued a horse in Tehachapi and saved a lot of money. I didn't want to be working a plow or buggy, and most of all I didn't want to be slaughtered, so I should have been happy just to be here.

The oak tree in my pasture was my only shelter and it stood next to the barbed wire fence that encompassed my living area. I used it to stand under it with my back end to the wind. It offered some shade from the hot summer sun, but no protection from the winter sun when it lost its leaves, and no protection from the cold and wintry mountain winds, which were often brutal and relentless. It was a beautiful day in Stallion Springs when I arrived, but little did I know the winter winds would soon be coming to the mountains, winds that were cold and unrelenting. I originally thought when I found out I was going to California, that it would be warm like it was when I raced in Santa Anita. Consequently, the winters of Ohio and Pennsylvania didn't look so bad now. Stallion Springs was a mountain community and had an elevation of five thousand feet with winds of fifty plus miles per hour every time a winter cold front would blow in. You could actually see it approach as it crossed the valley beneath us. I really missed the green beauty of my Kentucky home and the serenity of the clear stream that flowed through the farm, as there were no streams here. I was at the top of a mountain and it was dry and brown most of the year. I also missed my friends and the beautiful countryside I grew up in, as I thought about it daily. Thinking of my past was like watching a movie, you could see it and you could feel it, but you couldn't walk into it and experience it; it was nothing but a mirage. I was homesick and heart-broken, but I had to accept reality. I knew my life would never be as good as it once was. Everything was changing and I had to change with it.

My mom's words; "Your life will never be the same," echoed through my mind over and over again as I scanned the dry barren hills and my lonely pasture. And the words; "But this will only be the beginning," made it hard to accept my new found fate and surroundings and made me wonder what else was in store for me.

And come the winds did. When a winter storm front would blow in, the winds would blow over eighty miles per hour at night sometimes on that mountain. The rain and snow would actually blow sideways and the wind chill driven by the cold air was blistering. All I could do was stand behind the trunk of the oak tree with my head down and my rear end to the wind, which was all the protection I had. In one snow driven storm, the winds were so strong that they actually blew the roof off of our neighbor's house, causing great alarm to the neighborhood that night. The roof opened up like a can opener opens a can and flew over fifty feet in the air before it came slamming down in an adjacent field. The wind and the roaring noise of the roof coming apart and crashing down of the house on the surrounding rocks scared me to death. When the winds would blow hard at night, I had to be extra alert because it was very hard to hear and see the predators who roamed the countryside at that time of day. It was also very dark in the mountains at night, darker than the city, mainly because we were in the country without any city lights illuminating the sky and not even a night light on the property. If you were a star gazer, you would be very happy here, because the sky would be brilliantly lit by millions of twinkling stars, stars that weren't visible in the city. Sometimes you could actually see the illumination of a satellite as it slowly flew by. But for me; I couldn't spend too much time looking at stars. Since I didn't have any protection, I had to be constantly on guard for predators.

All I had was the width of the oak tree trunk for protection from the elements, as the tree had no leaves in the winter. Sherrie would put a blanket on me at night, and if the weather was really bad, I would wear that wet blanket all of the next day. She couldn't ride me and she never walked me. She didn't have a horse trailer and never took me anywhere. It was almost as if I was confined to a prison, a small barbed wire enclosure without even friends or a shelter to protect me. On my lucky days, she would come outside and pull up a chair next to my fence and sit with me for a while. I'd stand there and stare at her while she sat and talked to me, sometimes for hours. I never had any exercise and there never were any other animals to play with or talk to, not even any in the neighborhood. I was sad and I was lonely. I was a trained and intensely high strung race horse without an outlet for my pent up frustration. The only other animals I saw were deer that would jump my fence and drink water from my barrel and the bobcats and raccoons that prowled the grounds at night. The first time I saw a bobcat I was scared to death, but soon found out they didn't want to hurt me. They were just as afraid of me as I was afraid of them; I had nothing they wanted. But mountain lions were a different animal and they were feared greatly, but thank goodness they were rarely seen. Sometimes an elk would lean over my fence and drink water too. The males were huge and had a large rack of antlers and scared me to death the first time I saw one. It was the first time I saw an animal bigger than me. But I soon found out they didn't want to hurt me either, they just wanted some water. They elk always traveled in herds, whereas deer would sometimes visit me by themselves.

"Didn't Sherrie know I was a herding animal and needed companionship too," I often wondered when I saw the deer and elk together. It seemed everyone had a friend but me.

Sherrie wasn't well, and as time went by, she began to spend less and less time with me. I know she loved me but I needed more; I needed companionship. When spring came, I was surprised to see a new house being built next door adjacent to my pasture, about fifty feet away. The house took over a year to build and I got used to the workers coming over to my fence daily to pat my head and give me treats of carrots and apples from their lunch. The new house helped block some of the westerly winds, but didn't help later on in the year with the bitter winter storms that usually came from the southwest and northeast. Steve and Andrea, the owners of the new house, used to buy a twenty five pound bag of carrots for me and feed them to me regularly; I used to excitingly run to the fence and greet them whenever I saw their car or truck drive up to their house. Andrea would see me and come to the fence and pat my head and neck when she came home from work and talk to me for a while. Sometimes, depending on how tired she was, she would sit at the fence and talk to me before she went in for the night. I really liked Steve and Andrea. They were very kind people and used to come over to the fence on their days off, with two chairs, to talk to me and spend time with me, sometimes for hours at a time. I really needed their company, kindness, and affection and appreciated it greatly. They would sit in the sun while I stood at the fence looking down at them and enjoying their company.

Then on a hot summer day, Steve surprised me by unexpectedly pulling into our driveway with his pickup truck full of lumber and building materials. He then knocked on Sherrie's door and surprisingly offered to build me a shelter. I heard Sherrie tell him she hadn't worked for a while and couldn't afford to pay him, to which Steve replied; "I'm not doing this for you, I'm doing this for Summer Storm; you don't have to pay me." Although she couldn't pay him, she stood close by and watched every step of construction, as if she had. I guess she wanted to be sure it was done right, as she asked him many questions. When he completed it, she was very happy and appreciative and told him that he was very talented and was surprised at how fast it went up and how good it came out.

I was so thankful. I loved the new shelter and the friendship with Steve and Andrea that only grew with each passing day. I now had protection from the sun year around now and the brutal winters were a lot easier to deal with. It was still cold, but at least I wasn't getting pelted with fifty mile per hour winds, rain, hail and snow any longer and I had some protection from the sun that was hot and unmerciful in the summer.

Steve and Andrea also had a pretty white Siamese Calico cat named Missy, who would become my friend. Missy would spend a lot of time with me during the daylight hours while Steve and Andrea worked. She was indeed a godsend, as she was the only company I had and lifted my spirits greatly, reminding me of little Princess back home in Kentucky. We both served each other well. She gave me the company I needed and I gave her company and the protection from predators during the daylight hours. She would sit in the shade of the shelter Steve built for me most of the day like Princess and Winnie did in my stall back home. The only time she would be gone is when she would occasionally hunt for gophers. When nightfall came, Steve and Andrea would call her and want her in the house at night because of predators. When she would hear Andrea's voice, she would go running to her, as I sensed she was afraid to stay out all night. We bonded immediately and we both looked forward to the mornings when she would be let out of her house to visit me for the day.

Spring soon came, and along with it the awakening of the hills, trees, and plants that were asleep all winter. The craggily branches on the oak tree above me would sprout their coarse green leaves and offer me some shade for the summer, as it loomed over my shelter. It was also the time of the year when the deer and elk herds would come up from the valley floor looking for fresh food and cooler air. The quail families would walk around in my pasture occasionally too, all in a long line, all following their mom and dad very hurriedly, and the majestic red tail hawks would sing to me as they circled overhead looking for their prey of ground squirrels, snakes and rabbits. Once in a while, a pair of bald eagles or condors would be sighted too, but they were rare. The condors were all tagged with a big white patch on their wing with a number on it. The small sparrows would sit on my back while I grazed, singing to each other and keeping the flies and bugs off of me. It is the prettiest time of the year in the mountains, when nature is reborn, but it doesn't last long, as the hot winds of summer soon follow. They would blow up from the hot valley floor beneath us and often reached one hundred degrees. And what follows is the browning out of all the hills until it rains again next winter. That's right, it doesn't rain all summer and most of the fall, which was the complete opposite of the weather in Ohio, Pennsylvania and Kentucky, where the summers were always green and lush.

On a hot, dry, and windy day in August, I was standing in my shelter trying to avoid the summer sun and the nagging flies that were relentlessly biting me. Sherrie had gone into town to buy some hay and to run some errands, and Steve and Andrea were working. Suddenly, my head turned and was directed upward as I heard two young hawks squawking loudly at me as they soared high in the air above me, as if they were warning me of something. As I stood there with Missy lying close by in my hay, I looked around the side of the shelter with my nose to the air and smelled a feint hint of smoke in the wind. It was a smell that instantly terrified me as it brought back memories of the fire in my barn and the horrid sound of my mom and the other horses crying out in pain, and the horrible memories of Princess and Winnie dying right in front of me. I hurriedly rushed out of my lean-to and looked into the wind and out over the large valley floor below us. I then saw a large plume of smoke and a roaring fire rushing up the canyon, heading in our direction and being pushed very rapidly by the wind. It was about two miles away as the crow flies and you could now hear the fire crackling as it quickly burned through the dry brush it consumed and you could smell the air, as it slowly became filled with blue smoke. My eyes began to burn and my unhealthy lungs became fouled with smoke as it got thicker and closer. Missy became afraid and started running towards her house for shelter, but after realizing that nobody was home and she couldn't get in, she panicked and ran up the street, evading the oncoming fire and smoke and leaving me behind. As I watched her run in fear, I panicked too and started running circles in my small pasture, my ears pinned back and my Arabian head and tail erect. It felt good to be alive again, but I was scared to death, afraid I might die. The fire got closer and closer very fast, and I began to feel the heat emanating from it. The sky grew dark with thick blue and black smoke that made it very difficult to see and breathe in. Deer and rabbits were running up the mountain ahead of the flames and right past my enclosure and up the hill and street that led from our house. I then heard the sound of sirens as a fire truck came out of the smoke and pulled into our driveway and surrounded Sherrie's house and another pulled into Steve and Andrea's driveway next door to protect their house. I heard the roar of helicopters flying overhead and saw them dropping something on the fire, as I nervously ran and continued to circle the pasture, wanting desperately to escape my enclosure. The flames coming up the hill were now reaching one hundred feet tall as they curled over the peak of the cliff behind Sherrie's house and were creating their own fire storm, its flames moving fast and driven by the wind it created. The flames looked serpentine like and were menacingly close, about only two hundred feet away now. They were doing the dance of death in the air, rapidly consuming everything in its path with loud crackling noises. The firemen ignored me completely and placed themselves between the fire and Sherrie's house; they were consumed in their work, trying to save the structures and trying to keep themselves alive while they worked.

"Can't they see me; why aren't they helping me? Come and get me. Please get me out of here?" I thought as the fire and winds got hotter and hotter and the noisy helicopters dropped water on the ever encroaching fire.

Although everything seemed to be happening so fast, my brain was in slow motion as I nervously paced the perimeter of my pasture, looking and finding an opening in part of the fence which was a little lower than the others. I then ran to it and leaped over the barbed wire and started running frantically up the street, away from the heat and the flames. The air was covered in smoke and burning embers from the wind were falling everywhere. Some people at the top of the hill tried to stop me and catch me but I ran right through them. In tremendous fear, I ran all the way up the big hill and down the other side; I ran until I couldn't run any longer. When I stopped running, I found myself three miles away in Cummings Valley, in a large pasture about two miles away as the crow flies with a large herd of cows and several other horses, with the fire and smoke far behind me. Cummings Valley was a beautiful community nestled all alone and surrounded by the oak tree studded Tehachapi Mountains, looking much like a post card.

I then lay down in the field as my leg was hurting and I was totally exhausted. My lungs were burning badly too, as I hadn't run in quite a while. It looked like the fire was starting to be contained at the top of the mountain, on the other side from which I came, as the sky was filled with helicopters and planes dropping water there. After a while, I got up and panted heavily as I walked, trying to catch my breath. It was after the adrenaline left me that I noticed my back leg was partially torn from the barbed wire; I must have injured it while leaping over the fence, or perhaps jumping into the cattle ranches fence, I don't know; I was so scared, I didn't remember where or when I hurt it. It was bleeding and hurt a little too, attracting flies now, but I was real happy that I was able to get away; I haven't been happy or filled with adrenaline in quite a while and it felt wonderful to feel alive again. As the rush of adrenaline slowly left me, my previously injured front leg began to hurt too; it seems I landed on it hard when I leaped the fence and it throbbed with every beat of my heart, as an artery ran through the affected area.

The very next day I was found by Sherrie and a rancher on the huge property I ended up on. It seems the owner of the property was an ex-Hollywood cowboy actor and everybody in town knew him. He was elderly now and got famous playing in westerns and was always the villain in murder mysteries when he was younger. He had retired to Stallion Springs several years ago and loved the quiet and remoteness of the area, as he was a loner. The solitude of the area encouraged him to paint and write a few books, while he managed his cow ranch. He told Sherrie he had heard about my history and said I could stay here for a while, until things quieted down on the mountain, but Sherrie being a loner, said thanks, but no thanks; she didn't want to inconvenience him and wanted me home. He told her it wasn't an inconvenience as he had over fifteen hundred acres, but it didn't matter. I was then put on his horse trailer and driven back to Sherrie's property and then later in the afternoon a Vet came out to doctor me. Sherrie was very happy that I was still alive and hugged me for a long time and sat outside with me for a while after that. But even though I liked Sherrie, I wished I could have stayed on that big ranch where they found me. I would have had a lot of company there. They had cows and horses there and the weather was also a little better down the mountain than at the peak, where I resided. I also needed company; I hated to be alone. Sherrie's house and Steve and Andrea's house were miraculously saved by the fire department, but the grounds surrounding the properties were charred and black. The majestic oak trees, my lean-to shelter, and my barbed wire fence were the only things standing in the charbroiled hills. It was so desolate, the deer and elk didn't come around anymore, and there was no vegetation for the rabbits and quail to enjoy either.

Missy was missing for three weeks and was finally found when Andrea posted flyers around town with her picture on them. We thought we would never see her again. It seems someone found her after the fire and took her in while they tried to find her owner. I was so glad to see her. I think we both cried with joy. She then walked around me and nuzzled herself up against my legs and purred for the longest time. My pasture and all of the rolling hills around us that were once dry brown fields were now black with soot and looked and smelled horribly bad. The hills wouldn't stop smelling like charcoal until the winter rains came.

Then just a couple of months later, in the fall and the weekend before Thanksgiving, a moving van unexpectedly pulled into Steve and Andrea's driveway. I guess the fire scared them pretty bad and they were moving back to the city.

"Why didn't they tell me," I thought, as I stood there and watched them closely.

I was blind-sided by this, as it completely shocked me. I stood there anxiously at the fence with a sad heart as I watched them pack and load up the truck. I knew they were moving away and I knew in my heart I would never see them again. The loading of the big truck took almost all day and the fog was dripping cold and as thick as pea soup when they both walked over to me carrying Missy to say goodbye. Before they left, they wanted to say goodbye and give me some carrots for the last time. Andrea tried to feed me, but I didn't want to eat. I just turned my head. I was sick to my stomach with the fear and anxiety of their leaving me and of me being abandoned again. Andrea cried and hugged my hung head, her tears running down my face, while Steve just stared at the ground and stoically told me "You'll be alright Summer Storm," and then told me to take care of myself, as he slowly turned his head.

"Why are you doing this to me?" I thought as I looked at them. "Don't you know I love you?"

I looked at them with tears welled up in my eyes and I hung my head low as Missy and I stared at each other for the last time. I think we were all sad, and each one of us let our emotions go in our own way. Missy turned around to look at me as Andrea picked her up and carried her away on her shoulder. She meowed loudly as they tried to put her in their car. I could tell that she didn't want to leave either; I could hear her crying loudly, even after their car door was closed.

"Goodbye my little friend; I'm going to miss you;" I thought while I stared at her looking through the window of the backseat.

I then begrudgingly watched them drive slowly away in the cold wet fog. My eyes followed their car out of their driveway and up the street until they disappeared into the thick cloud that consumed our mountain. I couldn't see them any longer, but I could hear their engine as it gradually became quieter and quieter with each foot it traveled. I knew they would never come back to see me and their departure felt like an arrow piercing my heart. After their moving van and car disappeared and the fog became quiet again, their disappearance sunk in. I then left the fence at the street and slowly dragged my feet over to the lean-to that Steve built for me and hung my head in sorrow, staring at the lonely straw covered ground where Missy used to lay and wondered why this was happening to me again. My eyes dripped tears and my heart ached inside that night, vowing never to get close to anybody again and I began to shut down. They say that your "eyes are the windows to the soul" and your "feelings are the words of the soul," and my eyes and feelings spoke volumes today. I was completely despondent. I was finding out that the joy of loving someone wasn't worth the heartache and the pain you feel when they are taken away. Abandonment is a dark deep hole that only gets deeper and more painful with each occurrence and this time it consumed me completely.

Winter seemed to come quicker this year to the mountain and it came with the usual cold wicked winds that escorted it in. The days were short and cold and the nights were long and colder still. It wasn't four o'clock and the sun had already gone down over the hills in the western sky, creating cold, dark shadows that only depressed me more. After every rain or snowfall we had, the thick wet fog from the remaining clouds in the valley below us would position and collect themselves next to the mountains we occupied for a couple of days and would leave me cold and wet and in a dreary depressed state of mind. You could smell the smog that was trapped in the fog that blew up from the valley below and you couldn't see further than twenty feet for days.

"Another cold winter was upon me. Could I last another few months in these conditions? I have to dig in somehow. I've got to muster up some energy and desire to go on," I thought, as I felt my depression sink in.

I thought I could, but I'm going to have to dig in hard this time, harder than usual because I felt myself getting weaker and weaker with each passing day. I knew I had to change my attitude, but didn't know how. "Attitude is everything," Lauren used to say when she would do something she didn't enjoy. I was so glad I had fond memories of her. She was always kind and encouraging. I think her heart was as big as mine.

Some days I wouldn't even leave my lean-to. I would just stand there with my head down, staring at the charred and barren ground all day. Food would lie there on the ground, sometimes for days too. And carrots? I couldn't tell you the last time I had a carrot or what they even tasted like anymore. My appetite was gone and I had no interest in anything anymore.

DARKNESS
BLUE MOODS AND NO MOON

Nightfall was always the hardest for me. I was alone most of the day, but when darkness hit, it magnified the feelings of despair that wretched in my mind. My days on the mountain were never kind to me and darkness brought out the demons that possessed my mind. It was the time of day that I really felt all alone. When I first arrived here, I didn't even have a shelter for protection. I was fully exposed to the harsh elements and the hungry predators who roamed the mountain at night. The shelter that Steve built for me was indeed a blessing, but it wasn't a barn, and was exposed on one side, to anything and everything. I had to learn to sleep on my feet, because I didn't want to lie down and become more vulnerable. My senses had to be acute. I always had to be ready. Thank God I knew how to rear up and present myself as being larger than life if I needed to.

Sherrie always went to bed early, and when she did she left no lights on, either in the house or outside for me. Steve and Andrea would retire early too, as they had a long commute every day. They left no light on next door either. Missy, my only friend, was also locked up at night. When the moon was visible and not obscured by clouds or mountain fog, I would have a slight advantage and be able to see any movement I might detect. But when there wasn't a moon, it would be pitch black at night. It was an astronomer's paradise, mainly because you had no aura from city lights on the mountain to diffuse the stars. Sometime I would gaze into the heavens and wonder where Mom and Lauren were, sometimes staring for hours at a time.

"Are you out there? Are you watching me? Are all of you together?"

I often wondered and pretended that they were indeed out there and they were always watching over me. Although the thought made me feel better, night was still a bitch. It was when I knew I was really alone; it was when I really felt it. The darkness of the night brought out emotions in me that weren't healthy and brought me down further. Sometimes I wished I would just die; I was tired of it all. But winter was the worst. Half of the day was dark and it started to get cold and dark late in the afternoon. I saw and heard things that Sherrie, Steve and Andrea couldn't imagine; things that literally petrified me sometimes. I knew I had to be strong, but I was so depressed and lonely that sometimes I just didn't care. Sometimes I would "smell" an intruder and walk the fence looking for it, putting myself out there and risking my life. The other side of me also felt that if I was active, they would fear me. Bobcats didn't bother me; I was too big for them. I had nothing they wanted. Raccoons had their own agenda and left me alone too. The deer and the elk just wanted water from my trough and sometimes would graze nearby, giving me company. But mountain lions and bears were a different animal.

It was winter when I first encountered a fear I had never experienced before. I've learned through the years that there are many forms of fear, but this one was memorable. On a dark and cold moonless night, after a long day of rain and fog, I smelled something pungent in the air. It was a distinct smell, a scent I had never smelled before. I couldn't see anything, but there was something about the smell that literally scared me and raised the hair on my neck. I walked out of my shelter to investigate and that's when I saw the cold look of death crouched in the weeds and staring at me. I didn't know what it was at first. I had heard about them, but had never seen one before. It was a huge mountain lion and looked about five or six feet long, his eyes almost glowing in the dark. He was motionless, crouched down and facing me, about thirty feet away, and staring at me with a menacing look. A stare I had never seen before, a stare that gave me the shivers and put me in a trance, almost hypnotizing me. As I stared at him, he crept forward, ever so slowly, continuing to freeze me as he crept. For the first time in my life, I was frozen on my feet and couldn't react. I could only watch him creep closer and closer, stealth like, quiet and sure of himself, his talons glistening in the dark. The fear I had inside gripped me. It was quiet tonight, way too quiet. I could hear myself breathing, but I couldn't move. He just kept getting closer and closer. Then he stopped creeping and lay there crouched down, just staring at me without blinking. He was still reclined on his haunches and his muscles were coiled and ready to strike. I couldn't move. I was petrified and frozen. The dark night, although quiet, was deafening in its own way. I could hear my heart beating and feel my leg throbbing from the pulse in my artery. I wanted to react, but I couldn't. I just stood there. My mind felt like it wanted to explode. I didn't know if it was fear that gripped me or the unconscious desire to die. Perhaps this was my bus ticket out of here, I thought. Maybe the ordeal on the mountain was over. Maybe the years long nightmare I had been living was over too.

Then I remembered what my dad had told me once; "You'll always be able to sense a weakness in your opponent. It's inherent in every animal. You'll learn how to read them and you'll learn how to take advantage of that weakness and beat them down."

His words echoed through my mind as I stood there staring at the big cat, shaking almost uncontrollably.

"Does he sense my weakness and fear?" I thought as he stared at me and drew closer. Although I tried to fool myself, I knew he did. He knew I wasn't healthy. He knew he had me for the taking; he was planning his attack in a way that prevented him from getting hurt. Getting hurt in this forest would be the death of him too.

Just then, I heard a car coming down the street towards our cul de sac and saw its headlights. The lights from the car then shined on us in a sweeping fashion as it made the curve in the road, illuminating us and the ground we stood on. The big cat turned his head to look, then stood up and immediately darted into the field, into the vast darkness of the countryside. The car stopped and pointed a flood light in my direction. It was the local police making its evening rounds. Apparently he saw the cat dart into the field and stopped to investigate. Big cat sightings occur up here every year, but this was the first time I experienced it. The policeman got out of his car with his flashlight and looked around for about ten minutes before he left.

Before he left, he yelled out to me; "Hey girl, you take care of yourself now."

I heard him and wished I could thank him. It was dark again. He got in his car and slowly drove up the hill, scanning the countryside with his spotlight as he went. I was more than happy he showed up when he did, but the adrenaline that flowed into my veins made it difficult for me to relax for hours. I was there; I had reached an excitement level I hadn't felt since my race days. I also didn't know if the cat was still watching me from a distance and would be back or not. It also comforted me that the police car came back every thirty minutes or so that night to check up on me. No one wanted that cat in their neighborhood, because it would not only eat livestock, but cats and dogs too. I had heard they attacked hikers and joggers too.

I made it through that dark and scary night, but every night after that the big cat was on my mind, making each night longer to endure. I would sleep lighter from that night on and would be acutely aware of everything. I soon found out that it was best to nap in the day and be awake at night. It was uncomfortable, but just safer that way.

"Would he be back? Did he always hunt alone, or were there two of them hunting in pairs?"

Scary thoughts went through my mind! The heavy darkness of night and the extreme quiet of the night didn't help either. But the cold and damp fog of the winter nights was the worst. Not only did the damp air chill me to the bone, but visibility at times was limited to maybe ten feet, making it very difficult to feel safe. Because of the dense fog my visibility was extremely limited, so my other senses kicked in, notably my ears and nose. Every night was an adventure I didn't look forward to, especially not knowing what weather conditions I might face, as the weather can change fast in the mountains. Wind, fog, rain, snow, sometimes four seasons in one day! But the winds; you could always count on those. If an animal approached me from upwind in the fog, it would be near impossible to detect him. Not only would the fog obscure him, but the rustling of the wind in the trees would disguise and hide any noise he may make and the "smell" they carried. I was literally scared to death every night!

Night time also played games with my mind. The loneliness of the night would consume me and on some occasions, in the dead of night, I could swear I could hear people walking up to me from behind the lean-to, their footsteps crunching on the frozen tundra and breaking the fallen oak branches as they walked. I would excitingly leave my lean-to and look around hoping to see somebody, somebody visiting me, but there never was anybody. It was just my cruel brain fooling me, making me think I had company, making me think someone was coming to visit me.

THE WHITE OWL

A little less than a year had passed since the forest fire and the departure of Andrea, Steve, and Missy, but it seemed like an eternity to me. Then more months passed and Sherrie's health seemed to take a turn for the worse, as she hardly spent any time at all with me anymore. She lost some weight and stayed in the house a lot and seemed to get weaker with each passing day. She isolated herself from the outside world and never had any visitors, no family, no friends, nobody. She was as lonely and depressed as I was. Then on a hot summer day, completely oblivious to me, she had a heart attack and died in her house with no one there to help her. At first I didn't know what happened and paced the pasture for two days without food until Sherrie's son, Eddie, came over one day to find her. An all too familiar ambulance then pulled up and silently took her away. I sadly watched her drive up the street too, out of my life forever. Death and heartache seemed to follow me with its hovering giant shadow that darkened my mood. It obliterated all hope I may have had and I hated dealing with it. After the ambulance left, Eddie then fed me and gave me fresh water and said he would come over every other day to feed me and check my water supply, as I wasn't eating all the food I had been given. The time passed very slowly now as the hot and dry winds of summer were upon me once again, but now I was really alone. No one lived at the house; Sherrie was gone, and Steve, Andrea and Missy had moved away to Studio City. The new owners of Steve and Andrea's house were young and had no interest in me at all. They worked all week and went away every weekend. When they were home, I was just another horse that lived next door that fouled the air once in a while and sent horse flies over to their barbeques. I soon lost my motivation and desire to go on and subsequently quit eating and drinking. Sadly, without that great spark that I once had, I waited to die.

Not very long after Sherrie's death, Eddie and his wife Marilyn drove up with an old horse trailer and took me to a horse rescue ranch in the Mojave Desert, which was down the mountain and about sixty miles away, near the city of Lancaster. He told me that I would be better off there and perhaps someone would rescue me and give me a good home. When we arrived in Lancaster, I felt that déjà vu feeling again, that same feeling I got in New York and the same feeling I got when I passed through this area on the way to Tehachapi a few years ago and didn't know how to deal with it. Although the area was vastly different than the mountain I just left, the same strange feeling I had in New York was still there. I smelled the air as I looked around and let my senses go. I couldn't detect anything harmful, but a weird and haunting feeling was there again and I didn't know why. It was an aura that touched my very soul and seemed to suffocate me. It was the dead of summer now in the desert, but a lot warmer than the mountains in Tehachapi. And although I was haunted by a feeling I couldn't escape, it was nice getting off that mountain with its harsh weather and non-stop winds, because I was a shell of my former self with no drive left in me anymore and not enough meat on my bones to keep me warm. Although it was windy in the desert too, at least there wasn't any cold damp fog there that hung around for days at a time, and the sun shined every day. It was also very barren and desolate. You could see sand and Joshua trees for miles, with the snow covered Sierra's in the background. Tumble weeds would blow across our fenced area and collect at our fence and the small buildings that outlined the property. It was not a place to be depressed in, because if you succumbed, the surroundings would suffocate you.

One hot and windy day, as I slowly walked past the sliding glass door of the shelter's office, I saw a different horse staring back at me, almost unrecognizable. It was skin and bone and looked nothing like the champion it once was.

"Is that me? Do I look that bad," I thought?

I hadn't seen an image of myself in years. The effervescent taste and boundless vitality of youth was gone now; it had trickled down and drained me of life, leaving me with nothing but memories.

"The rose had lost its bloom and dropped its' petals," I thought.

I stared at my reflection in the window and studied my deformed body for what seemed like the longest time and wondered how I became this way. The proud gait of my Arabian mom was gone as well as the erect cocked head and tail when I walked. The muscular frame I inherited from my dad had dwindled down to a sway back and I was now skin and bone, since I had lost even more weight since I arrived here. My legs, due to the lack of any exercise for years, had lost their muscular shape too. I was a mere shadow of my former self and I even had trouble breathing because my lungs had been burned in the barn fire and fouled again by the forest fire in Stallion Springs.

"Where have my body and vitality gone? How was it sucked out of me, leaving me a shadow of my former self? Why does the act of living drain you so?" I wondered, as I vainly stared at myself, waiting for an answer; from whom, I don't know. The longer I stared at my reflection, the worst I felt.

I then scanned the reflection in the window again and then cast my head down, as I finally realized my pride was gone too. You see, if I still had pride, I wouldn't have let myself get into the miserable condition I saw staring back at me. But even though I knew I was looking at walking death, I tried in vain to adjust to my new home. Something inside of me wouldn't quit. The heart in me that once won race after race was the same heart that kept me going now. I was surrounded at the shelter by other horses, all of them being in better shape than me, all looking for a home too. It was nice to be around others again, as I had been alone for a few years on that mountain, but all the horses were just as depressed as me. They all had their own heartbreaking story.

Sugar was a roan mare whose family couldn't afford to care for her anymore and eventually sold the farm she lived on. Buck was a

Clydesdale gelding that was used to pull a plow and, because of his age, couldn't do it anymore. Socks was still attractive, but had to be given up when her owner died; she was the youngest of all of us. We all travelled different roads, but somehow we all ended up here.

They just stared straight ahead with their heads down and their backs to the wind, almost listless, as if they knew their impending fate. None of them here knew of my former fame and glory and no one cared; I didn't even care anymore. I was just another skinny horse looking for a home. But, sadly, after seeing myself in the window, I also knew no one would want me this time; I was the skinniest of the bunch; this time my fate was doomed. I looked down at my bent and crooked shadow and then watched myself walk away from the reflection in the window.

"Perhaps I set myself up for this condition," I thought. "Perhaps my pride and vanity was the catalyst that doomed my fate. I think Dad was right."

Thinking of Dad made me melancholy and took me far away to the farm I grew up on. It was a nice thought and relieved me momentarily of my present surroundings. After looking at the desert landscape, I closed my eyes and the fields were green again, green with the smell of Kentucky Bluegrass. I then looked to the heavens.

"Dad, where are you now? Are you still alive? I wish I could see you again. You were always there for me. Time has not been kind to me and I miss you badly." I thought as I stood there with my eyes closed, wanting to cry.

The feeling didn't last long, as I was brought to my senses by the noise of a flatbed diesel delivering hay to the ranch. "Hay," I thought. I couldn't remember the last time I tasted the sweet taste of alphalfa and carmeled oats.

Some of the other horses sensed something was wrong with me because I wasn't eating and I never hung around with them. I didn't want company anymore, even though their presence was a strange comfort in itself. I knew I wasn't alone in this world anymore and that was enough for me. Socks tried to comfort me some of the time, but I was lost in my own hell, an internal burning that ate at my very soul and an external hell that wouldn't let my mind rest. The guilt I carried around for Lauren's death was like a ravenous cancer and it was consuming my spirit daily, little by little. It was a very dark time in my life that just kept getting extended. I was only thirteen years old now, but I looked like I was much older and was ready to die. I led the first three years of my life in happiness and bliss, but the past ten years has been a tormented hell, wretched with many dismal calamities that would have brought anyone down.

Matt, the veterinarian in town, used to visit the horse rescue ranch frequently with his young son Brody and his black Lab named Ozzie; they always hung out together. Matt was about 35 or so and had made a name for himself as one of the best veterinarians in the tri-state area. He was compassionate and up to date on the latest equine procedures. Brody was only four years old and very active. He used to walk around the ranch feeding the horses hay that he found on the ground. He was thin with black hair and looked just like his father. Ozzie was young and full of energy and used to run around the ranch while Matt worked. He tried to play with me once, but he saw I wasn't interested and quit trying. I always looked forward to their visits.

Matt was a good guy and noticed I didn't have any energy and that I wasn't eating and suggested to Michael, the owner of the horse rescue ranch, that I should be examined. He then took blood tests, X-rays, and examined me everywhere and couldn't find anything physically wrong with me other than my known maladies, notably my leg and my lungs. He was puzzled but said he's seen these symptoms before. He said it looked like I had a broken heart and didn't want to be here. He said it looked like I lost the will to live, as I just stared at the ground and looked weary and lethargic and had no appetite. My eyes, the windows to the soul, had no life in them; they were empty and listless and longed for love. Michael was informed to part of my history from Sherrie's son Eddie, when I was dropped off, and concurred with the vet. They both tried to help me, but I didn't have the fire in my belly anymore. My aspiration and desire were gone and my attitude stunk with sorrow. As I looked at them, they started to converse.

"Look at her Michael. This horse was once rated the best filly in the world. On a scale of one to ten, she was an eleven. Nobody was in her time zone. She was simply the best there ever was."

Mike stared at me and then looked into the sky, shaking his head, almost perplexed. He kicked the fence post in disgust and then gently patted my neck. A dust cloud, a dirt devil, formed around fifty feet from them and frightened me momentarily. Mike held my halter while they spoke, while Ozzie sat close by and watched it all as the dirt devil slowly drifted away.

"You'd never know it to look at her Matt. I wonder how in the hell she got this way? Of all places, I wonder how she ended up here? Lancaster is a long ways from Kentucky. I hate to imagine the pain and heartache she must have experienced along the way."

Matt, seeing Mike was visibly upset, put his arm on his shoulder and looked at the papers in his hand that he received from Eddie, searching for more information.

"Well, it says right here Mike. When she won The Triple Tiara ten years ago, she broke her Sesamoid bones in her right leg while crossing the finish line and killed her female jockey when she fell. God, I remember that. I watched it happen live on TV! It broke my heart watching her standing there all alone in the rain, overlooking her dead jockey! Because she would have been so valuable for breeding purposes, her owner made the decision to spare her life that day in favor of potential riches she could bring later. Every other race horse had been put down with this type of injury, including the great Ruffian. Then later on they unfortunately found out she was infertile and couldn't make any money for them with breeding fees. It was a disservice keeping a horse with such a severe injury and a horse with so much spirit alive in the first place. This horse was bred for racing and now she even had trouble walking. A couple years after her injury, she was involved in a suspicious barn fire in Kentucky that seared her lungs, and together with her leg injury, made her unable to ride. At this time, the authorities discovered she had been drugged by the Mafia, which probably led to her injury and being infertile. She then was purchased and went on the road as a sideshow attraction, making money for someone else. When the economy took a hit and that failed, she ended up at a horse rescue farm in western Pennsylvania, in Amish country. Her past owner, who was on vacation from Tehachapi, saw her and rescued her, shipping her to Stallion Springs where she ultimately ended up in the front yard of a mountain home. Then a few years later, her new owner died too, and now she's here. It's no wonder she's tormented by demons. She's been all over and seen a lot of death and heartache in her life. If you can say anything about her, she is indeed a survivor."

Mike shook his head again and continued to rub my head while he listened. With a strong desert wind blowing tumbleweeds and dust all around them, he spoke again.

"Wow, from the rich bluegrass meadows of Kentucky to the dry hills of Tehachapi; what an unfortunate turns of events she's been exposed to! Man, isn't money the root of all evil? But, you know Matt, I've been caring for horses for a long time now, and it seems there is something else at play here. I know she's been awfully unlucky and has had a debilitating injury, but she has no interest in anything anymore. It's as if she has a broken heart or something. You can look into her eyes and see she's not here, there's nobody home. Her heart is physically sound and her blood work indicates that her organs are strong too. This has to be mental. What do you think?"

Matt studied me while he spoke and came to the conclusion that I was indeed empty inside, much more than they usually see in other "rescued" horses.

"Well, if horses have a soul like we humans; it's apparent to me that she feels bad and misses something, perhaps somebody or something. I don't know, but her heart is definitely broken and her spirit is gone. After all, she has had a tormented past with many pitfalls. You're right about her eyes Mike. There is nobody home."

"Okay Matt, the best we could do for her is to keep her alive and hope she snaps out of it."

"What do you propose buddy? Something has to be done or she is going to die. I'm sure of that."

"Let's put her in the new stables that were just finished and start caring for her like she may have been cared for back in Kentucky. She'll have company and I'll have my daughter brush her daily and see to it she gets fed well. I'll also have her lead her on walks around the ranch. Medically, she will be pumped up with vitamins and nutrients. This will take care of both her physical and emotional needs. Then we'll see if there is any progress and whether her spirit has returned. What do you think?"

"It's worth a shot Mike; let's get started on it tomorrow morning. She was once a magnificent animal. It's a shame to give up on her. She has lived through a serpentine chain of events, but yet somehow survived. How come the brightest flame always blows out the fastest?"

I heard their conversation and when they finished Mike let go of my halter and I slowly walked away. The new ranch with other horses for company and their plan to rehabilitate me wasn't enough to stop my endless downhill spiral at this point. The genie was already out of the bottle and you couldn't put her back. Too much time had passed and I just didn't have the heart anymore; it had bled way too much. Nightfall soon came on that hot and windy desert floor bringing me down even further. Night was always tough for me anyway. It brought out the demons that ravaged my mind. I couldn't relax, so I strolled the long and sandy perimeter of the fence and reminisced and thought about the past again. It seemed I did a lot of that lately. It was a great escape from the guilt, pain, and turmoil I experienced on a daily basis. Horses sleep on their feet sometimes and I got used to sleeping on my feet because of the predators in the neighborhood on that dark mountain in Tehachapi. I always had to be alert while I was there. It was either pitch dark and without a moon, or cold and foggy with zero visibility. Nevertheless, the wind always blew, coming up from the valley floor, and the predators were always active at night. The drop off at Sherrie's and Andrea and Steve's backyard was actually 3,000 feet to the valley floor, with their property bordered by the famous Tejon Ranch. The wind blowing up the canyon made it hard to hear predators creeping up on me at night, but at least my nose still worked well, as wild animals had a distinct odor and their smell always alerted me. Because of all of that, I didn't miss my time on that mountain in Tehachapi at all.

Competition consumed and inspired my former life. I lived it and breathed it. I was addicted to running and winning, and then rearing up in triumph after each race I won. I was an alpha female, the best of the best. But as I selfishly look at myself now, the fame, the spotlights, the adoration of an adoring public, and most of all, the intimacy and closeness of my best friend's love was gone. My foolish pride took it all away and the guilt I carried was slowly killing me, eating away at my very fiber. I was a shell lying in the ocean of life without a pearl. I was empty.

Although I had walked the fences at night many times before, this night seemed eerily different. The full moon was hidden tonight by ominous clouds, the lightning flashing in the distance, an indication of a summer storm blowing in; locals called it monsoons. The darkness hid the scattered Joshua trees and the barren desert landscape I stood in and barely exposed the majestic snow capped Sierra Nevada Mountains in the distance. In the other direction and west from here I could also see the wind mills on the Tehachapi Mountains and reflected on my time in Stallion Springs too. The Mojave Desert is vast and empty and covers thousands of square miles, and can be quite scary at night. The low dark clouds made the aura of the city lights of Palmdale and Lancaster seem brighter than usual, making it a surreal moment.

Just then I heard and saw a huge lonely white owl flying high above and circling me overhead. It looked almost majestic with its large white wings outlined by the dark blue sky. As it screeched, the darkness and the still of the night awoke my senses and brought out emotions in me that hadn't existed in a long time. It was almost as if the owl was calling out to me, as if the owl was occupied by another

and damp bluegrass and the rich caramel oats that Lauren would feed me out of her hand. I dreamt about all the wonderful experiences we shared together and all the places we visited and all the races we won. It all seemed so far away, but somehow they seemed closer tonight, almost close enough to touch.

I could hear the race announcer on the loud speaker saying; "It's Summer Storm by a length, it's Summer Storm by two lengths. Summer Storm is running away from the field again. She may be the best race horse that ever lived," as I pounded my way down the track, all the while Lauren patting my neck and the crowd roaring noisily in approval.

I dreamt fondly of all the time Lauren spent with me too, the quiet trips to the winding creek in the woods and the closeness we shared no matter where we were and wished I could be with her again. I knew there was more to our trips to the country than just going for a walk. I was making memories back then and I knew it, memories that have kept me alive but yet continue to haunt me. The dream was so rich and vivid that I could see the sun filtering through the majestic magnolias and actually smell the flowers that grew along the creek. I could also hear the stream bubbling and the red-headed woodpeckers pounding the trees above me. The frogs croaked in the background as I felt her long and silky hair touch my wet nose. She hugged me and looked into my eyes and I wondered if I would someday be with her again. I remembered too the Christmas morning she got engaged to Bryan and how happy she was. How she jumped with joy and told me I would never be out of her life, even though she would be getting married soon. Then I saw Princess with her pretty little babies playing in my stall and my bud Winnie lying there close by and watching everything. It was a wonderful night that made me so very happy and seemed to last forever. I dreamt of Roberta and Kate and the trips we took and how I thought they only wanted the best for me. I dreamt of our fame and glory, the crowds that roared in appreciation when they saw me and how proud everyone was of me. I dreamt about Patrick too and how he tried to make my life better in Ohio, and I dreamt about Sherrie rescuing me and trying to make my life better too. But, unfortunately, all the trouble I had on that mountain in Stallion

Springs was depressing and brought me further down. I know Sherrie loved me and meant well, thinking she rescued me, but it was a rough and lonely time in my life. I was in a desolate place, surrounded by barbed wire, wild animals, and brutal winter weather without friends. It was a living hell, encapsulated by barbed wire that framed my loneliness. I also dreamt about Steve and Andrea, the big hearts they had and all the time they spent sitting with me by my fence. I saw the shelter Steve built for me and I could taste the carrots that Andrea fed me. I also remembered how bad I felt when they drove away into the fog. I missed them dearly, as they were my last gleam of hope. I saw little Missy sitting on my hay in my shelter and felt the comfort she brought me on a daily basis. I could still see and hear Missy crying as they drove up the street, into the dense grey cloud that enveloped us, and out of my life. That foggy day was a symbol of the clouded life that lay before me. I saw it all as my whole life passed in front of me.

I then quietly drifted to another time, another place, where I was free again, free from the inner demons and the guilt that had haunted and destroyed me on a daily basis. I dreamt all night in a peace I had never experienced before, a euphoric peace that took me away, far, far away, to a place where pain and loneliness didn't exist anymore either. It was like sleeping in my stall as a young filly, with the indescribable comfort of knowing Winnie and Princess were there with me and Lauren would be spending time with me the next day. What a wonderful feeling of peace and security.

Suddenly, everything changed. I then saw Lauren and my mom waiting for me under a beautiful huge magnolia tree alongside the creek at the farm in Kentucky we used to walk. As I slowly walked up to them on a gleaming golden path that glistened from a ray of light streaming through the trees in the summer sun, they both smiled at me with love in their eyes while Lauren extended her arms out to me. The golden path was very intense, almost blinding me and shining ever so brightly as I got closer. I turned to my left and saw Princess and her babies playing on the bank of the stream while Winnie just ate in the woods nearby and watched. Missy then came out from under a bush and nuzzled and purred against my injured leg, her back arched and her tail erect while she rubbed against me. I felt a tear of happiness run down my face and saw it drop on her nose, as she looked up to me. My dad was there too, standing tall and proud, smiling and overlooking it all from a knoll in the woods behind my mom and Lauren. The vision was in color and oh so beautiful. I then felt my inner demons leave me, freeing me from the pain and guilt that encapsulated me for so long. When I walked up to my mom, she rubbed noses with me and Lauren put her arms around both of us and hugged us tightly, with her long beautiful silky hair flowing into my eyes. She then pulled back from her hug and looked into my eyes.

"Summer Storm, we have all watched you suffer without us. We watched you suffer through that terrible barn fire and thought you would join us then, but that great heart that won races for you was the same great heart that helped you survive that horrendous tragedy. We have watched you for a long time, but we patiently waited for you, and now we're all together again. I'm just sorry you had to endure so much pain and it took so long for you to get here. You had to learn that pride and vanity is a sin, and you had to pay for it. You'll soon find out there is no such thing as time or pain here, only love and happiness."

I took a deep sigh of relief and put my head down in joy as I felt their comfort. I then lifted my head high and took a deep breath, uncontrollably gritting my teeth as tears of bliss ran down my face onto my mom and Lauren's face. The dream was too much to bear. I was extremely happy as I felt I was finally free of my tormented past.

But just then, as I was enjoying this wonderful and enchantingly, delightful, blissful moment, a sudden violent chill and a surge of goose bumps quickly radiated throughout my body, freezing me where I stood and rocking my very soul. I blinked when it hit me and my lights went out as it hit me so quickly. My legs then crumbled from underneath me and I fell hard to the wet desert floor.

A quiet calmness came over me as I then left my body and slowly drifted skyward, staring down at my lifeless scarred and skinny frame lying there alone in the hot and barren desert sand; Heaven's Gate had opened. I instinctively looked up and saw my friends and family atop a golden ladder with outreached arms calling out to me. The beautiful white owl was still soaring and circling high above them in the wet night air, still screeching loudly and calling out to me as I slowly climbed that golden ladder.

I died that night on that warm and muddy desert floor in Lancaster and was relieved of the physical and mental burden I had carried for years. I was born in a summer storm and I died in a summer storm; I had gone full circle. I soon found out that the beautiful dream I had did last forever and I was indeed reunited with my family and friends and happy again at last. I would be there with them through eternity as we shared the memories of our relationships and continued to have good times together. We took over where we left off and I was finally free.

We all reach the end point of our lives in a different way. Though the paths we take are often varied, we are all subjected to various degrees of love, joy, pain, and sorrow. How we deal with them sets us apart and differentiates us from the pack. Through it all and what it all comes down to is survival. That is the one constant.

Everybody thinks they know my story, but the way I see it, it's only just begun. But before I go, please remember this. The next time you drive by a farm or ranch and you see a horse standing out in his pasture all alone, his head hung down, staring at the ground with listless eyes, remember he is not a dumb animal. No one knows how he came to that point in his life, but he has feelings like you and me, feelings that perhaps have been numbed by the passage of time. He lives and breathes, feels joy and pain, and has a soul. He needs to be loved and wants to give love in return. If you only knew what we can see and feel, you would respect us more and perhaps treat us better. Maybe you would treat everyone better.

I hurt myself today . . . . to see if I still feel;
I focused on the pain . . . . the only thing that's real.

What have I become . . . . my sweetest friend,
Everyone I know . . . . goes away in the end.

And you can have it all . . . . my empire of dirt,
I will let you down . . . . I will make you hurt.

I wear this crown of thorns . . . . upon my lyre chair,
Full of broken thoughts . . . . I cannot repair.

Beneath the stains of time . . . . the feeling disappears;
You are someone else . . . . I am still right here.

What have I become . . . . my sweetest friend?
Everyone I know . . . . goes away in the end.

If I could start again . . . . a million miles away,
I would keep myself . . . . I would find a way. Trent Reznor